A SOUL CALLED
RIVER

Love Can Hold Us All And Bring Us Home

John Tweedy

Many thanks for taking the time to read this

Peace and Happiness always

Johny Tweedy.

To all those who allowed me to share their lives and walked with me, at times carried me, on my journey.

To all the anonymous people — you know who you are — who shared their lives, strengths and hope with me and showed me what love really means.

For my two 'tricky' princesses, Italia and Daejah. You have bought fun, smiles and innocence to my life and I will love you always.

To my sister — no words will ever be enough, except to say I am blessed to have you and always have been. May we share more memories and laughter throughout the years.

To my dad — who showed what it means to be loved. Your hugs I will always miss. Your love, courage and relationship I will carry close with me every day; bless you and thank you, my old mate.

CONTENTS

ACKNOWLEDGEMENTS

To the girl who inspired this book, you know who you are. You inspire passion and a desire in me to be better each day. May the sun always shine on your life as you find all that you need as you walk with every breath. peace always 'princess'... For whatever reason you came into my path, provided the passion, the soul in me into writing this – over seven years later we are still close – fly and dare to dream, and know a smile I carry belongs to you.

Love, Peace and Happiness to you always. x

And to my publishing team at KINDLE BOOK PUBLISHING, thank you for your help and support.

And to those I work with now, my colleagues, I am blessed and grateful for your presence in my life. We have shared much, and we have watched people change before our eyes... surely the greatest gift. The ripples of your dedication and work move into many people's lives... so thank you.

And for those I hurt, abandoned and left because of my fall into addiction. I will never be able to give back enough to make up for all those times I left you in despair. This book is for you as much as anyone else... I treated you in ways now I could not comprehend and one day maybe I can make those full amends to you all... thank you.

CHAPTER 1

Like twin brothers bound together...

"Can you hear that, did you hear that," – she lifted her head and looked up to try and see who had spoken.

There seemed to be no one around but she heard the voice again, even softer, **"Did you hear that, can you see that... Sound, shape and a colour... of a feeling."**

She looked around again and saw no one. The beach was deserted, the ocean waves came in and out again. A gentle soothing motion which held her gaze as she thought about the voice and what it said, 'shape, colour, sound of a feeling', the words walked across her mind and she found herself thinking of all the positive feelings she had. Gentleness, compassion, grace, love of her family – all beautiful things which made her smile and feel peace inside. Each of them a blessing, as she felt blessed when she connected to that place deep and safe inside.

She got up and walked towards the water's edge. The sea felt warm and healing on her feet and she dared to walk in a little deeper than she had done before. She went further, up to her knees and let her hands fall by her side, her fingers running through the top of the surface water. She moved them and watched how the water danced with them, patterns came and went and she followed them all. She then heard it again, the voice. ***"What's it like to touch that feeling? Let it touch you?"***

She looked back at the beach but there was no one. Surprisingly for her, she was not scared. The voice and its words were as comforting as the warm waters she continued to walk through. She lifted her gaze up towards the distant horizon and beyond the sun which blazed there, far away. The air shimmered, the haze drifted and she felt her thoughts drift away with it. She felt herself moving from one thought to the next in her mind, not stopping to concentrate or focus on anything in specific. Words began to form in her mind things that she had never felt before – beyond the waves and beneath the haze of the day she left that place spiritually.

She floated above the physical form of the world and found herself relaxing more as every second went by. It was like the best meditation she had ever known, her breathing became shallow and her mind clear of the debris she often wanted to leave behind. It felt like she had left part of her on the beach, or something had been left there she did not need anymore. She felt herself drift through time and space, the minutes almost waving as they flew by. She continued to drift and looked down at the landscape, the scenery beginning to change beneath her with every second. Mountain ranges, snow-capped and vast spread out below her one minute to be replaced by the lush green meadows of fields where animals grazed throughout the next. In the next moment she looked upon vast fields of sunflowers sitting amongst streams which tumbled and twirled across the countryside feeding into lakes where birds drifted across the top of the water.

A voice entered into her consciousness, ***"You need to come down and be here."***

She found herself slowly descending towards a lake which was fed into by several streams. There was a clearing surrounded by pines and the smell of them intoxicated her senses as she landed softly at the side of the lake. Walking slowly she noticed that where the streams converged there were several large rocks which sat half in and half out of the water. On one of these rocks she noticed a man sitting alone staring at the water. She looked around for somewhere to sit and found herself drawn towards a flat area of grass close to the rock where he sat staring at the water.

She walked over and slowly sat down looking up to see if he noticed her or even acknowledged her arriving. He did neither and continued to stare intently at the water as it tumbled past into the blue crystal waters of the lake. She adjusted her sight to the surroundings and looked round slowly trying to see exactly where she was and what lay around. It was strange that despite never ever setting foot in the place she felt calm and peaceful and a strange sense of belonging to it. Blue and yellow flowers populated the water's edge and trees lived alongside them, their branches provided shade where necessary from the bright rays of the burning sun. The trees branches did more than that though as they also acted as silhouettes which allowed the light from the sun to filter through onto the areas around both the grass and the water. They reflected onto and into the water and lit up areas where flowers grew wild and free throughout the clearing.

"When you look into the abyss, you become a part of it."

The voice came from next to her and the man who sat, staring into the water as he spoke.

"I'm sorry I didn't…"

"When you look into the abyss, you become a part of it, I said."

"Well I don't know, I've never looked in there, can't say if that's the case or not," she said trying not to sound too knowing.

"Like twin brothers, bound together, entwined, connected."

3

She thought for a moment she felt fear rise, a desire to run, but something made her stay, held her enough to let her say, "I don't know, I don't think I've ever looked."

The man lifted his gaze from the water and glanced at her quickly before returning his eyes to the hypnotic waters, "I looked into the abyss too long, held its gaze longer than I should have."

She felt she wanted to move away and that the peace and tranquillity of what she had just experienced would be shattered and disappear if she stayed and continued the conversation. Her mind raced to find a way in which she could get up and move somewhere else but she heard the voice from the beach once again.

"Don't leave him, he needs to speak and needs you to listen."

She felt that this was the last thing she wanted to do but sat and said, "Like twin brothers you said."

The man didn't respond immediately and simply sat staring. Time passed, minutes went by until he spoke again.

"Yes like twin brothers or blood brothers. I stood at the edge too long and held its hand for what seemed an eternity. I looked into it, stared, and could not pull myself away. It saw me and I saw all of it and for a while it tempted me."

She thought about what the man had said and the way that he spoke in such a short and punctuated way, as if he was delivering a poem. "What did you see in there?" she asked after a considerable amount of time.

"Despair, desolation, emptiness, and a pit of fear which went on for ever. I know that now, what it is, a reflection of my insides. The abyss smiled at me and pulled me close, but I didn't give in to its call," pausing slightly, "until now."

She felt the words, icy and cold upon her skin, "Until now… but you're here and not staring at it now. It's beautiful here."

"Is it beautiful, I will have to take your word for that? My eyes and mind can only focus on what was left behind by that time," slowly pushing his soles onto the rock and lifting himself onto his feet as he spoke again, "I think it's time now."

She was instantly alert, "It's time now for what?"

"Time to go, time to finally jump and find out if it is all that I want it to be," he said looking up and then down at her.

Then he jumped feet first into the waters of the stream below the rock, disappearing straight away into the cold waters.

She got up quickly rushing to the edge to see him and help pull him clear of the rushing waters as they tumbled down towards the bends of other streams. She looked into the water but could see no sign of him – nothing at all. She ran along the bank and looked further down the stream but again nothing. She ran back to where he jumped in and stared intently at the spot that he entered into the water. There was nothing there, no sign of any sort. She stood up and turned to the rock itself, where he had been sitting, and saw a book which had writing across the front and had the words "From the Inside" written across the front of it.

She walked over and picked the book up, holding it carefully as she did, and opened it.

She started to read.

CHAPTER 2

Innocence was laughing...

Inside the book there were pages and pages of notes, scribbles and drawings. Some of the writing was neat and tidy and presented in an orderly way and the sentences flowed from page to page. In other places the writing was more disorganised, lines of poems written haphazardly across the page, overflowing onto other pages. As she thumbed through the book certain ones hit her full in the face.

"When I die and my corpse lays rotting in the earth... Feel like I'm imploding today from inside to out... Loneliness eats through me tonight... When you're not here the devil has my ear, he whispers, he taunts, he creates and he haunts."

She continued to scan through the pages and found similar themes all the way through it and every space which could be written in was filled with something. She was about to put the book down when her eyes were drawn to a single line written at the top of the last page, "I think it's time now!!!!!" She was struck by these words, they were the last ones the man said before he jumped and disappeared. She looked back at the water as its surface rippled with the wind that softly blew across it. There was nothing there, he was not there.

She felt suddenly cold and looked up to see a single dark cloud pass across the face of the sun. She hunted for her bag and pulled out the jumper she always kept in it and quickly put it on. She felt the wind increase and the waters of the lake and streams rise to meet it. She pulled herself into her jumper and tried to bury herself deeper into its warm depths. It wasn't working and she felt as if someone had just walked across her shadow or her grave as the saying went. She looked around to see if there was anywhere which could offer some warmth and shelter from the cloud which seemed to be sitting directly across the middle of the sun and not moving. The wind continued to increase and the tree branches shifted uneasily above her head.

She picked up her bag and started to walk towards the rock face looking for entry into any nook and cranny which may offer her some form of shelter and respite from the coldness which threatened to consume her. She walked along the face of the wall and found herself a small crevice which offered her some protection from the wind and huddled, trying to pull every part of her together to get some warmth. The wind whistled in amongst the tress which shook angrily under its pull and the waters of the streams chattered and whispered to each other as they ran across the rocks underneath its surface.

"He had to go you know. It was time he stopped thinking and did what he needed to. Sometimes you can't save everyone, they have to save themselves... if they want to," the voice whispered to her through the sound of the rustling leaves.

Since hearing the voice on the beach she had no thoughts of speaking back. It felt like she was there to listen and conversing was not on the table; she was to listen and not speak. But the unexpected turn of events, the man jumping, talk of an abyss and the rising noise of the wind seemed to change all of what had gone before.

"What did he need to do? I don't understand," she cried out into the nothingness of the darkening day.

There was no response; the voice remained silent and the clearing stayed empty. The winds died, the cloud disappeared and the full rays of the sun returned.

She came out from where she had been sheltering and felt the warmth of the sun return to her face. Her spirits lifted at its touch, like a lovers soft fingers on her cheek and she raised her head to stare directly into it for some time. Her jumper discarded she walked over towards the stream which ran quiet now and bent down to wash her face in its waters. The waters may have been still but she felt moved inside with a sense of loss for someone she didn't know who had jumped. What was his story, his history, his life? Why could he not have stayed and what was it that he had to do? She scooped another handful of the refreshing water into her hands and threw it across the back of her neck feeling its coldness trickle down her spine.

"Will you play with me now?"

A child's voice, soft and calm, spoke from behind her.

Her head shot round and she started to stand up. The voice came from a boy who stood looking at her from a few feet away. She didn't hear him come up to her and for a moment she was startled. His hair was the brightest blonde and hung down over his small and fragile shoulders and he was dressed in a red tracksuit top, blue jeans and black boots which came half way up his slender legs to his calf. In his hand he held a red football, offering it out towards her as he stood there. He looked about eight or nine years old from his size, although his face showed wisdom beyond those years. The most startling thing about him, apart from appearing from apparent thin air, was his eyes. They were the deepest brown and surrounded by eyelashes so long they half covered their vivid colour. The thought which came immediately to her mind, from nowhere, was that was the colour that chocolate should always be.

The boy spoke again, pleading, "Will you play with me now?"

She tried to stay calm, giving herself time to adjust, "Well yes of course," before adding slowly, "sorry, forgive me, but I don't understand. Where did you come from?"

The boy looked at her for a moment before replying, "Here and there. My name's River, what's yours?" throwing the ball high into the air and catching it without taking his eyes away from her face as it dropped.

She felt herself relax, less fearful now, "Me! Well my name's not as nice as yours, its Sarah," bending down a little so as to appear less threatening.

"Yeah I knew that, but just wanted to check. They said you would come to play someday, but that seems such a long time ago I nearly forgot," spinning around again and throwing the ball in her direction.

Sarah caught it just before it hit her in the face and threw it back quickly. He caught it deftly, spun round two or three times and started to walk towards the water's edge himself. He didn't stop at the edge, smoothly stepping off into the water itself. He started to walk up against the current singing softly to himself.

"You staying or coming?" he shouted back over his shoulder at Sarah.

He was ten yards away from her in a short space of time and Sarah started after him. She was afraid of him being in the water after what had just happened, although he seemed more at home than any other child she had ever seen. She hurried after him trying to catch up.

"River wait, slow down please," she shouted at him, more in confusion than discomfort at his unexpected arrival. Sarah needed him to stop and talk to her. She needn't worry River suddenly stopped, turned round and looked past her and stood staring at the rock where the man had been sitting.

"Where's Tony?" he said, craning his small neck to look around her now.

"Tony, who's Tony?" she said trying to hide any knowledge she might have about who he was speaking about.

River had turned now and started to walk back towards her, speaking as he did, "Tony, sits on the rock all day staring at the water. I've never not known him being there. Where is he?"

She tried to maintain her ignorance, "Sorry I don't know a Tony," trying to sound convincing.

He stopped, almost level with her now, looking directly at her, the smile he had worn since he had arrived gone from his face, "Sarah, please don't."

She shifted her eyes from his, looking away as she spoke back, "Don't what, River?"

"Please don't lie to me or try and protect me. I don't need protecting here ever… Never ever. Where is Tony?"

Sarah lowered her head, her voice lowering with it, "He jumped into the water and I haven't seen him since."

River looked at her, his face fell and his eyes closed momentarily. He opened them again but the light which had reflected off them before seemed to fade, sadness entering into them. It contained a depth and intensity of sadness which Sarah had never witnessed before. River lowered his head and stood still for a moment before finally speaking.

"Did he say anything before he jumped?"

Sarah paused, looking at him and searching to offer comfort with anything she might say, "He said he needed to go, that was the last thing he said."

River lifted his head and his gaze and scanned her face to see if this was the truth. He found what he needed and started to slowly smile again whilst the sadness remained in his eyes, "Thank you."

He walked slowly over to her and put his small and fragile arms around her waist and held her close to his face before releasing her and taking her hand in his. He lead her back towards the rock where Tony had been and made her sit down with her back against it, following her and doing the same once she was settled. They sat there for a while, his hand in hers on top of his knee as the sun held them in its warmth and the trees sat silently with them, as they paid them no mind.

River spoke slowly after moments of silence between them and the world, "He used to play with me every day. We used to play here for ages and I was so happy when we did. He used to watch me play on my own also and write things which were so nice and made me laugh," he paused and then continued after a time, "He said that I reminded him of something long gone. He was always writing and sometimes would share what he had written. I always wanted more but he said some things are best not heard, that they are better left unsaid."

Sarah listened intently and felt the emotion in the words that River spoke. She looked at his delicate features and found a beauty and grace that she had never seen before. She only felt she could offer him something after a time had passed.

"That sounds really nice and its good you got to play together," watching his face for a reaction. "What kind of things did he write and tell you?"

River spoke looking out across the stream and lake as he did, "I can't remember all of what he wrote but he watched me playing one day chasing butterflies and frogs and I remember what he wrote on that day, well some of it."

"That sounds like a good day," she said. "What can you remember form then, what he wrote?"

"It was one of the best and he was smiling all day. I think it went... across a cloudless sky, innocence was laughing at a butterfly – resting on a child's hand, and as they talked they found beauty...

There was more but I liked that best so he taught it to me before I went for the day," River replied smiling slightly now as he remembered the memory.

Sarah didn't speak immediately. River was right it was beautiful and she could imagine him running around chasing and catching butterflies whilst Tony watched, smiling. She found herself smiling in response to River's and the feelings around them lifted slightly.

"River, that is beautiful and so sounds like Tony, liked you," she said after a time.

River lifted his head and looked at her, his eyes speaking without words, "Tony loved me and I loved him. That's the most important thing, he knew I loved him," he paused to let the words sink in for Sarah before adding, "read me the rest of that poem."

Sarah's face showed her puzzlement and confusion, which was shown also in her words, "Read the rest of it. How can I do that River?"

"Look in the book, it's in your bag. Please find it and read it to me. I'm sure he won't mind as it's for me."

"Sorry, River, I don't have Tony's book in my bag. It was on the rock and I did look at it but it's not in my bag," Sarah said directly to his face knowing that the truth was all he wanted.

River kept on looking at her, his smile growing, "Sarah it's in your bag, just read it please."

Sarah looked at him as he raised his eyebrows and nodded towards her bag. She looked at him again and his smile grew bigger. She turned and reached down into her bag and looked for what he said was there. It was. She pulled it out and looked at him knowing that she had left it on the rock and having no idea how it got there. But then again she had no idea how she had got where she was and should have been ready for the unexpected by now she thought. She opened the book and drifted her gaze over the pages to find what he wanted read to him.

As she searched, River got up and stretched his limbs upwards, stretching towards the sky, before disappearing, running around the other side of the rock, out of sight. Sarah heard him run off and followed the sound, slightly anxious now, her defences rising. He reappeared on top of the rock and moved towards the edge of it, dangerously close.

Sarah saw him for the first time since he had run off and instantly panicked. She got up quickly, yelling as she did, "River, please be careful, keep back from the edge."

River laughed at her anxiety, long and loud, "Sarah, don't worry nothing can hurt me here. I don't have fear, I don't have experience to hold me back from what is natural. Look I will sit down whilst you read it to me just to keep you happy," which he did as he finished speaking.

Sarah felt her heart relax inside her chest, her normal breathing return, "Thank you, thank you I appreciate it."

"Hurry up then, what you waiting for, Christmas?" he said still laughing.

She continued to look through the pages until she found what River wanted. The pages where the poem was written were the only ones in the whole book which had nothing else written on them except for the name River at the top of the page. It was written out clearly, neatly and fitted onto the whole of one page.

"Gonna read it then, are you," his voice bringing her back from her thoughts. "Can't sit here all day just to ease your fears, Sarah," adding jokingly as he looked down.

"Ok wait a second, let me get comfortable," she said settling herself on the grass next to the rock where he sat.

She took a deep breath and tried to calm her heart, before starting.

"Across a cloudless sky, life was – smiling, a deep resonance of sheer simplicity. And as it walked it found Innocence."

She looked up to see River staring out across the water, seemingly lost somewhere in the distance.

"And…"

"Then it's your bit, the words you remember."

"Ok… after that then what?"

"Across a cloudless sky," she started, "beauty was infinite, around and within, it simply 'was' – And all together, they found… love."

River sat still, continuing to stare out across the water and into the far horizon, "Anymore?"

She looked back down and started up again, "Across a cloudless sky, love was there, it had found Life, Innocence – Entwined with beauty inside. Inside a cloudless sky," she finished and read the words Tony had written in small print at the bottom to herself only. "For River, who lights my smiles," before looking back up towards River and where he sat.

River was no longer looking out across the top of the water but rather straight into the water at the bottom of the rock, at the exact spot that she saw Tony staring into. River spoke, more so whispered really, "You forgot to read what he wrote at the bottom… for River who lights my smiles," he looked down at her before adding, "why did you leave that out?"

Sarah lowered her head, embarrassed slightly, "Sorry, I don't know really."

River forgave her in an instant, "Sarah, don't worry I know it was there because he read that bit to me also at the time. Do you really think I would not remember that bit – it was the best part, then and now."

"I bet it was," Sarah replied trying to avoid eye contact for the fear of displaying her own sadness and as a mark of respect for the depth of feelings that obviously existed between Tony and River.

"Sarah, thank you," he said, slowly getting up and looking over towards where she sat, her head bowed trying to avoid his eyes. "I think I need to go to him now."

River jumped straight into the water, feet first, exactly in the spot where Tony had jumped.

For a moment Sarah was stunned, thrown off guard completely by what had just happened, out of nowhere. Then she was up, without a second thought, she threw herself into the waters, feeling its icy touch invade her every sinew. She dived under, she thrashed, twisting and searching, desperation in every movement. She dived deeper each time, but to no avail, she could not find him. She returned to the surface to catch a breath, she was crying, tears adding to the waters flow. She searched, she dived, and she found herself sobbing each time she returned to the surface for air, tiredness eating into her until she could hardly keep herself afloat, let alone look for him. Eventually the tiredness claimed her and she fell sobbing onto the bank, her hair matted to her head. She looked up and found her eyes drawn to the ball that River had with him when she first saw him. It sat still, unmoving, un-played with.

Sarah's emotions consumed her. She wept. She screamed out. She sobbed.

The water was still and silent, River had gone.

It started to rain.

With the rain came the wind. A wind that tore leaves from the trees and stirred the waters of the recently quiet streams to a frenzy. The waters rose and threatened to burst out, across onto the grass and flood the area where Sarah lay. She couldn't move the only sign she was still breathing was the movement of her back as her sobs continued in severity.

She lay in the same position, face down, for what seemed a lifetime. That thought went through her mind; I need to lay here for the length of River's lifetime. All that did was increase her sobs even more as the wind tore across her back and the rain left her hair matted to her head. I will lay here and not move until the length of River's lifetime has gone and then I will just lie here for that time again. She had never known grief, despair and loss on such a scale. Even the pain of losing her father who she was so close to could not come close to what she was feeling inside.

It was like someone had got the biggest stone, or boulder, they could find and forced it down her throat and it lay now in the middle of her stomach whilst someone trampled across her heart. If there were a God why would they let this happen to this little boy? What did River mean by him needing to go now and get him? He couldn't save him from death or where he had gone, could he? The fear that River didn't have would not save him there. Tony had made a decision and the ripples of it now had caused River to jump in after him and now he was gone too. From the depths of somewhere, she knew not where, something told Sarah to drag herself up and get under shelter and away from the elements that continued to throw themselves at her and the whole of the world itself.

She slowly moved to rest on her knees and then slower still moved from that position to one where she put her weight on her feet and eventually stood upright.

From amidst the wind and the rain, a voice came, **"You can get through…"**

Sarah didn't even think before answering, shouting back, "Don't even think about it, don't even try and speak."

The voice tried to speak in between her words but she carried on, "I do not want to hear another single thing that you say, ever," looking up, turning round and shouting as she did. "Go away and stay away from me, forever."

She snatched her bag up from the grass and threw her jumper across her shoulders and ran. She ran for cover, she ran away from the place where all things had changed, she ran to where she knew she would find somewhere she could escape, at least from the wind and rain.

She ran to the alcove.

As she came to the alcove and where it sat in the rock face she saw that it had changed. It had become bigger, allowing more shelter away from the weather which continued to fall in its lament for River. Now, above it and across the front there existed a network of branches covered by large leaves which allowed the area underneath to remain dry. It was on the floor where the biggest change had occurred. On this there lay a bed of what looked like fresh dry straw, fluffy and appealing on the eye, and comforting enough for anyone's feelings of grief. A blanket or two lay on top and Sarah quickly bent down to pull one of them up and put it around her wet and freezing shoulders. She shivered and moved to lay down throwing her bag and its occupants casually to the side under a nearby rock. She lay down on her side and looked out onto the scene which now lay outside.

The rain was coming down in torrents and the wind threw it at the trees, water and rocks of the nearby clearing. The waters of the nearby streams could easily be heard as they made their way across the valleys, chattering angrily as they went by. All the sounds clashed together like Sarah's feelings as she lay there – all of them spat out grief, spoke of loss and mourned the going of the child – their child, River.

Sarah's tears continued to run slowly down her cheeks, her blouse soaked by the rain but more so by the tears. She reached for the other blanket and turned round to face the wall. She turned her back on the world and its grief and wept herself. She wanted no part of anything anymore and turned her back on time and its healing. Her thoughts turned to River, her mind turned to his eyes, his face, his laugh and sleep came and found her, whispering soft words of comfort to cover up her grief and despair.

CHAPTER 3

My soul cries out for her...

As soon as Sarah succumbed to sleep bought on by the tiredness of grief, the rain stopped, the wind relented and night came to the clearing. It was a night lit up by the lights of a million stars, each one sparkling in a fight against the others to be the brightest. The moon was out watching their personal fights, full and bright, a spotlight on the greatest stage of all – the summer night's sky. The clearing was peaceful and still, illuminated by the lights from above, resting from the tragic events it had been a witness to, the loss of two departed souls, one of them a child.

A nightingale sat within one of the trees and shattered the stillness, its song rising and falling across the air for all to hear. With it came the hands of time, trying to step in and heal the wounds laid out before it. But it had misjudged the moment, it was far too soon, and it quickly vanished. It left feelings behind to twist and form in the night air, coming to rest softly on the blanket around Sarah's slender frame.

On the rock itself, something moved and shifted slightly, a shadow or a figure, not easily identified at first glance. It was a figure of a woman. She sat, her head resting on one knee whilst the other leg lay at right angles underneath her. Her hair hardly recognisable in the night, due to its colour hung in ringlets down to her waist. Her hair was the colour of coal, from the deepest seams of the earth. Her head was bowed and from any distance it was not easy to see if she was either sleeping or simply resting. What could be seen though was her stillness, the way she sat and waited, for what or whom no one knew. Her hair reflected the light of the moon as she sat, sending small silver diamonds out onto the rocks surface.

She lifted her head and looked straight over towards the sleeping form of Sarah and whispers of healing escaped her lips, "Sleep and be comforted, rest and be refreshed and let your dreams hold your grief, my sweet child of grace."

Her words finished she lowered her chin back onto her bended knee and bowed her head.

The woman was not seen by a figure that choose at that moment to make his way into the clearing. A lithe and athletic figure, he moved gracefully and softly through the grass, hardily treading on the softness beneath his feet. His features were distinguished, handsome, and rugged and on his head light brown hair fell down to his shoulders. He wore clothes which fitted loosely around his frame and he moved easily in them as he entered the clearing. He looked up briefly, as if to check his way, and made his way over to the shallow waters of the stream, bending down on his haunches to scoop up the cold waters into his mouth two or three times to quench his thirst. He remained in this position as he turned his head to take in the surroundings and his eyes strayed towards the rock and caught sight of the figure silhouetted against the night sky, instantly alerted, rising to his full height, ready to attack.

The voice, soft and calm, eased his fears as it spoke.

"I don't think there's any need to be scared of me, is there?" she whispered throwing soft thoughts out into the air, across his mind.

He paused before he spoke, unusually apprehensive, "Just cautious, and not scared."

She laughed, slowly lifting her head, "I thought you would be here sooner. I've been waiting a while."

He paused again, his expected arrival confusing, "You have been here waiting for me?"

Her eyes followed him for a while before she spoke. "For longer than you think, maybe even a lifetime," her head dropping back onto her knee this time on her side, so she could still look at him from a different angle, before adding, "your lifetime of course."

He was totally lost and confused now, "Sorry I don't understand. How you knew I would be coming at all. Even I didn't know that. I got lost," walking over to the rock where she sat as he finished speaking.

She sighed, a sound that he followed as it left her mouth, "Lost, found, knowing or not knowing where you are going... what's the difference. You're here and I'm here, alone together in the dark. No one around," looking away quickly then straight back at him. "The possibilities are endless."

If he was cautious before he now found himself as nervous as a deer caught in the open as wolves closed in, shifting from one foot to another and trying to look away. He couldn't move though from the spot, there was something in her voice, her eyes, and her sheer presence... just her. She was hypnotic and he was caught in her gaze. His senses reeled and smashed, crashing against each other, until they fell in a heap at her feet.

She laughed, more music to his ears, before she spoke again, "Don't worry I'm just teasing," her laughter continuing for a while until she added, "although possibilities are endless, don't you think?"

He looked at his feet, shifting once more, "I was just looking for somewhere to sleep," ignoring her laughter and teasing at his expense.

She ran her fingers through her hair, playing with each strand, "Here in this place, alone with me, and you want to sleep," her eyes closing and then opening, wider now.

"I'm just tired and need to rest, it's been a long day. I just want to lie down and sleep," he replied trying to sound convincing.

She looked straight into his eyes and spoke, "You want to sleep… So you can dream," throwing the words out between them, a hint of a question at the end once again.

If she didn't before, she had his attention now, and they both knew it. His voice betrayed him as he stuttered a response, "Yes… to… dream."

"What is your name?" she asked, her voice soft and inviting.

"Ty, my name is Ty."

"Tell me what you dream, Ty."

He looked at her and dissolved, giving in. He needed to be on the ground suddenly, he glanced around and found the same area of grass that Sarah had and moved across to sit cross-legged, looking up at her.

She asked him again, in a voice that was barely audible, "Tell me what you dream, Ty."

He sighed and spoke, "I dream of a girl every night, the same girl – she is stunning in every way. Her looks, the way she moves, speaks, smells. Every night she holds me, she talks to me. Her smell is like… like… nothing else," he stopped briefly as if remembering it and then added, "she is in here (tapping his head), and in here (holding his heart tightly). My soul cries out."

"Your soul cries out – for what?"

"Her. It cries out for her," Ty added.

"Ahh, she has you then," sighing as she spoke. "Are you lost in her?"

He replied instantly, "I've never thought of it like that. I'd be lost if I didn't dream of her," pausing before adding, "what I want is for her to be lost in me."

She watched him closely, his eyes betraying a trace of pain, "Sounds, and looks, like you do. Maybe you can get lost together... and find each other."

"I have found her but... " he stopped, as if his mouth had finally caught up with his thoughts, and didn't finish the sentence.

She looked across at him, concerned for a moment. "But what?"

Ty continued to look down and spoke, "I don't know what she looks like."

She was on her feet quickly, rising gracefully from her seated position, across the rock and jumped swiftly down, without making a sound. She crossed the space between them to where he was sitting, lost in his own world, his sadness, the loss, and his dreams. He was so lost he was totally unaware to where she was now, next to him.

She spoke, her breath so close to him now, "You see her every night in your dreams, you want her, are lost without her but... you can't remember what she looks like. That's not good?"

Her voice bought him back and he became aware that she was now sitting with him on the grass. He could smell her hair, see the moonlight bouncing off her skin, it was mesmerising, "It's not good. Every night I pray before I lay my head down and sleep. I ask to remember her before I drift off to her. I dream... I wake up... and she is gone. The image, the smell is gone as she has gone too."

She looked at him and put her hand out slowly, resting it on his forearm, "That sounds so painful and so sad."

He let her touch his arm and felt the softness and warmth on his skin and for a moment he felt something he knew, "It is painful, it feels like the worst pain. I want to remember so that I can think of her during the day and hold onto through every waking hour also."

She smiled, feeling his emotion, "Hold onto her in the day, like living the dream," she added casually.

He was confused again by her, "But I'd be awake so it's not a dream; you can't dream while you're awake."

She moved her hand and bought it up to his chin, lifting his head slightly to look into his eyes, "You can't dream while you're awake. Now that is painful."

He looked into her eyes, so close for the first time. They were almond in shape and matched the colour of her hair, deepest black. But despite their colour they were not dark, they were soft, warm, inviting, shining and full of light, most of all they were full of peace.

"I remember her name though, I can remember that," he said after a time.

She smiled directly at him and he melted. His sadness and loss dropping away like the setting sun, "That's a start then, a name for her face, for her. I am intrigued now, what is her name."

One word escaped his lips, "Princess."

She dropped an eyebrow and looked at him quizzically, "Princess. Is she really that?"

"Really what?"

"A princess," she replied holding his gaze.

Ty felt suddenly misunderstood, as if he was a cause of humour for her and he wanted to be somewhere else, "No that's my name for her," his voice rising in tone slightly.

She refused to move her eyes, "Princess is a title. It's not really a name."

Ty moved and started to rise up from his seated position, angry, "It's a name; it's her name and I gave it to her." He was standing now, above her almost daring her to taunt him more or say something else.

She stayed seated but lifted her head in reply, "Can you really give someone anything they don't ask for, even a name?"

Ty looked down and then around. He was lost, no idea where he was and where he was going. Here in the open, in the dark of night who was this girl? The tiredness he had felt when he entered the clearing seemed to rise up and draw its cloak around him. It consumed and moved him forcing him to sit down as his eyes nodded encouragement to do it. He needed sleep, craved sleep and he wanted to find to go to her, he wanted his dreams.

She had seen how he had reacted and wondered momentarily if she had gone too far. Her honesty was her gift to all but at times its use had been problematic in the past. She bought herself back to him as he did move away from her but simply to find a place comfortable to lie down. The air was warm and relaxing and the breeze cooling as he lay his head down, his hands slightly under it, offering some support.

She knew it was time to go and softly moved over to kiss him gently on his sun-bleached hair and then got up to move away. She started to move slowly towards the forest and the trees that signalled its beginning, some way back from the clearing itself.

Her kiss and her presence so close, woke him from his drifting, "Thank you."

She heard him but continued to walk away without thinking of replying or turning to go back.

"What is your name?" he added before she disappeared from both sight and sound.

She half stopped and looked slowly up towards the night and the cloudless sky, the stars spread out like diamonds across a purple canvas.

"My name," pausing and continuing to look upwards towards the sky, "is Princess."

He heard the words, he heard her name, but tiredness would not allow him to lift his head, although his eyes opened wider from beneath their sleepy lids.

"Princess," gasping for words and breath now, "and what do you dream of?"

She stopped, turned and smiled, the softness and lightness of her nature raising his hopes. She held out one hand and offered it out towards him.

She laughed before speaking, "I dream of you of course."

She turned and began to walk away as she finished speaking, her laughter left behind, her hand moving back towards her side as she disappeared from view.

His tiredness overcame him and he drifted off to sleep. He left to walk with the Princess in his dreams as she left to walk towards him in hers.

CHAPTER 4

Faith's left home...

Sarah had been awake for some time, woken both by the raw emotions of grief and the voices barely audible above them from somewhere close by. She had turned round to try and both see and hear the voices clearer and gazed on two silhouettes against the backdrop of the forest. The voices were merely whispering but she saw an arm reach out and then soon after a kiss and a girl walking away. Her movements gentle and soothing on the ground and for a moment they had the same affect across Sarah's breaking heart.

The thoughts of despair and hopelessness soon returned and smashed through breaking the stillness and the respite that she had felt briefly. Her sleep had been fitful, filled with despair, and nothingness held onto her body as she lay unable to move. Sarah always had faith that through the bleakest of times, however deep the hole, that something would carry her through it. She felt that when her dad had passed away and the long months which followed with a hole the shape of him etched inside her. She felt he was always there but his physical absence was the biggest barrier to her fully being able to recover and move forward. She had eventually settled on an uncomfortable uneasiness which sat and walked with her since that time. There had been moments of respite from that but they had been all to brief and the emptiness and meaninglessness soon returned with a vengeance as she tried to carry on.

She recognised those feelings and emotions now and knew if she lay where she was any longer then there was a chance she would never get up. She stretched out her limbs and became ready to try and stand and move out into the open. She moved slowly and lifted her aching limbs from where she lay, hoping that in the process the grief she felt would drop and fall also and she would feel lighter. That didn't happen and it simply stayed making every move worse than the last. She still held the blankets around her as she stood trying to hold onto some kind of physical warmth against the coldness of her grief. It didn't work and she stood there shivering despite the warmness of the night air.

The girl she had seen had walked away into the trees on the far side of the clearing. He still remained, lying sleeping on the grass area where Sarah had originally sat talking with Tony. She had forgotten about him, Tony. Her grief had been purely for River and now there was another person. The feeling was different though and tinged with anger and resentment. It was Tony who had been the main reason that River had jumped. River's love and need to be with or save Tony had been the reason why he was now gone. How could Tony have allowed that to happen? What hold did he have over River which reached out and extended so far, even beyond his death, that River would sacrifice himself for Tony? There was no way that Tony should have that hold of River, no one should have that hold over anyone let alone a child's life.

Her thoughts straying to Tony reminded her that his book was in her bag and she reached down to find it. Maybe somewhere in there, amidst the words, lay a clue that would throw further light on the relationship that had been between them, how long and how deep it ran. She felt round for the book and pulled it out. The cover was battered and worn and Tony had obviously owned it for a long time. She ran her fingers across the cover and felt each mark and indentation separately. Each one felt like it had its own story and she tried to imagine what some of them would be. She opened the book and if fell open to a page which took her straight back to the conversation she had with Tony.

It helps me, seems a cure.

Makes me, wakes me
It helps me, forget to live
It heals me, opens my eyes
It sees through the abyss
Reveals all, tells all
It knows me…
Really knows me.

What was it? Could he be talking about River? Healing, seeing through an abyss, knows me, really knows me. She moved on flicking through the pages which held words which hit her hard. Shame, hurt, pain, anger. So many negative words and emotions attached to them. If Tony had shared all these with River then she would have been both disappointed and angry. She continued to flick through the pages, most of them the same a jumble of words written across the page. They followed no rhythm and no rhyme and at times Sarah found them extremely hard to follow. Her heart was heavy and now her head was also from trying to de-cipher the ranting's of what seemed like a demented soul. She looked up and out into the night sky and across the heads of the trees which seemed to offer protection from the rolling expanse of the hills beyond. Her eyes wandered across the landscape, flitting from one thing to the next, none of them holding her gaze until she found herself returning to what was close by – the rock. Just looking at it sent a chill of recognition down her spine. A coldness represented by her feelings and the likely touch of the water into which River had jumped without a thought for his own safety. She held the book in one hand and the blanket around her shoulders with the other and slowly walked out and across towards it.

As she moved towards the rock she passed the sleeping figure of the man. As she drew closer to she trod carefully so as not to wake him. None of this was done for his consideration but more so that she could be left alone. The last thing on her mind was to enter into any form of contact or conversation with anyone. The only thing she was on talking terms with at that moment was her grief and that was difficult enough. She came to the rock, stopped, and looked for the best place to climb up. She decided on the route which River had taken himself which entailed walking round to the other side where the face was less steep and the holds more frequent. Still managing to hold onto both the book and the blanket she half scrambled up its side feeling the cold surface as she went through the light of the moon. She reached the top and positioned herself facing out across the stream leading into the lake and beyond that to the hills in the distance. Despite her low mood she had to admit that the view itself provided a sense of calm and a better perspective of reality. It was little wonder Tony sat here every day. If she was here she would have done the same.

The contrast between the view and Tony's mind hit her and that things must have been pretty awful for him to feel like he did facing a view like this. Then again when she met him he never looked up, he was always looking into the waters of the stream that ran beneath the rock and out towards the lake. She looked down and found herself fixated by the shapes and movements of the water. It took her back to her hands running over the surface of the ocean at the beach before she had been transported here. The beach seemed an age away, a lifetime. The words lifetime bought her back to where she was as her feelings struck up once again smashing their way through to her heart. A lifetime… it was a lifetime ago.

River's lifetime.

From nowhere her grief for River escaped and she was bought straight back to the time of her father's death and the feelings which had sat dormant for so long resurfaced, kicking at the shirt tails of River's. They were so close together and so closely entwined that for a time Sarah was unable to work out which was what and who was who. They twisted and tumbled through the whole of her body, dancing a tango of grief across her tortured mind. She was consumed by grief and pulled the blanket up over her lowered head to try and confront the intensity of feelings which threatened to overwhelm her. She closed her eyes and tried to concentrate on her breathing to calm her racing heart. She knew that if she didn't, she would be overcome and there would be no escape. Slowly and gradually the thoughts and mixing of the grief's separated and drifted apart and her focus came towards her dad and what had come to pass back then.

He had not been well for a while and had been in and out of Hospital for many months. The last time he went in was to have an operation where the chances of success were rated as fifty-fifty and Sarah's last night with him before the operation came back to her. They sat and spoke and held each other until it was time for her to go. They didn't speak about what was to come or what could possibly happen but it was on both their minds throughout that time. The thoughts and words unsaid held them both and they could hardly pull themselves apart at the end of the visit. She remembers not being able to sleep, fearing the worst but hoping against hope for the best.

The next day came and she waited outside the theatre at the Hospital alone and praying to whatever deity may exist for her dad to get through it. He came out and went into Intensive Care and the next twelve days were spent in a room with nurses coming and going, time passing slowly and her dad slipping in and out of drug induced sleep. She held his hand, she kept on talking to him but things did not get any better and he slowly started to drift away. Every day Sarah went to the Chapel in the Hospital to sit and be still and pray for her dad. The Chapel became a place over the next week or so where she went just to get a break and to try and find something within herself to pull her through it. More so to try and find something to pull him through it. When she was in the Chapel Sarah felt that God held and comforted her, showing her the path to stay strong and positive. It also bought something new, an emotion every bone in her body tried to throw out and reject – being close to God bought gratitude. In that Chapel she found some hope maybe even some faith. That word itself was something that she had always fought against as it was beyond her own head's understanding and workings. She did not know then that faith is something that the head will always have trouble with. Faith was a gift of the heart not the head and at that time Faith was a gift that Sarah found hard to receive.

"Faith comes from unlikely places," the voice had returned, trying to come at her from a place which she may find healing and identify with.

Unlike earlier when she had shouted at the voice and told it never to speak again or even try and speak to her she heard the words and sat with them for a while. The anger which had initially rested inside had withdrawn leaving her grief and sorrow and she had lost all fight inside her to respond in a similar way. She sat looking at the water and for a time all was still and the only sound was the waters constant journey past the bottom of the rock.

Sarah eventually spoke, from a place inside she knew not, "Faith's left home at humanity's cost, grief's in control… and I am lost," she spoke in a faltering tone.

"Princess?"

The voice had left but another had spoken. In normal circumstances and everyday life it would have startled her, but Sarah as she normally existed was not there. Her grief held no fear within it, just nothingness.

"I'm not Princess," she replied flatly.

"Sorry I thought… " Ty tried to add.

"She left as you slept," Sarah quickly interrupted. "She walked away when you fell asleep, in that direction," waving a hand in the general direction of the forest.

Ty followed her movement looking for signs of something, an essence, that may have remained, but there was nothing, "So she has gone again, as soon as I wake up, she has gone," he said solemnly, the tone of his words matching the feelings of his heart.

"Everyone goes, they all leave," Sarah added simply, staring down into the waters which drifted effortlessly under her gaze.

Ty had remained lying down but started to lift his head, his body following, "But she will return," he said as he finally got to his feet and stood up.

Sarah lifted her eyes from the water and turned her head so she could face Ty.

"Once there gone, that's it. No one ever returns," her eyes blank and lifeless as her words. "Not even the ones who leave before they should, just to save someone else return."

She held Ty's gaze for a time before returning her eyes to the water, drawn to its dance and movement, like a moth to a flame.

Ty stood and looked at Sarah and felt her words sweep across his body. They bought a sense of uneasiness and dread coupled with the twin cloaks of despair and loneliness which made him shiver and look longingly at the blanket wrapped around her shoulder. He felt he should say something but sensed that whatever he did would not be welcome. He stayed still for a moment and then dared to move over towards the stream both to drink and also to splash water across his face to help him wake up. He moved slowly not wishing to disturb what already seemed a fragile part of whatever was going on with Sarah.

Sarah's head remained still but she followed Ty with her eyes, without him knowing, seeing him move closer to the water's edge. Her senses heightened, sinews of anxiety rising inside her body. It seemed as if every nerve ending and muscle within her went on edge and she felt fear grab her beating heart with both hands.

Ty had got to the water's edge and squatted down to get easy access to its clear and refreshing charms and scooped two or three big handfuls up into his mouth, savouring each one as if it was the first. He looked out across the water and then at the changing sky. The dawn was rising in its pace, the textures of night retreating under its subtle gaze. He felt a need to wash fully and swim in the crystal-clear waters in front of him which reflected back the colours and shapes of the surrounding area.

He stood up and took a deep breath and dived into the water, deep and long.

Sarah was up and on her feet in an instance, dropping the blanket from her shoulders. She half scrambled and half fell down off the rock onto the grass and she threw herself into the water,

"No. No. No. What are you doing, don't go in, don't go in, get out, get out, come back, come back to me," she shouted and screamed as she moved.

She thrashed around in the shallows of the water and dived down trying to find Ty who for a while was gone and lost from sight. Sarah was crying and sobbing as she continued her frenetic search for him. She got lost in who or what her search was for – Tony, River, her dad, and Ty or maybe even her faith.

She stood in the water, her feet searching for solid footing underneath and screamed, "No, why would you do this. Why?" her head turning towards the heavens as she did.

Ty resurfaced about twenty yards from where Sarah stood screaming at the sky above. The instance his head broke the surface of the water he was moving towards her using the current to take him quickly to her. She was still screaming and smashing at the water with the palms of her hands as she did. The sound carried across both the stream and the lake and hit the hillsides on the other side and bounced back with increased intensity.

Ty got to Sarah and reached out to grab at her just as her feelings started to draw her under into the dark waters below the surface. She was still screaming and sobbing hysterically. He pulled her up and moved towards the bank, holding her close to him, the full weight of her exhausted body resting against him as he made short work of the distance to the bank. He climbed up and carried her towards the rock and looked around for the blankets to try and wrap around Sarah's shivering form. She was still crying and although she was aware of someone holding her she was not sure who it was. All she knew was that she could not carry on anymore and that this grief had beaten her and all the fight had left her body. Her soul seemingly turned inside out and then back again within that fight.

Ty lay her down on the grass and briefly left her to collect up both blankets. He returned and sat next to her, pulling her head up and across his knees as he attempted to cover her with as much of the blankets as he could. Sarah's eyes were closed and her breathing shallow. Her tears had slowed considerably since she had been bought from the water but they remained close to the edge. Ty pulled her up and held her firmly in his arms, her head resting on his chest as he smoothed her matted hair and stroked it as she continued to lay there, grateful for the warmth and comfort he was giving to her.

She may have felt comforted but for Ty it simply felt painful. He knew he had to do what he could to help and support and be there. Something told him to stay and be there for the girl who was broken and adrift. He felt his heart being torn into different directions.

Ty knew he had to stay but for him there was only one person he wanted close to him and she was not there. As he held Sarah to his chest his heart and soul called out into the air – one word cried out, Princess.

His words reached out into the unknown, into the night, He got no reply back.

CHAPTER 5

Emptiness sits alone, in a crowded room...

Sarah fell asleep. Her grief, the physical tiredness bought on by it and also her search in the cold waters for Ty had left her emotionally and physically spent. Ty felt her breath slow and let her lay there for a short while before he slowly lifted her head and moved out from beneath her. He rested her head gently on the soft grass and pulled the blankets up close to keep her warm. He paused for a moment and looked at her lying there and could see that whatever had happened to bring on her sleep it was painful and full of so much anguish and despair.

He got up and walked towards the water's edge once again. The sky had continued to change as he had comforted Sarah and the clouds, which sat within in drifted slowly by on a breeze, which was gentle and warm. Their fluffy white shapes chased each other across the sky and Ty watched them pass by with interest but also a semblance of indifference. He looked back quickly to check on Sarah, who lay sleeping still, and wandered around the sides of the rock where he had first seen her. She had been pre-occupied by the waters running beneath and he decided to get up on the rock and see what it was that held her attention there.

He swiftly climbed up its glassy face and found himself ten feet above the ground looking out at an expanse and view which was beautiful in the least, and captivating at its extreme. He stood there silently taking in the colours, shapes and sounds of what was there and felt peace move inside his heart to a place he knew well. It was the place he often went with Princess. She bought stillness to his heart which he found hard to find anywhere else. It was a simplicity that was mixed when he was with her. It also held a desire and passion which made it race and beat twice as fast whenever he held her. The contrast never failed to amaze him that one person could do that to him. When he lay with her nothing else mattered, all thoughts and worries disappeared and he was present for only one thing, to be with her. At this moment though he sighed, deep within him, her absence stirred regret and pain and he looked down and away from the beauty, which had previously lifted him.

As Ty looked down he found, close by a book. It was battered and torn lying as if casually dropped or discarded by someone in a hurry to be rid of it. He bent down and picked it up examining the outside with his hands, the imperfections feeling like cuts across the fairest skin. He turned it over and found the reverse the same and looked casually over at Sarah to check she was still sleeping, sitting down as he finished. Ty was curious as to what was inside but also felt that he shouldn't open the cover and read through the pages inside. From somewhere inside him a voice told him to look whilst another told him not to. Two voices which battled against each other until his curiosity won through and he opened the book to the pages inside.

What he found was very much not what he expected. Across the pages he found the same as Sarah had. Words, sentences and ramblings – some in order and written neatly others scrawled as if the pain behind them had actually held the pen and wrote in a style which showed what was behind the words – experience which had heartache underpinning it all, the current that drove the words written. The word current came to Ty's mind and he looked down into the waters and watched them spiral and twist beneath his gaze, patterns coming and going as he did. He bought his focus back to the book and continued to move from page to page, reading the words out in a silent whisper to himself as he did.

"All rhyme and reason, has flown this nest... He longs for love, and fills with hate, hopes for serenity but it's much too late... nice place to die, where lake meets the sky... Emptiness sits; empty, in a crowded room, and feels, really feels, there is no end to the void evoked, to which it runs and contemplates the... EMPTINESS."

Ty stopped reading and let his thoughts run across the feeling now rising from his chest. The word emptiness had struck a chord deep within him and he felt himself shrinking as he looked out from the pages to the lake, which seemed so vast and endless now. The waters there seemed to his fearful heart full up with everything; freedom, opportunities, possibilities, love and beauty whilst the waters of his soul trickled with what had been written, emptiness. He felt empty without her, without purpose or reason, and little hope in moving beyond those feelings. For a moment he sat and reflected on his life outside the dreams and outside of laying with her and tears began to flow, falling from his cheek onto his chest. A chest which felt so empty without her head resting across it. The sweet smell of her hair filling his senses, leaving him as it always did intoxicated. He sat crying for what seemed an eternity, an age, before they ran dry and he wiped away what was left of their journey and returned his attention to the book.

As he flicked slowly through the pages the themes and words continued in the same way. All of them seemed to hold little faith and no passage of hope in the existence of anything beyond the worst things. The despair, isolation, sadness, loneliness and desperation at and for others. He continued to read, again whispering as he did, "confused messages, from a soul that's dead... What is

God's will, where is my will? No-one cares, no-one shares... a princess will come from his every dream, searching... Words they mean nothing at all... actions, looks, thoughts in the mind, they mean everything... they are everything... Sometimes it feels hard, to take a breath in as if the very act is too much... I am worth nothing, I have no value."

Ty stopped suddenly and scanned back over the pages as his heart caught up with what he had just read. He found the words that his heart had alerted him to, "A princess will come from his every dream... searching."

He read the words again and jumped to his feet. From his recent memory came the words that Sarah had said and what she had seen. She said she had seen Princess. Sarah said that Princess had been there right in the spot where he had been sleeping. Princess had been by his side. If this was true and what Sarah had seen been reality then it meant only one thing. Princess was not bound by the confines of a dream of just his. She was real, she had been there and Sarah had seen her also. This and the words in the book meant that whoever wrote them had seen or knew of her too. It was not all a dream or a flight into fantasy; she was real and existed outside his dreams and had been there just a short while ago. She was not a figment of his imagination or simply a dream anymore and only one thing existed in his head and heart. He must find her.

Ty jumped down from the rock and ran towards the place at the edge of the clearing where the forest started. This was the direction that Sarah had pointed towards that Princess had last been seen going. He moved into the trees, woken from their night's sleep by the shouting of her name as he searched amongst the dense canopy and the cover it exerted on the floor of the forest. He continued to shout as he moved from one place to another in his frantic search for her. Nothing answered back, nothing moved except the branches of the trees above in the gentle dance of the morning breeze. The sun came through the branches in spaces and lit up the flowers, which grew widely here and there, their colours throwing out smiles to any who could see them. Ty was unaware of them, blind to everything else apart from his desire to find her. His mind and thoughts on nothing else except the search for the girl of his dreams.

His shouts had been loud and widespread and alerted and woke anything that was still asleep or dozing, Sarah being one of those. She was walking towards the forest, blankets wrapped around her slender frame as she did all the while hearing the sounds of Ty's calls which came from deep among the trees. She didn't call out just listened until eventually he returned battered and blood stained from where branches and thorns had pierced and cut his skin.

"What is it? Who are you shouting for," she said quickly as he returned.

"Princess. You said she was here, that you saw her?" he replied distracted and turning around back towards the forest and the forefront of his mind.

"Yes I saw a woman, if that's her name then yes, I saw Princess. What is the big deal?"

Ty stopped and turned towards her, pausing to catch his breath as he did, "Princess is someone I know only from my dreams, all of my dreams," he paused to let it sink in, "if you saw her then she is not just a dream, is she?"

Sarah looked at him, bloody and obviously lost and distracted, somewhere else, "No obviously not. I'm sorry I didn't know that until now, otherwise I would have said something to you... sorry what is your name?"

"Ty, my name is Ty."

"Ok Ty, I'm Sarah by the way," she added in the event he was interested which at this time seemed a remote possibility.

From somewhere inside him Ty suddenly felt normality return smashing him in the face. He remembered that before he had read the book Sarah had been sleeping. He must have woken her and he felt troubled by this, "Sorry, you were asleep. I woke you didn't I?"

"Yes but no matter, I wasn't sleeping deeply," Sarah said looking around her at the forest, her mind captured and held by the colours shining from it fleetingly.

"I'm sorry for that, I just was thrown. I was sitting on the rock reading a book I found there and came across something which said Princess would come from a dream searching and reminded me that you had seen her. I didn't even recognise that when you said it, but the book did."

Sarah looked at the book, which Ty held in his hand and knew straight away whose book it was and some of what was inside. The grief and despair, which had been held and numbed by sleep and her rude awaking, came back and she felt the heaviness of both of them on her shoulders. Ty saw her change in front of his eyes.

"What is it Sarah?" he asked with eyes full of concern.

Sarah didn't speak to begin with but waited, trying to compose the emotions welling up inside, "I've seen that book and I met the person who wrote what's in it," she paused. "I also met someone else who knew that person."

"Where did you meet them? Here? Where are they now?" Ty said watching her movements and the slowness that was captured in them.

Sarah started to walk away without answering. She walked back to where she had been sleeping and Ty followed her keeping a distance which he felt inside was what she needed.

She sat down and after a time began to speak, "I met them here yesterday separately, at different times. One called Tony whose book it is and the other a child called River who appeared after Tony had…"

she couldn't finish the sentence immediately, her emotions rising.

Eventually she felt able to speak again, "After Tony had jumped into the water and disappeared. River came and he stayed for a while and then he…" the sentence catching in her throat as grief grabbed at the words about to be spoken, pulling them back and leaving her speechless.

Ty both saw and felt her pain. He guessed the rest but allowed time before he added the words which she was unable or unwilling to say, "He jumped also and disappeared," whispered as quietly as he could manage but loud enough for Sarah to hear.

She looked up at him with tears flowing, pain in her eyes and simply nodded. She wanted to be alone earlier but Ty being here now certainly helped just simply by sharing it a small slither of grief had been quietened for a while.

Ty bent down next to her and held the book out towards her, "Here you have it back, you found it."

Sarah wanted so much just to grab it from Ty's hand and throw it into the waters where Tony and River had jumped. She wanted it to be gone in the hope that she would forget without anything physical there to remind her. But something held her and she reached out and took it gently, nodding her acceptance and appreciation towards Ty.

"So what are you going to do now about Princess then?"

Ty was not expecting the question said so flatly, so plainly or so quickly. He hadn't really given it a thought until now after being lost in Sarah's short and painful story. The name from Sarah's lips bought her back to his heart and what lay inside it.

"I have to go and find her. I can't rest now that I know she is here somewhere. But I am also puzzled?"

"Why?"

"Because she left. If she wants to be here and with me just as much and it's not a dream why leave. I don't understand that part?"

Sarah understood his thoughts but spoke from what she had recently witnessed, "She must have her reasons. The main thing is that she came and that she will come back. Sometimes people have to do their own thing which takes them away for a while. They are not measured by that but by their capacity to return. As long as they come back and you know there coming back then that is the most important part to hold onto."

"How do you know she is coming back, Sarah?"

For the first time in the last few hours something entered into Sarah's heart, softening it as it did, her face showing this outwardly.

"Because I saw how she looked at you Ty before she left. Believe me she will be back. As much as I can or anyone can, I promise she will return to you."

Ty was lifted and hope returned. He looked away from Sarah and out across the waters, to the sky and the hills in the distance and the mountains which dwarfed even those hills. The morning was coming faster now, nearly upon them and with it the suns warmth permeated the dark and coldness of the things which had passed and their hearts. His mind was made up, his heart and soul set.

"I need to search for her. My heart tells me that I have to and if we are to be together then it will not be here in this place. I have to find her."

Sarah knew Ty was right but the thought of being left alone with the feelings running inside, in this place was too much that she could handle.

"I will come with you. If that's OK?"

Ty was pleased that she had said it. He knew he had to try and find Princess but leaving Sarah was something he did not want to do, so her words were welcome and much needed at that time.

"Sarah, I think that its meant to be for now, you and me together, for whatever reason."

They spoke no more but turned their attention to moving and moving fast. Sarah stood up quickly and gathered up the bag and blankets whilst Ty collected his belongings, which had been in the same place since he had met Princess. With a last look around them and with the heaviness already starting to lift through they turned and took their first steps into the forest.

They began the search for Princess.

CHAPTER 6

Nothing hurts more than an invisible wound…

Tony sat in the corner of the room. His knees pulled up tight to his chest with his head resting forward on them. He had been in that position for hours, days, weeks; maybe even eternity. It was hard to tell or know exactly how long. The room which he had arrived in was painted only one colour, white. That colour was almost all gone now, taken up by the black markings of words and pictures which had grown in volume and intensity in the time he had been there. The floor was a cold concrete base on which he could find no comfort and certainly no warmth. It was icy to the touch and the room empty of anything except him sitting in the corner. No furniture and no comfort and a voice inside his head which gave him no rest. A voice which mocked, taunted and whispered depending on the level and ferocity of its assault. It manipulated and pulled at the strings of his heart offering solace and comfort then pulling it away as quick as it had been offered or given. The one small window which had first lifted his heart continued to show the same scene outside. It was a window out onto a barren and desolate wasteland. A place where nothing lived or moved or could be seen except a single tree. The tree was as empty as the earth that held its roots. The branches withered and wasted with every breath of the air outside, as if that air itself was poisoned. There was no point looking out. Tony had come to understand that it offered no comfort or release. He had to look inside and that view was worse but it was all he had.

When Tony jumped into the water he thought that would be it, instant relief, and he would be lost – gone and forgotten. But that idea and desire even was quickly smashed and proved to be untrue. What followed was hours of hell after the initial impact which knocked him out. After that he found himself falling, spinning, and twisting, out of control as he fell through the icy waters into the deep and darkest depths beneath. When he sat on the rock every day and looked into the water he thought he could always see the bottom, shimmering away beneath the surface, maybe ten metres below. The jump itself had been another four or five metres and he felt that at the least he would hit his head on another rock beneath the surface and that would be it – gone and forgotten.

When he did wake from unconsciousness, Tony found himself sinking further and further beyond where he thought the bottom was and then even further. His whole body felt under pressure. A force so great that he felt the air sucked out of his lungs as his head seemed to shrink in size as the water got deeper and heavier. He continued to fall beyond thought, time and even memory of the world outside. As he fell the story, the journey of his life, twisted and turned with him as he fell to an end which he had no knowledge of. He had written that at times he had been in love with death, but if this was it then that love was short lived as the pressure increased and the shock took over. He tried to close his eyes to help stem the thoughts going through his head but he could not focus, all of that was lost. He had jumped and nothing could turn the clock back on that now. Once he took that step he had set in motion a sequence of events of which he was no longer in control. He had often spoken about powerlessness and the real meaning of it, spoken and written so much about it. He now knew what it meant and to feel its full impact. No control, no influence on what happens next and no knowledge of the ending. He did not know how long he had been falling out of control except that the water got darker and the pressure inside his head increased to such a point that he fainted, and for a time he knew nothing else.

He awoke cold and wet lying face down on a concrete floor. His head ached, his limbs felt battered and his heart was empty, nothingness had re-doubled its attack since he jumped and now he felt its full force. He attempted to lift his head but there was no energy and no life in any movement. His eyes were open but no life existed within them either. He could see and feel the floor but little else. He couldn't feel his arms or legs but felt by instinct they were still there. Then he heard it, something he knew so well, a voice which attacked him with the bitterness and contempt which he had long lived with.

"So you jumped, after all this time, you jumped. Came to see what had captivated and held you for so long. You stared at me and I stared back and you thought why not. You have no idea what I am capable of."

In just one single sentence Tony knew. He should never have jumped. He thought he knew pain but didn't, until now. He had said that nothing hurt more than an invisible wound. The wounds he had were numerous but not invisible once he wrote about them. This one would be totally invisible as there was no going back, this wound would remain unspoken about and unresolved. Tony did feel some kind of life coming back into his limbs and he managed to lift his head from the floor and look around more. However this did not help. All he saw was one small window on a wall which was painted white along with the other four walls. There was nothing else in the room, just him and the four walls and a voice which he knew was there to torture him. This was the Abyss that he had dreamt up – alone, cast out and blankness.

"What does lie within? Is it friend or monster? A wolf in waiting ready to lead me, like a child, to the edge, the Abyss," the voice came back and trampled through his brain, *"remember those words do you?"*

Tony remembered them, he wrote them, and many more similar to them. He had been sitting as normal on the rock and it was the first day that he had met River. The word River bought sharp pains to the side of his chest, stabbing pains, through his very heart.

"That name is not known here, it is gone, as he has gone. No memory of him here for you," the voice was back taunting now, whispering in dulcet tones, *"You left him alone to who knows to what fate, when you jumped."*

This had pretty much been the same story minute after minute, day after long endless day, until the point that Tony sat in the corner with his knees up to his chest. There was no concept of time in this place. No change in light, no sounds from the bird's dawn chorus, nothing changed. Tony had come to understand that this was an eternity without change in it. The worse thing that he had to live with though was that it was an abyss of his making and the thoughts of his demented mind and ravaged soul. An eternity in a room with no colour and light. No smell or sounds and only the consistent pain which reached its hand into his chest and held onto his beating heart. He had been in a room like this before in the darkest of his days and it was the abyss to him then and he had named it that. Now when he could no longer hold out it had become that living hell transported to another dimension and sphere. He had become a reflection of it and worse, he had become an extension of it.

The voice started up again, it had been silent for a while, "Do you feel like your imploding, from inside to out. Like a tin can, crushed by the force inside. A wound, invisible to the eye, imprisons body and soul. Not just here, not just now but for all eternity... I wonder how long an eternity feels like," the last *words said with a finality that made Tony lift his head.*

When he did lift his head he saw black markings start to appear on the wall opposite. At first they were faint but grew in size and clarity as he watched. His eyes narrowed and he tried to work out what they were, what was appearing, but his eyes failed him and he simply stared as the markings continued to come in and out of focus. He thought he could be hallucinating and closed them briefly before opening them again, this time there was no mistake as to what they said.

I am a Prince
Who would be King?
A man in waiting
I am a God
And I know everything
All there is to know
And much best not to
Remember.

For Tony, the words seemed familiar although he couldn't quite place them. They touched something inside of him that he had a sense of, but not quite the feel. As if he connected to them personally but then again possibly not. They were a part of him or maybe just a part of someone else he may have known, at some point.

"Familiar to you, that's what you're thinking. Or is that my thoughts that are there, we are twin brothers. Try and connect them, try and remember them if you can. But most of all remember this," the voice said before more writing appeared under what was there.

There's no faith in this hope
No point to this amen.

The words had the effect that was intended, what they had been written for. Two lines which grabbed Tony and shook him to the centre of his core as the room began to close in. He remembered now where he had seen those two lines, what they had meant and where they had lead him to. Tony dissolved and slumped to the floor, knowing now there was no going back and even crawling into a ball could not save him from that again. He screamed out in anguish. He was right back to the time and place when he had lost all sense of reality and all sense of purpose and he started to rock.

The pain had simply just started.

CHAPTER 7

Dazed by your face...

Princess had not wanted to walk away from him but she knew that there was something she had to do, somewhere else that she had to be. Her heart was heavy but not in a way which contained sadness or longing. She knew that she and Ty would be reunited somewhere along each other's path but that time was not now. As she walked away her step was light and her heart echoed this. It was always the same whenever she met with him. She would leave with a feeling of contentment and peace which stayed with her. Her heartbeat slower than anyone else's as it was, it was a gift given to her, but after seeing him it slowed to such a rate that alongside it the world slowed also to its soft and soothing beat.

She walked away into the forest, the light dim and shadows lurking, but it held no fear for her. She never walked alone and had spirits, guides and other angels which always matched her step with step. She moved with such grace and beauty that the grass beneath hardly felt the impression of her passing. The only sign that she had been there was a renewing of colour and depth in anything that she walked across. She moved as if she was dancing with nature, a long slow graceful dance, like two lovers meeting for the first time. Her gentle touch and nature had always been the thing that others noticed about her at a first meeting. She had always possessed that gift even as a small child when she could bring peace to the most crowded of situations. She would walk into a room and the noise levels would lessen, she often thought it was because others were speaking about her. However she learnt as she grew up that it was a unique part of her personality and her presence stilled the parts of others that they could not still alone. She had watched her mother have the same impact and when they walked into a room together it was like watching two angels floating through the doors of heaven. The name Princess sat easily on her slender shoulders and she grew to love it along with her life.

As she moved easily through the forest she looked, sensed and saw glimpses of her spirits and guides as they ran ahead of her on the trail. They ran, they floated and some simply walked next to her as she made her way. They usually kept themselves hidden but today they remained in her vision, to help ease her mind and that of the person she was going to see. She may not have shown it but they sensed a change in the rhythms of her heart. They felt the uneasiness and dread in each of her steps towards her destination and a slowing of her pace in getting there. Anyone else would not have seen it and been oblivious but they knew every movement of her body, every change in her breath and the increased ripples of her beating heart. Princess did not show fear normally but it was there today as her eyes narrowed in pain at the thought of where she was going and she longed for a gentle touch and some re-assurance.

"Princess, why do you worry? Life is stronger than you think," a gentle soothing voice came from next to her, a voice she knew so well and longed for every day.

"I knew you would come, you always do just when I need you," she replied.

Her heart felt the touch and feel of her mother on its surface.

"You knew but doubted at the same time," her mother said before laughing. Her laugh climbing up, reaching out into the forests canopy, ruffling its hair as it did.

Princess laughed with her but at the same time did not look across at her. She didn't need to see her Mother to be able to picture her. It was an image that she held inside her heart since her first breathe and she would never lose it. A Mother's gift to a child. They walked for a while in silence, as they often did, no need for words, no need for conversations out loud as their connection lay deeper in the streams of consciousness, which were denied to others. The new day's sun flickered and played through the branches of the trees round which they walked. There were no paths that lead them to their destination just a way, a way covered with love and care and unselfish devotion to heal the pain of others. Even the flowers seemed to bend towards their coming, moving away from the sun's eyes to the warmth of their way.

"Is there any reason that I can give for why this doesn't have to happen," Princess said after they had been walking for some time.

"I'm sure there are many that you could give, but none are valid here. Fate, destiny, a journey. Whichever way it's put it's not yours to decide a reason for another not to do something," her mother said in response.

"I can make that reason. I can change this and stop it," she replied instantly, before adding, "Or go myself."

Her mother stopped walking and stood still looking up as two eagles soared high above their heads before speaking directly at her, "Or go yourself?"

"What would be so wrong with that, I've done it before remember," Princess said as she carried on walking, not wanting to stop and wait for her mother.

"Yes you did but this is different. Being allowed to do it once does not make it possible to do it again, you know that," her mother said as she started walking again following the exact path that Princess had taken.

"I can save anyone," Princess said turning to face her mother for the first time.

Her mother continued walking slowly up to where Princess had stopped to face her. She came close and reached out to touch her face with a single hand. Princess pulled away, looking down as she did.

"You can't save anyone who has gone too far or someone who doesn't want to be saved. All of us must find the desire inside ourselves to save ourselves from anything. We must choose it and not others. This is something else that you know also.

Her mother spoke slowly so that Princess could take in every part of what she said. As she did she lifted her face back up and found Princess was crying. She reached out and held her, letting Princess dissolve totally into her arms.

Even her mother had misjudged the intensity and emotions which had been stirred up inside Princess. She did not fully understand that what was being asked and for Princess it was the hardest thing she ever had to do. She was being asked to let someone go where she could not go herself and that was alien to her. She was being asked to let someone go knowing what they would go through and she was unable to go instead of or with. They would be alone to face what was ahead of them. Princess could not understand how things how been allowed to come to this point. In the end it was her mother who read her feelings and broke the silence between them.

"My dear child, you feel too much for others without regard for what it does to you. Everyone is stronger than you think. Sometimes things happen which cannot be explained and seem unnatural and at odds against all that you are. It is life. It is nature and it is death. It is the will of something so much greater than you. The world cannot be shaped by your touch all the time. Letting go is hard but in letting go other things are found."

Princess pulled away, wiping her tear-stained cheeks as she did, anger flickering across her face and in her eyes. "Other things, other things. You know where this will lead; you know what they will go through. They will not recover."

"They will recover and they will be stronger. Each of us has to go through stages and parts of our life when the road is narrow and the way ahead masked by uncertainty. You know this better than most Princess," her mother said before adding, "never doubt the strength which lies beneath all of us, what we know?"

Princess looked at her for a moment and was calmed for a while before she answered, "We don't know anything, we don't know anything about someone else."

Her mother's face softened even more, any lines disappearing with it as she spoke again.

"We have our experience which tells us, that come what may we will be ok, that we will survive and move on. We are never given anything more than we can cope with in a day, your experience tells you this and reminds you. That we are all looked after by something which cannot be explained through books or in classrooms. It is something we feel when we are still when we let our hearts beat in rhythm to the sounds and breaths of the world. We feel peace and we see beauty and we just know that something is there. Something holds us when we cannot hold ourselves and keeps us safe."

Princess closed her eyes, letting the words and her Mother sooth her. When she opened them, her Mother was gone, as Princess knew she would be.

Despite her need to continue the argument, Princess knew that her mother was right. When she was a child she had terrible fights with her sisters which would leave her alone and isolated and she would cry through the frustration of it all. But inside of her even at those times she found a place to be herself and to have her emotions without striking out against others and more so herself. A place where she felt comforted and held and which belonged only to her. She also knew, which comforted her most, that the person she was going to see also had this, even more than anyone else she had met. It was something she saw in them at their first meeting and it was a common bond which joined their hearts, even their souls. It was also the reason why she was being asked to go and do what was needed. The person trusted her, they loved her, and no one else would be able to offer and give what Princess would give.

Someone had said that to Princess once, "She was a gift that kept on giving."

Her mother was still standing opposite her, her eyes sparkling from the light of the sun above, and she moved forward to cup Princess's cheek with one hand, "When you was a child I used to watch you sleep, every night, dazed by your face. I thought that you were so beautiful and that really I had only borrowed you."

Princess's face changed and she laughed, "Borrowed me?"

Her mother laughed and learned forward to kiss her on the cheek and whisper in her ear, "Yes borrowed from God. Your gentleness and compassion made me believe you came from God."

And then she was gone, as Princess knew she would go.

She closed her eyes and willed her back, just for another minute, just another kiss. But it was pointless; she knew that for now she had gone. She also knew that she had nearly reached the end of her journey and that around the next bend she would find what she came for. Her breathing increased and her heart missed a beat as she thought of what she had to do and how she would have to let go. It was the hardest thing that she had ever been given to do and she knew that she would have to hide what she felt deep inside. If she didn't the other person would see it and all would be lost. She opened her eyes and walked around the bend treading softly so as not to give away her coming.

She slowly made her way forward and stopped next to a tree which sat on the bend. She had seen him sitting at the bank of a small stream which made its way through a small set of rocks, where they had first met. Every time she saw him she always had to do it, watch him for a while without him knowing. He was so beautiful and such a part of everything he touched and felt. There was nothing which did not seem to come easily to him, running, walking, laughing and crying, he did them all with such naturalness and little sense of it not being the right thing to do. She knew he would be here and so did he.

He sat with his boots off and his small legs dangling in the cold waters as it slipped slowly by, his feet submerged under the water. He was laughing and kept pulling a leg at a time up and then quickly putting it back in to the water. Princess had stopped, standing there watching him, peace and a sense of innocence running through her veins. She felt it every time they were together, only Ty made her feel a similar way, but this was different.

"The fish they keep nibbling my toes," laughter punctuating every word. "Come on, Princes,s put your feet in, it's so funny." He finished what he was saying and turned round to face her.

She dissolved instantly, her heart broken. She sighed and wept inside, but stepped forward.

"Hello, River, it's so nice to see you again."

CHAPTER 8

Does time change me, or do I change with time...

Ty and Sarah left the surroundings of the rock and the streams with a firm stride and a sense of purpose, both for different reasons. Ty was eager to search far and wide, if necessary, for Princess whilst Sarah just wanted to get as far away as possible from a place where grief had consumed her. The sun was high in the sky and its warmth stretched between the trees and illuminated the way. That is if they had a path to keep to or knew the way. It seemed at times they were just walking for the sake of walking and the general feeling that at least they were doing something, anything, to forget about their twin feelings of longing and despair.

The forest was dense in places with tree after tree, next to each other, almost on top of each other and a clear path could not be seen for the most part. They picked their way through the forest and Ty at times reached back to check Sarah was ok and put out a hand of help or an arm of comfort if she showed signs of stumbling. Sarah took his hand where she needed to but felt little comfort in its physical touch, which failed to pierce the sense of deep emotions she walked with. Her heart was heavy and at times it seemed to weigh her down as if she was carrying a 50 stone weight in a backpack along with her.

The whole walk and the areas it went through were covered with intense colour and natural beauty, but Sarah's eyes remained closed and hidden to anything else. She could only picture River hitting the water and her search for him under the surface, her unsuccessful search for him. At times she walked crying softly to herself and Ty could hear her behind him. He was at a lost what to do but felt any word or asking if she wanted to stop for a while would not be welcome. He just adjusted his pace to try and take into account her state of mind and the tiredness that he knew grief bought.

They had just succeeded in getting through a particular dense area of forest where the tress sat tightly together when they unexpectedly came upon an area where there were no trees at all. In front of them was an area of grass or more so a meadow, which was lush and coloured a dark vivid green by the rain, which must have fallen there overnight. The heat of the sun had burned the rain from the meadow but the colour still remained and it was a welcome sight to both of them after the intense and suffocating nature of forest they had just come through. It seemed the perfect time, to Ty, to rest and look around and maybe decide on a joint course of both action and direction. He had no idea where he was going, it just felt better to be on the move in any direction. His experience of Princess and the faith he had in her gave him the general sense that it was the right thing to be doing, moving along.

"How're you doing, Sarah? I think maybe it's time we found a place to just stop for a while," Ty said half-looking behind him at Sarah.

It was the first words spoken between them in over an hour and the sound of them seemed to awaken Sarah from a walking sleep. She lifted her head up, sheltering her eyes from the bright sun.

"I think that would be a good idea, somewhere out of the sun."

Ty looked around and half way up the meadow there sat one tree, alone, almost as if it had been made for them to rest at in the shade, with branches hanging out low and wide across the meadow,

"I think there is as good as spot as any," he said pointing up the slight slope towards the tree. Sarah nodded her agreement and they made their way slowly up the hill until they half collapsed under the trees welcome arms.

They both had water they had collected from the banks of the stream before they had left and drank long and fast from their own bottles. They finished and sat there, both of them with their backs leaning against the main trunk of the tree, looking out in different directions across the meadow. Ty closed his eyes and pictured Princess walking towards him and reaching down to take his hand as she softly bent over to kiss him.

Sarah's thoughts were somewhere else, but she felt a shift in the air around them and glanced over at Ty, guessing where he was at that moment.

She thought before she spoke, finding the words hard as they tumbled out, "It must be nice picturing something, or someone, so comforting?"

Ty came back from where he was, and spoke but with eyes still closed, "It's a nice picture yes, but not something that has come easily to me. It's taken time and its only now that I know she is here and not just my imagination or a dream that I can actually picture her. Until this moment I could never remember what she looked like once I was awake."

Sarah was surprised by this but tried not to show the fact, "It must be nice knowing that she is there for you, wherever that may be."

"It is now after reading the book and you saying she was there. Until then it was not pleasant all the time. The only thing good about each day was sleep and her in my dreams."

"Do you love her?" Sarah asked flatly and without any real

emotion, as she continued to look out away from where they sat.

Ty did not respond straight away, it was some time before he said anything at all, "I think the word love is the one word I would not use to describe what I feel for her."

Sarah felt the potency of what he said and the feeling of intensity behind it, "What is wrong with the word love?"

Ty paused again before half-turning to Sarah, waiting until she looked at him also, before he spoke.

"It's just one word, with four letters and goes nowhere near being able to describe how I feel about her, or what it feels like to be with her."

Sarah was intrigued now and turned herself more towards Ty. She had used the word love so much over her life and used it in so many different settings. For her it was enough but now Ty was saying it wasn't enough, not even close, and she was interested.

"Why is love not good enough then?"

Ty turned himself fully towards her before speaking, the importance not lost on him of what was being asked.

"Eskimos have fifty words for snow, fifty words for snow alone. Do you know why?"

Sarah looked at him, without emotion, before answering, "No idea."

Ty continued, "They have fifty words for it because in their life it is so important, its life and death, safe or unsafe – eating or not eating. They have fifty words to describe its depth, the type of snow, its feel and texture, the colour. They have fifty words for snow. We have one for love, which is meant to describe a set of emotions that I would struggle to pin down into one word for Princess. Many easily say the word love and it brings heartache and joy in equal measure but I would never say that I love Princess. So in short the answer is no, I don't love her."

Sarah listened to Ty and could understand where he was coming from. She loved her father and knew what that meant. Equally she had said many times that she loved swimming and going shopping but the feelings were totally different to what she felt for her father.

"So love is a word thrown around which has lost its meaning because it says a lot without really meaning anything."

Ty responded instantly, "Love for me is more of an action than a word. I can say a lot but if I don't then act in that way what is the point in saying anything at all. When I think of Princess and try and describe her I could use many words, passion, grace, beauty, stillness, elegance, sweet even, peacefulness, serenity, enlightened even. All words which could give a sense of her but it's to be with her that really is the key."

Sarah liked the way he spoke about Princess, there was emotion and passion itself behind his words, but it was his eyes which showed how he felt, alive yet at peace, full but hungry, "What is it like to be with her, to hold her then?" she asked.

Again Ty paused before he spoke, and when he did, it was passion which was delivered with a whispered voice, "Around her and holding her I can feel my heart soften, as if she had reached inside and stilled it herself, not with touch but through her just being there. When she lies on my chest and I hold her hair in my hands it feels like I am holding the streams of time, alive and filled with the most intense emotions, each one containing the radiance of her smile and the beauty of her soul."

Sarah liked how he said that and used different ways to talk about a girl she had only seen in the shadows one night, but felt like she knew her already and leaned back against the tree, "Keep talking about you and what she does for you, it's relaxing to hear."

Ty saw her lean back, and knew it was providing some form of relief for her, "I hold her hand in mine and slowly let it go, playing with each finger, dancing and moving slowly from one to another sometimes. I look and watch them playing with each other, connected to us, but also disconnected as if they were currents of electricity trying to find a point to ignite. She ignites something inside of me, which cannot be denied, my heart is drawn towards hers, like magnets in a field of dreams."

"And now that's in a field of reality. Even better than a dream," Sarah responded, eyes still closed.

Ty was at peace. Either being with or talking about Princess always bought that. Something inside which could never be bought or sought, it came as a gift when it did but it could never be forced or achieved through any means if it was unnatural. After a while he spoke again, "Sarah, what are you searching for?"

Sarah's heart froze inside and the feeling of ease slipped away as quickly as it had come and she felt herself set on edge. It was not that she felt anger towards Ty but maybe just wanted relief for a little bit longer before having to go back to the grief.

"Relief and answers to why River went into the water. It's not even about Tony it's about River. I spent hardly any time with him but there was something else there."

Ty listened, happy that Sarah had felt able to say something about what she felt, "You felt something else between you," he replied. He himself was searching for the meaning behind her words.

"Yes something else which was there. I can't put my finger on it but there is something else there which at the moment I cannot link. As if I know him and he knows me. In fact I am certain he knows where we fit or have met before but I am not. I have seen his eyes and his smile but cannot pin it down. It's bugging me in truth. He also said something through his eyes when we were together which I cannot work out."

"What?"

"Does time change me, or do I change with time. I don't know if he was talking about himself or asking me?" Sarah responded.

Ty was interested by this and the connection that Sarah had felt although she was still unsure of what it was, "It's an interesting thought but also that you say he knows where you have crossed before. That would say that there is a reason for what has happened and you coming together, it's part of a bigger plan or picture maybe. This is a good thing."

Sarah was for a moment gripped by the colour red, anger, "A plan, what kind of plan would let him do that? How could that be part of any plan?"

Ty had ignited something inside her and connected her to the emotions that boiled inside, he knew treading carefully and speaking softly and slowly was important, to think before each word, which he did before answering.

"In my experience we are all part of something greater than ourselves. We are put into each other's path for a reason; sometimes we do not understand the reason, even after the event has happened. But if we hold onto the knowledge that behind it all is a loving and caring power greater than ourselves then all will be well. As time passes more is revealed and the picture becomes clearer, the jigsaw takes shape. More importantly the reason for each of us being in each other's lives becomes apparent and it makes sense. If we hold onto that it brings comfort for when it's needed. No one knows why we are here together at this point in time but we are. I don't know why but I'm glad I'm here with you now."

Sarah's anger fell away and she felt herself fall back against the tree, grateful for its presence holding her up at that point, "I'm happy that you're here also, although as you say I don't know why either. I just don't understand why there has to be such pain in a world that's supposedly directed by something loving and caring."

Ty understood where she was coming from, "Life is suffering, so Buddhism tells us. But it's not all suffering and not all attachment brings it. I'm attached and joined to everything but I don't suffer from that attachment always. I only suffer when I forget about the price tag which comes with freedom."

Sarah half-laughed, something which felt uncomfortable for her at this time of her life, laughter, "A price tag, what's that then?"

Ty smiled with her and felt the uneasiness she felt by laughing, "The price tag for any freedom is acceptance. That if I choose to be free then I also have to accept that I don't control people or events. If I crave and desire real freedom I have to give up controlling both. It's hard and difficult to achieve and I have struggled with it but freedom is so important that I will take acceptance any day of the week."

Sarah listened again, but struggled with what Ty said, "Acceptance is a hard and costly price as far as River is concerned for me, too high a price for freedom."

Ty did not respond, he knew that what Sarah said was more to herself than to anyone else who may be listening including him. After a while she spoke again, "Do you have any idea where we are going Ty, or where to find her?"

Ty had been looking around the whole time he had been sitting, his mind already out walking and searching for Princess. Sarah's question was one he had expected but had no real answer.

"Something inside me is pointing the way, most likely my heart, but the short answer is no. I think we should just carry on up this hill and walk through the meadow and find what we find. It's not a plan but it seems the thing to do."

Sarah was happy enough with the answer. Ty had bought some companionship and also some diversion from her own head, and that itself was a blessing. She sighed and got up swiftly, reaching down to collect up her belongings and looked at Ty.

"Come on then let's go. Walking moves my grief around and doesn't let it settle too much which is a good thing. I am sure that Princess is waiting for you somewhere, it would be rude to keep her waiting."

Ty smiled at the mention of her name and got up quickly, "Sarah, I think that something more that Princess is waiting for us both, of that I'm more than certain."

Sarah looked at him and forced a smile. There was only one thing she wanted to find, River, and the chances of that were non-existent but she forced her feet to move and with it they set off up the hill.

They set off again in the search for whatever it was that they would find.

CHAPTER 9

Alone to face, what or who...

For Tony, the walls had started to move, to close in, and the shape of the room he was in changed. Before the room had been uniform, all four walls the same size and colour. The only difference in any of them was the one small window set at eye level on one side. The rest was the same throughout. It was changing around him now as he lay curled up in a ball, as small as he could make himself. He longed for release from what he was going through or had been through since he jumped but more so release or a pause in what he knew was still to come. The walls continued to move, the writing with them, closing in and finally settling on a shape similar to that of a hallway, two longer walls and two shorter one. There were doors in all of the walls now but no windows. But they were doors without handles and no way of using them to get away from where he was.

Tony was now trapped in a smaller room with doors but no way of using them to escape. He was also aware that inside his head the thoughts that were there began to take over. His mind and head scrambled with a million different threads, none of them leading to something which was helpful. The voice had been silent for a while and he was anxious for its return. Not because he craved its sound but anything was better than the isolation and the madness, which was now going on in his head. All through his life, since he could remember, he had sought seclusion and somewhere to be away from the world, something which brought fear to every breath. He thought that seclusion and isolation were his friends but over time they turned against him and rendered him incapable of moving out of his flat. They spoke to him and led him to believe that anything else could not be trusted. All intimate relationships were doomed from the start and that trust was something which did not exist. He listened and allowed himself to be manipulated by these twin voices until he could not leave them behind. They understood him; they knew him and they held him. They held him with arms, which never went or left him. They offered empathy and sympathy in equal regard and he knew no other way then to listen to their every word. It was this false belief harboured over time, which had forced him into a place where he knew nothing apart from the darkest thoughts and beliefs about the outside world. He stayed in and allowed them to manifest into something more sinister and darker than anything he could ever have imagined. His perceptions became projected beliefs onto the world outside and nothing could change this.

"You remember that time now. When we came and held you, so loving, so caring, so easily led you were by us," the voice whispered to him. *"We would have left if you had asked us to, but you didn't and we stayed."*

Tony did remember how he invited them in because he failed to seek help for all that was on his mind. He had people around him who cared but he could not open his mouth to ask for help. He surrendered instead to the first thing that came along and offered him an ear, his own despair and emptiness.

"Alone to face, what or who. You made yourself alone you know, others tried but couldn't reach you because of your own ego. Your ego bought you here, and it's left you here, alone to

face, what or who," the voice continued to taunt.

Tony had started to uncurl himself from the ball he had been in but the sight of the hall and the walls covered, without a place left bare, was not something that offered or bought him relief. He was naked now, his clothes gone and he was left cold and alone in a place, which he knew well, a place which he had run to, run to away from his whole life.

"Where is God now? Where is his will? Or are you just following your will again. God has deserted you because you deserted him for so long. You choose a path which led away from truth and honesty and only into self-pity, and this is where you are now, through your own will." The voice laughed after it finished speaking, a laugh which sounded like the bells from hell welcoming the sinners into its arms.

Tony for the first time found a voice from inside himself, which shocked him as it came out, "I may have deserted God a long time ago but I came back and he knows that," he said, standing now and turning around as he spoke.

The voice stopped laughing, "You want to have a discussion now, a conversation, here and now. Don't look for God here my twin brother. God exists where faith exists. You have no faith in anything other than yourself. The boy had it. But you no!!!!! You let go of that a long time ago alongside its other twin brother... hope. There is no hope here and there is no faith here, not inside you at least. Read the words, you wrote them, and there's no faith in this hope."

The mention of the word boy was the only word that Tony really heard. His memory had left him during his time after he had first got there but the word sparked something across his heart. He tried to pull the emotion and feeling to the surface but his mind grabbed it, tearing it from his heart. The boy, a boy, did not exist here, for Tony it did not exist anywhere. Children represented innocence and there was no innocence in the place he was.

"Time enough for sitting and talking has passed. There is only one place left to go," the voice counted.

Tony looked down and saw what had appeared in his right hand. He knew it was coming and was not surprised. A sense of resignation and defeat had come over him and he had known for a long time where it was all leading and the end result. In his hand sat a marker pen, black in colour. The memory's came back and he knew that he was naked now for a reason.

Many years ago he had been in a similar place. The voices of seclusion and despair had done their work and he was ripe and ready for what was to come. Any hope or trust that he had placed in others had disappeared in the sounds of girl finishing their relationship. He knew it had been coming, his bizarre behaviour and obsession with her had culminated in her not being able to stand it anymore and she had left, to have a break. He knew what that meant but held onto the hope that maybe it was a break and that she would return. He hadn't been able to sleep for days and hadn't eaten anything of value for a week. He was tired and he was in the place where anything was going to tip him over the edge. Her voice on the end of the phone was enough and it proved the catalyst to what he did next.

After finishing the phone call he remembered throwing the phone across the hallway and falling to the floor in a heap, sobbing. He stayed in that position for what seemed an eternity until something moved him to get up. He entered into the lounge and looked for something, anything, to break or to throw. He found them easily. All the pictures, all the mementoes of his childhood and his family sat there ready for him. He picked every single one up and threw them, smashed them and broke them until the glass lay shattered on the floor and the pictures sat next to them, ripped to shreds. But that wasn't enough. He remembered picking up a pen, a black marker pen and writing on the walls of his flat until there was not a single piece left uncovered. He wrote about the girl, about life, about God, about death. He just wrote until there was nowhere else left to write on, nothing else left to cover with the demented ranting's going on inside his head.

All those feelings and thoughts rose up in him now as if he was back in that same place. It was on him, raw and as if it had just happened. He was transported back in time in his head. He had nowhere else to go, nothing else left to do, except do what he did then. He started, slowly, but increased in pace once he got a feel for what he was doing. He started to write all over his body, any place that he could reach he used as a place to vent what he was feeling. There was no end to his thoughts, no end to the levels that he would go to simply just to feed the despair inside his heart.

This for him was the Abyss, the place he never wanted to return to, a place he had tried to avoid but wherever he went it remained within him. It was a place fuelled by drugs and the paranoia and psychosis that it fed on. He continued to write now and more disturbing to him was the feeling of it being something he had missed. A part of him had sought it out again and now he got a sense of gratification from doing what he was doing. Eventually he threw the pen down and stood there, arms outstretched, laughing demonically to himself. It was laughter born from defeat, a giving in, too what had been hidden inside him for so long. It had slept as he had lived. He thought it was under wraps that it would never return but it had simply lain dormant. Sitting, waiting for its time, which it knew would return.

"So we are here again, where we both knew you would return. To our arms, our warm embrace, our care. You have come back home, now and forever," the voice taunted, *laughing, screaming in joy.*

Tony collapsed and found himself withdrawing to a corner, crying in desperation, sobbing with defeat.

He curled up into a ball once more, and waited for who knows what to come.

CHAPTER 10

When God sighs, you can see His cry's...

Princess had sat down and at River's suggestion had put her feet in the water, alongside his. Since she had done this he had done nothing but laugh and talk to himself. The water was crystal clear and they could see the fishes as they swam up to and then away from where there feet paddled in the cold waters. Princess was not interested in the fishes or what they were doing, her attention and her eye was on River. He seemed oblivious to her and anything else around him except what was going on at his feet. His innocence was enticing and his laughter infectious, although her heart struggled to see both. She was aware of why she was there but was unsure if he knew. The uncertainty and the not knowing eat away at her and she struggled to pull herself from being consumed by it.

After a time, she spoke, softly but loud enough for him to hear above the laughter he was displaying, "How long have you been here River?"

He didn't answer immediately, happy enough to giggle and splash his feet in and out of the water. She knew he had heard her as after a time, he answered.

"Hours, days, weeks, I don't know. I don't really care. I could stay here for ever," before glancing up at her to smile and add, "as long as you stayed here to."

They held each other's gaze for a moment before his returned to the water and started laughing once again. Princess knew that they spoke to each other through those moments and the meeting of their eyes, others may so soul. What she did hope was that he could not see into her soul fully and what lay inside, today at least. If he did it didn't show it, then again you could rarely tell with him. His was named River by his parents for a reason and why he always gravitated back to the place where they sat now. The still waters in River ran deep but they carried with them a message which those who met and knew him never failed to recognise or see.

"Of course I would stay here with you, River, we could stay and live. Just you and me," Princess said, trying to cover up the sadness she felt inside.

River heard, as he always did, what she said, but waited to answer, "What about Ty, wouldn't he get jealous?"

For a moment Princess was perplexed, she had never spoken with River about Ty, but somehow he knew. She thought about her answer before saying, "I'm sure he could come and visit us, if that would be ok with you."

River laughed, "You pass the test again, Princess, you always do," he said.

"What test?" she said instantly.

"The truth test. You pass all the tests every time I see you," River said swishing his feet from side to side as he spoke.

The word truth from River's lips at this time was hard for Princess to hear. At this precise moment she felt that the honesty that all could see in her and what she bought was being disturbed, almost hidden by what she had been sent to do. It was uncomfortable for her to keep hiding and knew that River would be able to pick up on it, sooner rather than later.

"I know why you are here, Princess?" he said startling her from her thoughts but hitting straight at the middle of them.

"You do," she said quietly.

"Of course. I know everything," River said looking straight at her, the smile falling from his face.

Princess looked at him and then down, her shame and guilt forcing her to keep it this way. Her heart already breaking, ripped apart.

River saw this and spoke, pushing his words into her to shore up the pieces of her heart as they shattered and fell apart.

"Because you love me."

Princess kept her head bowed, tears starting to fall easily. It was some time before she managed to stem the flow and lift her head.

River smiled an enormous grin and said, "See told you I know everything," and laughed long and loud scaring the birds from their surrounding nests up into the blue sky.

Princess reached over and grabbed for him, as he tried to roll away, "Alright you that's it, can't have you giving away all my secrets."

They rolled and laughed and grabbed onto each other as Princess tried to tickle his sides. River giggled and they continued to roll around until she held him tight to her chest, not allowing him to move. He was silent, still for the time being, and content simply to hold onto her and be close to her breath and heart. His head resting eventually just under chin. She could feel her own heart thumping, desperate for release, but more so she could feel his. It had not changed or missed a single beat, a slow almost non-existent rhythm which settled between them. It seemed to reach out and into her and she felt a physical sensation, as if their hearts actually touched, and her own heart slowed to match his. He made no move to get away from her, he never did.

This time she heard his breathing slow down even further and she looked down, adjusting her head so she could see.

River had fallen asleep.

When River had jumped into the water, physically he had instantly been asleep. The spirits and guides and all the universe would not allow him to go through that part of the journey as he followed Tony. Whatever else happened or where he may have to go he was spared that. Although it could easily be said that others were spared the knowledge and feelings that he would go through that. It was not easy to know the difference, except he was transported somewhere else, to where he was now, before he would leave. What he was doing and where he was going could ultimately not be decided by others.

River made his own decisions, but it could be managed to limit the chances of damage to him. River was the golden child of the forest and there were too many things watching him to let him go through that. So he had been lifted and taken to a place which he loved. The stream, the fishes, the beauty around it and also taken towards her – towards Princess. It was in her hands now. She and River alone would decide when he finally went to get Tony. The outcome was uncertain for Tony and also River and it was this that they all struggled with, Princess the most.

She lay there, listening to him breathing and holding his head in her hand, softly stroking his blonde hair which shone even in the fading light. She thought of the day they first met when she came upon him pretty much in similar circumstances with him sitting by the stream. When people meet for the first time normally there is a sense of discomfort or awkwardness, a sizing up. With them it was different it was the same as it had been today and every other day, natural, warm, loving and filled with laughter and peace. The connection was strong, respect and love mutual, and they knew each would be in the other's lives for ever. It was only today that Princess had realised that today may be the end of that. Today could be their last day together.

He awoke gently, stretching and yawning, taking time to open his eyes, letting them adjust to the evening's dusty light. She had moved her position as he slept so that his head was now cradled in her lap, so when his eyes had adjusted and they were open he was looking straight up into her's. She smiled down at him and he grinned back.

"Sleeping makes me so hungry."

Princess knew what this meant, but teased him none the less, "It's too dark to go there, we won't be able to see anything."

River knew she was teasing and refused to play along.

"With our eyes we see everything. Even that which wishes to remain hidden," before adding with a slight change in tone, "And I see you too."

Princess was alerted to something different picked up by the change of tone, but tried to mask it through humour, "And I see you too little boy," reaching down to pinch one cheek.

River would not be so easily distracted, pursuing the truth, "I see you, inside and out, Princess."

Princess started to get up, gently holding his head and not letting it fall to the floor, distracting herself from his eyes and his pursuit of her insides.

"Come on then let's go, otherwise there will be no peace I imagine," she said turning away from his gaze just to give herself time to compose her feelings.

River was standing now, eyeing her with amusement, comfortable with her being uncomfortable. He was the only one who could make her feel like that, even Ty did not have that effect.

"Princess, it's OK, I know why you're here, but let's eat first and then we can sit and talk as we eat. That's why you're here isn't it, to talk to me?"

Princess continued on her course of distraction, "Well lets go and pick first and this time I get first go, you always take the best ones and I'm left with what you don't want," finishing and slowly beginning to walk away.

River ran after her, closing the gap quickly, and reached for her hand as they moved away from the stream, its smallness fitting easily into hers, as it always did.

"Princess, it's OK. I have no fear of what I can't see. But if you have fear of something then let it go, as I will fear it too," he said as they walked to the place where they could always find food.

She remained silent happy to feel his hand in hers for however long that would be.

Whenever they were there they would always end up at the same place, amidst a dense part of the forest where the bushes grew in tangles and the grass came up to River's knees, forcing him to push his way through it, like walking against the current in a fast-flowing stream. He had shown her the place where every berry you could wish to eat grew, ripe and lush, and always ready for picking, but more importantly for eating. River always got in first picking large handfuls before she even had chance to grab a dock leaf to hold the harvest and this time was no different. He laughed and teased her as he picked and ate at the same time, his hunger and desire for both insatiable. For a moment Princess forgot all about her reasons for being there and what was to come until eventually they had filled their leaves and moved back to the stream to eat.

The day was now fading, the light of the moon and stars rising, as they sat by the stream in simple silence, happy to eat and look at the wonders of the night sky unfolding. They had done it often with Princess telling him stories of her travels and which star was jealous of the others and the reasons for it. He always listened in awe and wonder at how she knew everything about all of this and grew to love her more each time. He not only grew to love her more but also wanted to visit the places she spoke about because she described them with such passion and intensity. He felt the bond between them grow every time they met, as she did too. River would have spent every waking, and sleeping, moment with her and understood why Ty was searching for her. Any man would have gone to the ends of the earth to spend time with her. River was the lucky one, she always sought him out. It bought him peace and a secret smile inside whenever he thought of it. After a time sitting and eating, River spoke.

"Do you remember when you told me about God crying," looking up at the heavens as he did?

She did remember, "Yes I do, when we sat here one day trying to shelter from the rain. It rained for ages that day didn't it?"

"You said, when God cries, you can see his sighs, it rains to show his pain," River repeating exactly what she had said during the rains.

Princess looked down and smiled, the memory of it providing the motivation, "I did say that Yes, because it's true."

River looked directly at her, their knowing eyes meeting each other.

"It rained after I jumped didn't it?"

Princess sighed deeply, her eyes changing colour and depth also, the sadness bursting out from their sides.

"Yes it did. The wind blew, the trees shook, the rain fell in torrents and the streams threatened to run over. I think God cried a lot then," her voice softening to a whisper.

River looked down for a moment, seemingly concerned, "Is God angry with me?"

Princess was in awe of this child. He even wanted to look out for God, her heart melted once again.

"River, he would never be angry with you. It rained so much because he was sad, very sad."

He continued to look down, "I hope God understands. I couldn't leave Tony, I have to try. If I don't who will?"

Princess reached over and put her hand round his shoulder, pulling him into her side, feeling the warmth of his gentle soul.

"Any of us would have gone for you River, but we can't take that from you. But we will be here waiting for your return."

River had never actually thought about returning. He didn't really know where he was going. He jumped because his heart told him to; he alone could reach Tony. After a while he spoke.

"My return is not a definite though. I see something inside your eyes that tells me that."

Princess was lost for words momentarily, knowing that she never had or could lie to him, he would always know, "You and I River both know that nothing is ever certain."

He smiled back, "Except that you love me, that's certain isn't it, Princess?"

It was not a question, and she pulled him closer.

"Yes, River, that one thing is certain, no doubts there. I will love you till the end of time and beyond. I think I even love you more when I'm away from you, if that's possible."

"Really," he replied giggling.

"Oh yes, really. Remember that wherever you are, even in the darkest of places that Princess waits to see you again. To hold you, to walk and sit with you, remember that, in here," reaching over and putting her hand on his heart, keeping it there.

River felt her touch and reached his hand up and put it on top of hers, as they sat there together, communicating through touch.

"Tell me one last story about one of the stars, to take with me," River asked after some time had passed between them and the world.

Princess felt the word 'last' kick deep inside her stomach, but moved beyond that feeling and began.

"Well do you see that star right at the back, past the moon, sitting there all alone," pointing far up into the night sky as she spoke.

River followed her hand and its direction, "Yes I do, it's so far away, it must be lonely."

"It is," she continued, "it's there because it got too big for its boots; bossing all the other stars around, telling them what to do and where to shine. All the other stars got so fed up with it they decided to teach it a lesson."

"What did they do?" River asked, a smile all across his face.

"They had a meeting and got some cheeky monkeys to go up there. They were very good at playing tricks on naughty stars," she said, knowing that River totally adored monkeys.

"What did the monkeys do?" River asked, eager for more from her.

"They got a load of elastic bands and tied them together, making one enormous one. They then told the bossy star that they could wrap it round him and fire him closer to the earth, so that he would be the brightest star that everyone could see, and the closest. The star loved that idea and couldn't wait for it to be done and asked them to do it that night."

River was starting to laugh, imagining the monkeys tricking the star and then climbing around it to fit the elastic band in place, "Come on what happened then?" he added in between his laugh.

"Well the monkeys climbed around the star and put the band in place. They pulled it back, right back until it was nearly breaking, then they counted down from three, as all the other stars watched, knowing what was going to happen. Then whoosh, they let go of the band and the star went flying off, quick as a rocket," Princess could see River's face, mesmerised by the whole story.

"But how did it end up there then and not closer," he laughed not understanding.

Princess looked down at his face to capture the image to hold onto before he went, "Because the monkeys had put the elastic band on the wrong way, without the star knowing. That's why it flew off backwards, shooting past the moon, right to where it sits now. They had tricked the bossy star."

River fell over onto his side laughing, hardly able to stop the tears flowing, "The cheeky monkeys… I bet they laughed… "

"They did laugh, so much that they fell off the star itself and onto each other, smashing their heads together, and laughing more at that," Princess added joining in with his laughter.

River's laughing had fresh impetus and he fell back onto his side again, picturing the monkey's falling over each other and smashing their heads together.

They laughed together, looking up at the star, beyond the moon that had been tricked, by the cheeky monkeys.

It took a while for River to stop laughing but eventually he did, sighing as he finished.

"That's a good story, one of the best," he said, before pausing to add, "a good last story to have."

The word 'last' had the same effect on Princess and her laughter ceased as quickly as it had begun as realisation kicked in that the time had come. She was even more surprised that it was he that spoke first. If he was ready then she knew that she had to be also. Instantly alert to his will and need to be gone, to find Tony.

"Are you ready then River?"

He nodded, reaching out for her hand, both of them holding tightly, as they stood up at the same time.

Anything that went on between River and Princess was never

planned and this was no exception. They both seemed to know naturally what to do, it came easy, especially when they were together and all their movements were rhythmic, slow and seemingly effortless. They had not spoken about where they were going to, they simply walked in the same direction.

Away from the streams and towards the forest that started approximately fifty yards away. They walked as slow as they could, a tortoise who may have been in a hurry would have easily passed them. They didn't speak to begin with, simply walked and held onto each other's hand, maybe just a little bit tighter than they did before.

Eventually they reached the start of the forest and it was Princess who stopped, and bent down onto her knees so that her face was directly level with his, eye meeting eye. Or they would have if River's head had not been slightly bowed, for the first time a sign of apprehension for what may come ahead. She felt it and he knew she did.

Princess put her hand forward and gently lifted his head from under his chin, and his eyes met hers. The only thing recognisable across both sets of them was sadness and regret at them having to leave each other, with no certain time or day of their next meeting.

Despite his anxiety, apprehension, fear even, it was River that spoke.

"Thank you for coming, it's been the best time ever."

Princess looked at him and smiled, awe written across every part of her face.

"No, it is I that should thank you. Not many people get to spend time with you, but I get it more than most. I feel so special and so privileged. When I'm with you it's like nothing else matters. It is only you and I, and it's what I want more than anything."

River smiled back, peace and ease returning to his previously sad eyes. His eyes said so much to her, gave her so much.

"When I come back you will still be here, waiting?" he said quietly.

"Waiting, longing, hoping to see you soon. All of those plus so much more. Yes, I will be waiting, even if the earth stops turning, I will stay and wait… count on it."

River didn't speak he just put his hands out and placed them gently on either side of her face, bringing his face close to hers, placing his forehead lightly against hers, their noses brushing softly.

"I have never had or could have wished for a better friend," he said, as they stayed that way, "You have always shown me so much, shared so much, I will love you until tomorrow and then again the day after."

Princess laughed, it was what he always said when they left each other, and he knew it would touch her.

"And I will love you beyond both of those and into next week," she replied, giving her normal response.

He threw his arms around her, pulling her close, so close, as if they were simply one person joined together – two hearts beating with one single breath. They stayed that way for some time until again it was River who made the first move and let go. She felt her heart racing, her breath coming in short gasps.

He put his hands on her cheeks again and started to kiss her, first on one check, then the other and then finally on her nose, saying as he did, "This is for later, this is for tomorrow and this is for right now," his final kiss like a butterfly's wings on her nose. He hugged her one last time and slowly turned and started to walk the final steps towards the beginning of the forest.

As he did, a single drop of rain fell, and landed on his cheek. Princess looked up as he did to and they both knew.

He was now at the start of the forest, the trees standing above him, making him seem even smaller. River turned and looked over at

Princess who was now standing, her hair swept back, her eyes ever alert, totally focused on him. He smiled, the biggest of smiles, the longest of smiles and put his head to one side simply to exaggerate its intensity, and then poked his tongue out at her.

Princess laughed, even in this moment, he was trying to ease her feelings, reaching out with what he knew, innocence and playfulness. Her eyes softened, her smile remained but inside her heart fell to pieces.

It lay smashed and battered, inside her soul which held it there in comfort.

River simply turned and walked away, as he did, he seemed to get even smaller until he disappeared and he was gone.

Princess continued to look towards where he had been, a whisper escaping from her breaking heart.

"Take care and travel in peace my sweet child – I will be here waiting for when you return."

She bowed her head, the tears falling softly down each cheek.

Only one thing happened then.

It started to rain.

CHAPTER 11

Spoke to me through twilight's gaze…

Sarah and Ty had been coming towards the edge of the meadow, towards an area, which was sparse but yet overgrown, when it started to rain heavily. There was no wind to speak of but the rain was icy, torrential and full of feeling. They both set off at a run towards the shelter of something, anything, which may have lain ahead and able to offer that. The rain snapped at their heels and lay ahead as they ran, the clouds built like a wall across any blue sky that existed behind. They both seemed to sight the same thing and ran towards a small set of trees, which although small promised some kind of respite from getting wet.

They arrived within seconds of each other, gasping for some kind of breath, and pushing their wet hair from their foreheads and wiping faces covered in rainwater. They looked out from the cover of the branches, which although sparse, gave some kind of shelter. Sarah got the feeling that in this place she was constantly getting wet. The sky was blue enough and the warmth of the sun inviting but the rain had a similar intensity and feel to it. Whatever nature seemed to throw at her in this place it was always at one end of the scale, never sitting in the middle of mediocrity. She looked over at Ty who stood tall and still, his face wet, eying the scene outside and the heavens which for the moment remained hidden by a blanket of grey cloud. She was glad to have him here and nearby, offering protection and company for her.

Ty himself felt closed in, both by the rain and lack of direction and clarity about his search. It seemed a good idea at the time just to simply set out and try and find Princess but they had been going for some time and he was fresh out of ideas and any inspiration he had at the beginning was starting to wane. He was also hungry and tired and aware that soon night would really be drawing in and felt he needed to find somewhere for both him and Sarah to lay up and rest for the night.

"It doesn't look too good does it," Ty said peering out and moving a little away from the branches to try and see further.

Sarah watched him but didn't follow, "No, this looks set in for some time. Although its eerie, there is not a breath of wind."

Ty had noticed that too and Sarah was right, there was no sound apart from that of water hitting ground or tree above, everything was silent, "Yeah it is eerie, I can't hear any other sound. It's like everything is holding its breath, afraid to make a noise for some reason, as if it will break some kind of spell."

"Or bring bad luck," Sarah completing the sentence.

Ty had moved back in under the shelter and stood next to Sarah. The protection of the branches was not great and they had to stand pretty close to each other to both find any of this. Their bodies gave off steam from the rainwater now drying and their breath could easily be seen in the air. They stood for a while watching the rain fall steadily, not letting up but not increasing either. It was a time when they had to make a decision and they both knew it, Ty speaking first, as he surveyed the route ahead, "It looks like the ground continues to climb up that ridge, but beyond that it's hard to see what lies ahead."

Sarah followed his eyes and spoke, "There is no chance of knowing if it's bad or worse than here, it's a gamble."

"I will go ahead and look and come back and let you know, will you be ok here," Ty said after some moments of deliberation.

Sarah's heart skipped a beat; the mere thought of being left, bringing panic to her system, "No, I will come with you. Don't leave me here, I'm not ready for that yet," her eyes and face showing the anxiety of what this meant for her.

Ty looked at her and realised he had misjudged the timing, "Of course, sorry, I didn't mean to scare you. I just thought you could stay here and be dry."

"The rain does not scare me, not having you here does. Being alone is not an option for me at the moment. I don't trust this grief with me, it's too far reaching and consuming. If it was left to me then I would just sit and wait until the end of time," Sarah said, surprised at how she needed him here and also that she could say it.

Ty both heard and saw her honesty, it was something he was becoming to admire in her, it reminded him of Princess and that was a good thing. He looked up at the sky again and could see no break in the blanket of cloud, "Let's just go, there seems no end to the rain at the moment. We may be here for ages if we wait," he said looking over towards her.

"Let's just wait for a short while, all I seem to do in this place is get wet," Sarah replied trying to laugh as she said it, "At least it gives us a chance to catch a breath also, and just rest," sitting down as she finished.

Ty did not want to push her despite the feeling inside that he wanted to press on. He knew that if it was just him walking he would have made faster progress but his heart was somewhere attuned to her feelings and the grief inside and he knew that he was needed by her, for the moment. He nodded his agreement and sat down a respectful distance away.

They drank and rested a while as the rain fell down, far and wide, across the rolling landscape that they had both crossed and were still to see. After a while Ty spoke, "You said that you and River had met, or at least you had some kind of feeling you had. Has anything more come to you?"

Sarah had thought of River and little else as they had walked but not the specific thing that Ty now asked. She continued to look out trying to bring her feelings under control at the sound of his name, "It is strange but no, I don't. River knows obviously and I keep trying to think back but nothing comes to mind. His words about time and change confused me. I'm not one for change, I like good old routine," she said continuing to gaze into the distance, lost in her own river of thoughts.

"You said you have seen his eyes and his smile, that's what you can remember," Ty said.

Sarah was aware that Ty was trying to help but the sudden mention of River's name and trying to remember when and where they had met only confused her, but she tried none the less, "His eyes are definitely not new to me. There is a part that's telling me they are from when I was a child but then logic tells me no as River is a child now. He can't always have been the same, we all change."

"Change with time," Ty said picking up the words that River had spoken to her.

"Yeah change with time, but is that just in appearance and age? Its physical but what about something else, does what we have as a child remain somewhere inside?" Sarah added trying to hear what she said in the search for further clarity.

"There's a part of me that has always been the same, since I was a child." Ty carried on, "Despite what life brings I try and hold onto it, although it's not easy."

Sarah turned to him, "What is that then Ty?"

"A belief that every day is a day that is different, nothing has to remain the same. I wake up every day as if new, like a child. It's a day to paint new colours, new shapes across life, across its canvas. I remember hearing it said as a child, spoken through twilight's gaze," Ty said turning also to look at her.

Sarah held his eyes. She admired his strength, the positive nature of his personality and could see for him that this worked, he had found both meaning and purpose for each day, each new day. She could see it in him but her grief, her recent heavy loss had clouded the part this could play for her. If she had a canvas in front of her now she would simply paint in the darkest black she could find. There was no light, no white clouds or blue sky, just despair and nothingness rested in her heart. She wanted to question him about hearing it and what it meant but the effort deserted her.

She sighed and Ty knew she did not want to speak anymore. They sat in silence for a short while looking out, in different directions with different thoughts across their minds. Eventually she spoke, "Let's just start walking again, to the top of that hill," she lifted her head up gesturing with it, "And let's see what we find when we come to the top. I don't care about the rain, it's raining inside anyway, so outside makes no difference. My grief sits with me and it walks with me, but walking at least takes me further away from the point where it happened and that seems a good thing."

They both got up and started out for the top of the Hill, to find whatever it was that they lay beyond it, as Sarah had said.

CHAPTER 12

I'll sit and wait…

Tony sat naked cross-legged with his head down. He had been in this same position for hours, the silence from the voice had been the same, and Tony knew that he was alone, at least for the moment. He was glad of the silence, the absence of the voice that mocked but also from the knowledge it had. It knew what he was thinking before he did. A chain or thread had started in his head and the voice finished it, cutting it dead. The feeling that normally followed crashing into the empty wasteland of meaninglessness which Tony was experiencing. Any thought of salvation and redemption had gone; all that was left was an eternity alone with a voice, which would never allow him peace. He knew that now but even this knowing bought no relief from the feelings he had inside – that this was it, he would never have or know anything more than naked emptiness and time that would never move forward.

"Are you just going to sit there then? Nothing to say all of a sudden. We used to speak all the time, I was your friend remember when no one would listen, I did. I'm ready to listen again, it's not like we will ever run out of time," the voice spoke teasing, menacing, revealing.

Tony had not said anything out loud since he had been there, any conversations had within the bounds of his head, the voice lived there and walked inside, it knew the way through his thoughts, having existed within them for so long. Tony felt he wanted to say something but felt that anything would just be twisted, turned around, and only add to the misery he felt.

"It's ok, I have time and so do you. Before the end, of which there is none, you will be begging to speak to someone and you will have no choice but to speak to me," the voice continued, "However long it takes, I'll sit and wait."

Tony screamed out, the voice would not let go, not shut up, even when it was not speaking out loud it was inside his head, walking and whispering through the sadness and misery, which had been self-inflicted.

"Scream, go on, and let it out. Better out than in... although no one can hear you and if they did they couldn't do anything. Even if they wanted to," the voice trying to be heard above the animal like screams, which came from Tony's mouth.

"Just leave me, go away, and stay away. I never invited you in. Why did you ever come into my life anyway," Tony had found his voice, from somewhere deep inside, hope had fought its way through, he was ready to fight, however fleeting the feeling was.

"Invited, gate crashed, you were open and ready. You craved attention, craved an ear, my ear, you wrote the words, I just heard them," the voice counted back, happy to have the conversation, allowing Tony hope, before it crushed it.

"I wrote what I did because it's what I felt. I didn't invite anyone in, I wrote from my heart," Tony shouted looking up trying to find a focus for his words. The voice's invisibility frustrating him as it hid.

"What are words you write except an invitation to be heard by those who read them? Your frustrated because you can't see

me, yet you hid away and its ok, others looked for you tried to find you, but you hid, for so long. Even the boy couldn't find you, then or now," the voice knew what to throw at Tony to make his misery worse.

The mention of the word 'boy' forced Tony's screams back inside. He backed himself into the corner, feeling the coldness of the walls on his naked skin. He pulled his knees up to his chest and sat their rocking, his head down, trying to find some comfort from deep inside. There was none. The word 'boy' bought no comfort, simply adding to his despair.

The voice knew this and laughed as Tony rocked himself, longing for release from the shame and guilt which overwhelmed him at the memory of what he had left behind; the memory of River.

CHAPTER 13

The child is here and there…

Princess had not moved from the moment that it had started to rain. She had stayed in exactly the same spot staring into the forest and the last place that she had seen River. Her hair was sodden, the rain flattening it to her head as it continued to fall. There was no let up, no respite, and the clouds above dark and endless, they mirrored the feelings that she felt inside. Her eyes never left the spot where he had been, as if they could wish him back safely simply by fixating on the place.

A soft and caring voice came from far away, Princess hearing its approach before it arrived, ***"Breathe and sit down, rest and be still, it is not time yet for him to return,"*** its soft tones reaching out to put their arms around her. Gently she felt a pressure that softly held her as she fell onto the floor. She sat with one knee raised her head resting on it, still looking into the forest.

She sat in a similar way to how Tony was currently. However unlike Tony, walls of despair and a voice, which showed no compassion, did not enclose Princess. River may have been the golden child of the forest but Princess was the depth of its colour and the face of its beauty. Without her, nothing would be the same and in times of doubt and anxiety the forest always closed around her offering protection in every step she took. It seemed that at this exact moment the whole nature of things as they were, stood in the balance; River and Princess were in need and the whole universe heard their call for help.

Princess may have been seated but her breathing remained erratic and the stillness, which normally was commonplace had left her, and this did not go unnoticed.

"Princess... Princess... Princess... let go and have faith," the voice returned its tone even softer, if that had ever been possible.

She as yet, could not hear, or concentrate on anything else. Her eyes and any power she felt inside her simply focused on just one thing. She was reaching out using all that she possessed to find River and let him feel her touch and hear her voice. She desperately wanted him to have something to hold onto in the hope that it would be enough and bring him back safely.

"He does not hear and he cannot see you for the moment. You may be fixed on him but he is focused on what he has to do. You have done enough and given him enough to hold onto... in his heart," the voice continuing, its desperation matching hers.

Princess stirred at the words, "Done enough. I should have gone in his place. I should have stopped him. He is a child and I should have protected him, you should have protected him," she cried out.

"You did do enough. Whilst you were with him he could not be reached. Where he is going knows that he is coming. They were searching and trying to reach him before he left. You protected him and did not allow that to happen, without you fear would have consumed him, his heart would have doubted and faith may have left him. You stopped that and gave him a

time that he holds onto deep inside, he will need that before the end," the voice persuasive in both tone and words.

"What will be the end? Will he return," she replied, her manner insistent and her words searching for something she could hold onto now.

There was silence for a while, no reply from the forest or the sky, until, *"Princess his fate is for him, what will be will be, you know that well enough."*

Princess had asked the question more in hope than expectation, she knew the reply she would get, but had asked it none the less. She was desperate, something which was alien to her, she walked with certainty everyday but today there existed barriers which she could not remove or breakdown. These feelings were hard even for her to control and she was unable to sit with the not knowing. The place she could go to and be safe inside surrounded by faith and courage and a sense of purpose would not sit still and Princess remained restless.

The voice spoke again, *"The impermanence of all things Princess, what is here now will come and then go, nothing ever remains the same, even people and places. When you have freedom you must also have acceptance."*

Princess was angry now, rising to her feet, walking towards the forest and where River had last been seen, "I will not accept that, I will follow him and bring him back, I will not let this happen even if you will," She walked purposefully, her mind set, her decision made.

The voice stronger now, insistent, *"Princess, do not get in the way of other's destiny. Growth comes from pain and from what people find in those times. Do not go, if you do, then that fate is sealed and all will perish and return to dust."*

Princess was nearly at the point where River was last seen; she heard the voice but paid it no mind. She was headstrong as a child and this had never left her and she pulled on that memory to keep her focused, her eye fixed firmly on River. She had just about reached the point when she felt a hand on her shoulder, and she turned, convinced it was River, elation filling her heart.

She turned to see her mother, her face twisted in sadness, tears falling from her eyes onto her smooth cheeks, it was enough to stop Princess in her tracks and for her to falter, it was the chance that they had waited for.

"My child, your love and desire to help River goes way beyond anything that could be hoped for. But you have been this way before, went when you should have not and it worked out. This time, if you go, that will not happen. Only River can reach Tony, there is a reason that is the case. If you get in the way now, to ease your discomfort and fears, all will be lost as will he. Whilst hope remains we must also remain… here. Look around you, remember, the child is here and there, wherever you are, so is he," her mother spoke, her tears falling steadily.

Her mother being there, her tears, her obvious love for Princess was enough to drag her back. She fell into her mother's arms and allowed herself to be held back. Her heart went out to River whilst her soul cried out for something else and someone else's arms.

She cried out for Ty.

CHAPTER 14

Beneath the mist...

Ty and Sarah had walked from the small area of shelter up towards the top of the hill, the last hundred yards a steep and exhausting climb with the rain falling. When they got to the top Ty pulled Sarah by her arm as the sheer effort of the last few yards took their toll and she struggled to stay upright. When they both got there and stood up, breathing much needed air into their lungs they gathered their senses and looked out. What met their eyes was not what they had expected.

The ground gently sloped down into a valley, some may would have said a rolling valley, filled with colours that for a moment took their breath away, just as it was trying to get into their lungs. For as far as the eye could see, on the ground, lay a carpet of flowers. So many different colours, so many different types – chrysanthemums, daffodils, tulips, carnations even rose bushes, springing up here and there, next to each other and around each other. So many different types of blues and purples the eye struggled to cope, whilst the smell was an intoxicant. The falling rain simply added to the freshness of the colours and the warmth of the smell as they stood there, eyes aghast at this new miracle that was spread out at their feet.

If this was not enough as the ground levelled out there was a small lake, much smaller than the one they had left, seemingly a lifetime ago. The water sparkled despite the lack of sun and the rain caused small ripples to wash out from the centre, so that the top of the surface seemed to be in a continual rolling motion. As they scanned the lake they saw over at the farthest corner, a small hut, shack even, with a balcony running round it and smoke rising from the chimney which sat in the direct centre of the roof. They looked at each other with this new development. They had been travelling for some time and apart from the sight and sounds of birds they had seen no other living creature. Now in this place, unexpectedly, they had come across not life but possible human life. For both of them it was not something which they were naturally comfortable with, life meant explanation and possible questions and neither was in the mood for it. They may have felt the need for rest and somewhere to sleep as the grey skies above began to be chased by the oncoming night but the need for other people was not high on their list. They had just got used to each other and strangers was not something they had expected or wanted.

"Let's go round the other way, bypass it," Sarah spoke almost urging Ty to agree with her.

Ty stood in thought and looked round the whole scene below, the flowers, the lake and then the shack. The first thing that struck him was that in amidst all the beauty and colour there stood a shack which just didn't fit in. It was a patchwork of wood, different colours and sizes and even from a distance he wondered how it was still standing upright. The balcony had chairs out on it, three, which seemed to signify more than one person, or at least the need for more than one. But these thoughts was also interspersed by the need for rest, somewhere dry and a place to sleep for both of them. He looked up and began to see the first signs of stars through the decreasing blanket of clouds and knew that further travel was not really an option. He was also aware of Sarah and her words, a plea almost, for them to walk round and go on beyond whatever may have been in the shack.

"Please, Ty, I know what you're thinking, but let's just go round, it's too much to even think about for me," Sarah spoke again, her voice matching the words with their desire and need to walk on by.

Ty turned and looked at her and slowly walked across the short distance between them, coming up close, "Sarah I hear what you're saying and if there was more daylight available I would have said yes. But night closes in, we need to dry off, to get warm, sleep even. There is something about the whole place, which is inviting, the flowers, lake, the smoke. It doesn't seem to threaten."

"It's not that I just can't deal with questions or talking, not tonight, not now, please," Sarah added looking up at his face, pleading through her eyes.

"There may not be anyone there and remember everything happens for a reason, maybe we were meant to find this place right at this time of day when we need it, hold onto that and I will deal with whatever else we come across… trust me," Ty said his softness of voice calming her.

Sarah could see and hear that Ty had a point. She was cold and tired and could do with the rest. The smoke would say that there was a fire and she had the image of lying down in-front of one, sleeping under a blanket of the deepest wool. Her grief forgotten about, respite for a while, however short that may be, "OK but please just remember, no questions," Sarah relented and placed herself under Ty's protective blanket for now.

"No questions, no talking, just rest," Ty said placing his arm on hers as they started to walk across the carpet spread out beneath them.

They walked slowly down the hill which although smooth and

even still demanded attention to their steps and an eye for each other, Ty for Sarah especially. They could not avoid stepping on flowers as there was no trail or path or area of grass to follow and keep to. It was literally floor-to-floor colour and as they walked their eyes struggled to cope with the assault they were given. The flowers were soft underneath their feet but disguised a springiness with every step. They lifted their feet and felt the flowers rise up again once they had moved on and when they looked back they could not even see from whence they had come. All sign of them passing was gone, the flowers simply came back up, renewed and in place. It was a sight that puzzled but excited at the same time. As if the softness of their step had barely brushed the surface of the beauty beneath them.

The ground levelled out and they found themselves at the water's edge. Sarah felt the hair on the back of her neck stand up to attention, memories of River and Tony and her time by the previous lake, flicking across her mind as she attempted to focus on anything else apart from the water. Ty sensed this in her and kept close by ready to offer support and protection if she faltered. Sarah was aware of his closeness but previously she had found this uncomfortable but these feelings had moved slightly and she felt reassured by his continued presence.

They continued to stay next to but not to near the lake, to align Sarah's anxiety, and moved round towards the place where the hut was located, grey smoke signalling to them to come in and rest. They came within ten feet of the balcony which ran round the hut and Sarah was on full alert ready to move away if there was even the slightest sign of something which she did not expect.

They both got what they did not expect just as they stepped onto the balcony, a male voice, gentle and warm, almost a whisper as if it was aware of the mind states of both of them, "At last you have got here, I've been waiting for so long. Come in, come in, welcome, welcome. Both of you must be so tied after what you have been through, so tired," its warmth and invitation like music to their ears, before adding in the softest of tones, "River said you would come one day."

All anxiety she had was stripped away and Sarah left Ty's side, bounding up the three steps onto the balcony and through the open door of the hut, Ty hurriedly regaining his senses and following her quickly.

Sarah had run in and found the inside of the hut so different to what she had seen from the outside. For her it had been drab and colourless and without the smoke coming from the chimney could not have envisaged it being warm in any shape or form. She was wrong the moment she went through the door and found herself looking at a man, about 60-years-old, who sat rocking himself in a chair by the fire, not even looking at her, or Ty who had now followed her through the door.

"How do you know River? How do you know we would come? How do you know what we have been through? Who are you?" she spoke rapidly firing her questions off at the man who stayed in the chair, rocking, looking into the glowing embers of the fire.

He laughed loud and long, the chair matching the intensity of his laughter, "I thought you said no questions, anything but questions, that's four I've counted in the space of seconds," he said, continuing to rock and look at the fire.

Sarah would not be denied and walked round the seats and table positioned in the middle of the room and made her way over to the chair, demanding to be seen and answered, "How do you know what I said?"

The man stopped laughing and slowed his rocking down to a gentle soothing motion as Sarah stood over him, not menacingly but with intent, "My name is Joshua, and I know what I know because you told me as you walked across the flowers. They can read the feelings in any step, even those which carry so much pain and grief Sarah," turning to look at her for the first time, his face still showing the last signs of the smile it had previously.

Sarah had never looked into a face which said so much and listened so much in her whole life. It was the eyes and the blue colour that they possessed inside. A deep blue, yet mixed with the light colours of aqua and turquoise across their surface. She had seen the Ocean and stared at it, hypnotised by its colour and rhythms many a time but these eyes put that to shame. In a moment, with just one look, she was calmed. Her heart rate reduced and her breathing evened out as Ty watched her physically change in front of her.

"Sit down, Sarah, be at peace, rest and be still," Joshua said, "There is food and warm tea to follow and then we will talk but for the moment, just be."

Sarah felt her tiredness, her grief heavy on her shoulders, the coldness of the rain on her frame and looked round for somewhere to sit, she had plenty of choices. She eventually choose a big leather armchair pulled up close on the opposite side of the fire from Joshua, its surface covered with a blanket which she was sure she had seen in her thoughts before they came down the hill. She slumped into, pulled her knees up to her chest and covered herself in the blanket. It smelt like a summer meadow recently visited by rain and the feel of it on her skin left her warm and content. She hadn't even wondered how he knew her name and for the moment didn't care. Any other thoughts apart from food and sleep disappeared as she sat back and simply sat in silence.

Ty moved forward from the door, having witnessed the exchange between Joshua and Sarah and her falling into the chair. He felt, for the first time, like a stranger but Joshua quickly dispelled this,.

"Come on Ty, sit down by the fire, rest and be still. Princess said you would come also and she would be disappointed if she knew I left you standing at the door."

Her name on his lips, the obvious knowledge that he had of her existence did exactly the same to him as Sarah, apart from the questions. He looked briefly round and took himself over to a similar seat to Sarah, a little further away from the fire, and sat there, content in body although his mind raced in every direction, all of them towards Princess and what Joshua may know of her. They sat there, both of them slumped in their chairs, covered in blankets, glad to be in the warm and way from the rain still falling outside. Joshua sat in the rocking chair moving slowly back and forth, the rhythm adding to the tiredness which had enveloped and consumed Ty and Sarah. It was the only sound in the room apart from the occasional crackle from the fire which glowed and threw shadows across the room, all of them offering warmth and sleep.

Both Ty and Sarah were content to stare at the fire and let the silence speak. They watched the flames rise, flicker and die forming patterns and colours as they did. The smoke coming from the fire seemed to be infused with a soft smell, jasmine or something similar. Both of them struggled to keep their eyes open, sleep calling them with every shallow breath they took. Joshua did not have the same struggles, the light from the fire occasionally caught his blue eyes, open, awake, alert, but still as the waters that ran through the quietest stream.

Sarah's eyes and heart were heavy with sleep but also filled with the twin sisters of grief and despair. She wanted to let herself just go and just drift off into dreams but the 'sisters' still had too much of a hold on her. She could not let go and trust what she had seen in Joshua's eyes – compassion, wisdom and care – and let that be enough for the moment. Her body like Ty's was tired but her thoughts were still walking and moving across the hills outside. So many questions unanswered, so many threads to link and tie together, her mind would not switch off. In amongst all of them, from the back of her mind, as her eyes finally began to close, she heard the voice, silent for so long, rise up and speak.

"The mill pond surface of the oceans waves, spoke to me through twilight's gaze, offered up a place, hard to resist, beneath the waves, beyond the mist."

Sarah's last thoughts before she fell asleep were of the ocean and the beach that she had been transported from, indeed her life that she had been lifted from. In amidst all that had happened she had forgotten that she had a life somewhere else and that all of this was not that life, or was it. The ocean, the streams, the lake and then of course River. Water everywhere running through her mind, chasing her down, relentless, her feelings overflowing, would there be no end to the cracks it could find within her soul, within her heart. She fell asleep to its sound, but for her it was the crashing of a waterfall onto the jagged rocks below, her body and her feelings smashed to pieces by the waters falling from above, from the River beyond that.

Ty was in a similar state of mind although his thoughts strayed out across the hills towards Princess. He watched the fire twist and turn, its colours inviting but dangerous. It reminded him of the first time he met Princess and the dangers he saw. They were not dangers to the flesh but more so from his feelings and falling to deep for her to quickly, to a place where he could not hope to return from. However it was mixed with the depth and intensity of her beauty, her grace, her obvious compassion and serenity. Words he thought he knew until he met her and realised he had no idea of them until he witnessed them in action. As his thoughts went to her and as his eyes closed an image came to him, an image of her. She was with her mother, holding on and sobbing, the sky was darkening around her and inside his heart he heard and felt the unmistakable sound of her voice, calling for him.

He was up, instantly awake, throwing off the blanket and gathering his belongings. He looked quickly at Sarah, asleep, for the first time that day her face peaceful and her breathing easy on the eye and ear. He turned to Joshua to speak, but was beaten to the words by him.

"She calls for you and you want to go, need to go. But you don't want to leave Sarah, your compassion and care comes through from the way you look at her. She will be ok, she needs sleep and she will find that and comfort within it. Go now and I will be here when she wakes, she will be safe here, within these walls she will find what she needs," Joshua said half-turning and looking up at Ty.

Ty could see that he had no reason to be concerned, despite only the short time they had been there it was obvious that the whole place and outside offered respite from despair and warmth to chill any coldness in the heart. He nodded and looked over at Sarah for one last time, and began to move across the room towards the door and the coolness of the night outside.

"Follow you heart Ty and think not too much of what direction. Her call, if you allow it to be, will guide you, may your journey be swift and your footsteps light. Go now and find your Princess," Joshua added as Ty slipped outside into the cold night air and started across the flowers towards his Princess and her call.

Joshua settled back into a gentle rocking of the chair, his eyes flicking from the fire to Sarah and then back again, "Go Ty and find her, time is short and she needs you now. River is nearly there and she will feel that in her heart. Here and now there is no time to sleep for you, speed is of the essence," he whispered into the stillness of the room and to the shadows which grew inside.

CHAPTER 15

They are everything…

"When I'm dead and my corpse lays rotting in the earth, will the shadow then lift from those I have hurt. Such drama and such passion, but there is no let up. No shadows lift from them as they do not even remember you being there. Gone and forgotten is more true. There is no death just this, day after day, year after year, a repeating of existence. If that's what this is, words, thoughts, actions, looks in the mind, they mean everything, there are everything," the voice was on a mission, loud, consuming and filling the space.

Tony could not attempt to move himself into the corner anymore. He was scrunched, huddled, into the smallest shape he could, naked, cold and alone, except for this voice which would not leave him alone. His skin was still covered in the markings he had written, words of nothing, in a place with no meaning written by a man with no hope left. The voice kept on speaking but he simply repeated the same thing over and over, minute after minute, hour after hour. Time stood still as Tony longed for release, longed for death and a place away from this hell. He had realised that him and the Abyss were never twin brothers, never connected. He had simply let himself forget what life meant and moved away from those who loved and cared for him. A movement for him towards solitude and towards the waiting arms of loneliness and desperation. A time when he was ready and open to listen to something that dwelt inside him as it did for others, everyone. But Tony had listened where others had not and he had been deceived by the gifts offered to him – he had a gift of desperation but had failed to use it properly.

"Yes desperation, the gift I gave you which you threw away and choose to simply ignore," the voice reaching into his thoughts and snatching them up to take, *"Gave you a way out, a chance to leave and you choose to stay thinking it was the right move, that you could cope by yourself. You thought you were being strong, coping alone, but that is where we wanted you. Afraid to make yourself vulnerable by asking for help, unaware that you can't obtain courage without walking through vulnerability."*

Tony was taken back to the time when he knew that he needed to ask for help, to reach out and put his faith and trust in something or someone else. He had nearly, he half-reached out, put a foot in but could never truly let himself go. He had people there who were asking him, seeking him out, but he could not take that final step. He got so close and then his ego pulled him back, letting him believe that he could cope and deal with it all on his own. As long as he wrote down what he felt then he thought he was getting it out, black ink on white paper was enough. He was unaware that it simply fuelled the fires and took him closer to where he was now. He started to rock, his tears flowing as he wished that he had been able to trust, to believe and let go of all that he felt inside. His tears increased and he started to sob, a never-ending torrent of tears which would not wash away that feeling of regret and despair that he could not take that final step. The realisation that he had bought himself to where he was now and no one else. The worst part of any self-reflection and self-awareness, the moment when he had to turn around and face himself. The sobs increased and his heart failed to stem the flow as he pushed himself more into the corner.

As he did this, he felt, as if from a dream, a hand, a gentle and small hand, reach out and lightly touch his shoulder, its warmth, its touch stopping his fall into oblivion, and then a voice, a child's voice, soft and soothing in his ear, he dared to turn slowly, and found himself seeing the hand and turning more to see the face of the voice that spoke.

Tony turned to find River at his side and his fall was complete.

CHAPTER 16

Tepid waters rise and fall…

Back at the stream, and in the clearing, where Sarah had met both Tony and River, the waters began to rise. They rose at a rate which would have been astonishing to anyone who had been there, but no one was there to see it.

They rose with an intensity and a passion which matched anything that nature and the waters of the universe could throw at anyone. They were stirred by a wind that would not be stilled by the hand of God or any other deity that had a mind to intervene. They rose up over the edges of the surrounding banks, overflowing onto the grass as they pursued a course towards the forest.

The trees answered in response, twisting in their roots, bending in their wills against the flood waters that moved towards them. The waters carried with them a voice, a crushing force that pushed it from deep inside, ***"We will not be denied, not now. He comes but he has no power here. Without your protection the boy is lost and fear will overcome him."***

The trees struggled in their response, held back by the roots that sustained their life, that sustained all life, their branches rattling and creaking in the winds which came at them, they answered in unison, a voice that held within it the wisdom of so many years, "He will not be lost, he holds us within his heart, that can never be taken away from him. He has the faith given to him by a million lifetimes and a hope which lives deep inside."

The waters continued to rise, pushing way beyond the banks now, a steady and sure progress towards the start of the forest and the small saplings that existed there, young and fragile, there youth providing a glimpse into River's soul, *"Faith, hope, those words have no place where he is. Hope left there a long time ago, and it will leave him just as quickly. He goes to save one who does not want to be saved,"* the voice from the Abyss, insistent and powerful riding on the waves which came faster now.

The rain started to fall again as the twin forces of water and wind stood there in the clearing, face to face, toe to toe with each other. Neither backing down, twisting and turning around each other, waiting for the other to make the first move, from opposite sides they came, with different agendas and endings in their hearts.

"Everyone wants to be saved, even those who don't know it yet. River has the force of us all behind him," two sentences that for a moment held back the tide from reaching the young saplings.

"Tepid waters rise and fall, as cruisers begin to drift, striding out on shifting sands, like pirates without a neck, there's no faith in that hope and no point to his amen," the waters and the voice moved forward and the bottom of the saplings were engulfed as the forest watched in vain.

The battle had begun.

CHAPTER 17

It's here inside me...

Ty had left the hut, jumped down the steps of the balcony, and he was off. His bag slung over his shoulder as he started off alone in his final search for his Princess. He was sad to leave Sarah behind but knew that she would understand and would be fine left with Joshua. Even just the short time they had been there convinced him of that, in a place that was so beautiful and still, nothing would happen to her.

Without Sarah, Ty picked up the pace. He ran, skirting the edge of the lake, the water glistening in the reflection of the moon that had come out overhead. The clouds had given way and the night sky lay vast and deep above him as he ran. He came to the end of the lake and for a moment paused trying to listen to his heart and the direction of her call. It was only a brief pause and he was off again, continuing the pace, moving away from the hut, the lake and the flowers which slept as the day had finished. Before Ty had felt so uncertain in the direction he was taking but it was like a new vigour and purpose had overtaken him. He was sure footed, precise and felt directed by something other than his thoughts. The words of Joshua kept going through his head, about being directed by her call and his heart, and he felt uplifted.

As he moved out from the lake the ground rose again, reaching away and beyond the valley, towards what lay ahead. He reached the summit of a small hill and stood there momentarily before darting off to the left towards an area of tress he could see in the distance. It seemed, in the dark, nearer than it might have been but Ty was sure and directed from within. The image of Princess sobbing and being held in her mother's arms called to him and his pace increased. He could not leave her there and not answer her call, he would never do that. It had never happened before so he knew the importance of it, he would answer her call.

Ty had not met her mother but knew how much she meant to her. Princess would often speak of her and about her and how close they were and also how similar, yet so different. She spoke of the spark and passion which her mother ignited in her and her desire to reach out and be with others. When Princess spoke of her mother her almond eyes always narrowed and the peace that always sat within them seemed to glow and resonate outwards. It was something he was always aware of and he often spoke about his desire to meet her mother.

When he did say this Princess laughed and said, "Isn't one of us enough, you would not be able to cope with two?" teasing him playfully.

Ty's pace never slackened as he moved across the open fields, sunflowers rising up on either side as he made his way swiftly through them. He stopped suddenly and felt an icy breeze pluck at the hairs on his neck. He stood still, the breeze more now, its chill forcing him to reach into his bag for a thin overcoat which would negate the chill without getting in the way of his pace. He put it on but the breeze threatened to be too much for the coat and for a moment Ty hesitated. Something had happened, or was about to. Doubt and fear raised their head and Ty was forced to stand still and let the icy breeze pass over and through him. He closed his eyes and tried to calm his breathing down, like Princess had shown him so many times before. He stood there, swaying slightly, trying to feel his breath rise and fall, his heart rise up and down. His eyes still closed, images came and went beneath them until something came into view, stronger and more in focus than the rest, an image that made his knees buckle, and his heart tremble.

The picture that came to mind, the images contained water, it was everywhere. Water rising up from the earth, out from the streams and lakes, waterfalls crashing down and amidst it all he saw her. Princess, on her knees, sobbing, crying out for help, her arms reaching out, towards him, away from him. He saw himself trying to reach her, the waters and currents too strong. He saw her falling, going under the water, him unable to get to her in time. He heard her words, words alien to him, words he had never heard the sound of from her lips, "Wound invisible to the eye, but it's here, inside me, piercing pain, turns my head, turns me, inside out, inside in." Her head going under the water and him unable to get to her, to protect her.

The image went as quick as it had come. The breeze disappeared and Ty opened his eyes. The night was still and Ty moved off, his pace quicker than before. He knew that time was running out and that Princess was now in grave peril. Only he could save her.

CHAPTER 18

All of them are friends… of silence…

Sarah had been asleep for some time now. Joshua remained where he had always been, rocking in the chair, his gaze alternating between the fire and her, then back to the fire. He got up and moved towards her. During her sleep the blanket had fallen away from her and her reached out to put it back in place and cover her more. Her face was at peace, the grief and despair forgotten in amidst all that had happened as she gained welcome respite from its depth. She moved slightly in her sleep as he touched the blanket but found another position and her shallow breaths told him she had not been disturbed by his actions.

Joshua moved towards the small kitchen area where food had been prepared waiting for the right time to serve it. He moved effortlessly expending little energy as he did, a gracefulness in all that he did and said. His face and eyes contained a wisdom which anyone who knew would know came from healed pain. An acceptance of life, the good and the bad, the beautiful and the painful. An acceptance of the impermanence of all things, including feelings of attachment. He busied himself amongst the plate and saucepans, a sixth sense telling him that what had been prepared would be ready soon and also needed.

He finished what needed to be done and walked towards the open door. It was always left open, day and night, an invitation to any who came by, including nature itself. It was cold outside, a chill in the air as he stood looking out into the now clear sky. He was keenly aware of the contrast of the cold air on his face and the warmth of the fire on his back. The sky was empty of clouds, the moon having risen high above the lake, sending its light out across the water and the fields of flowers. Nothing moved in the whole of the valley, a silence so deep it could be felt by all who witnessed it. A calm before the storm, a pause before the battle, and Joshua's thoughts went out to River.

He turned his gaze at the chairs on the balcony and remembered the times he sat there with River teaching River how to play chess, and his laughter as he learnt. The look on River's face once he had mastered the game and the first time that he had beat Joshua. The smile of joy as River realised that he was about to win, the excitement in his eye's at the final move. When the game had been completed and River's triumph was complete he ran round the table and flung himself at Joshua. His laughter matched only by the intensity of the hugs he bestowed on him, almost bear like. Such a wonderful spontaneous expression of love that Joshua struggled, at the time, to hold back his tears.

As he stood in the doorway and looked out, Joshua's thoughts, prayers and hopes went out to River, He knew that he was not alone in sending these, that the night sky, that night, was full of many of these exact same things. It was the main reason for the silence, if not the only reason. Although nothing moved seemingly, Joshua knew that everything moved in silence. The whole forest, the whole of nature and life outside was moving to kneel in prayer and reflection for River. The boy was loved by all for his innocence, his lack of fear and his faith and trust in others. It was hard to accept that he was beyond their reach. But the prayers were not about physical salvation but a message of love and support to the boy who jumped. River who dared to go where no others would, to face something that could not be seen because he could not simply look on and do nothing for another in pain.

"Where's Ty?" Sarah's voice punctuated his thoughts, although he knew it was coming.

Joshua turned to find her sitting up on the chair, at the edge yawning, the blanket wrapped around her shoulders.

"He had to go, Princess needs him and he could not wait any longer. He said you would understand," turning and walking towards the kitchen as he finished.

Sarah did not seem or act surprised by this news or concerned about being left behind with Joshua, a person she had only recently met. Her sleep, although not long, had allowed her some peace of mind for a time and it had provided some balance, relief and rest from the feelings that she carried with her during the journey with Ty.

"You must be hungry, come and eat. Afterwards we can talk, if you want to," Joshua said pulling a chair out from under the table, gesturing for her to come and sit down.

Sarah got up and walked slowly over to the table, sleep trying to pull her back into the chair, but she continued moving towards the food with the blanket placed around her shoulders, both hands keeping it in place. She looked down at the various dishes laid out before her, vegetables of different types and colours, all steaming hot and calling out to her stomach. She was hungry and tried to think of the last time she had really eaten but couldn't focus with her tiredness and quickly gave up on trying to.

Joshua sat down next to her bringing with him freshly baked bread which looked delicious and smelt heavenly. Sarah moved to help herself but something stopped her midway and she pulled her hands back looking at Joshua. He was sitting head bowed his eyes closed. He was quite, in thought or prayer. Sarah felt awkward for the first time, a little uncomfortable and unsure what to do. In the end she decided on sitting still and in silence, waiting for him to finish.

After a few minutes it appeared that he had, raising his head, opening his eyes and looking at her, "Eat, come on, dig in," he said smiling.

Sarah did just that, cutting a slice of the fresh bread and dishing up various vegetables and placing them on her plate until there was room for no more. She started to eat, amazed by the freshness and taste of the food, hardly waiting to finish one mouthful before stuffing the next one in. The bread was as good as it looked and she cut herself another slice and used it to wipe up the last of the food from her plate. Joshua eat in silence but his manner was the complete opposite of Sarah's. Each mouthful was savoured and chewed slowly, pausing between each one to drink from a glass of water. It was almost like a meditation exercise for him as he eat with little effort and apparent ease and skill.

When they had finished, they both sat back in their chairs, little need for talking as they contemplated the food they had eaten and its taste. After a while Joshua got up and started to collect the dishes up to take them over for washing. Sarah went to help but he refused her attempts and said there was no need, he had it all covered. She sat down at the table and watched him. His movements were busy but unhurried, each one planned and completed with balance and precision. In no time at all, everything was put away and the table was cleaned.

"Shall we go outside onto the balcony and sit. The night is cold but beautiful, it will be warm enough if you bring your blanket," Joshua said as he moved back towards, and then past, the table and where Sarah was sitting.

She followed him outside, he paused to pick up a blanket for himself as they moved out onto the balcony. They made themselves comfortable in chairs looking out at angels from the balcony. They were neither looking at or away from each other and the distance between them was enough so that she felt neither hemmed in or alone. They sat there for a while, blankets over each of them watching the night outside and feeling the beauty of the moment.

"How often did River used to come here?" it was Sarah who spoke first, breaking the silence between them and the night.

"All the time, not always up to the hut or to speak with me. I would often just look out and see him sitting by the lake or lying in the flowers. He loved lying in the flowers, for hours, staring up at the sky. His face a picture of contentment, his eyes closed. He always said that in those moments he found love, faith and God and that those things could not be found in noise or restlessness. He once said to me that all of them are friends... of silence."

Sarah looked at Joshua to find that he was looking at her also. His eyes sparkling, his face caught in a smile at the image if River lying down, of him talking. The words that he had said were truly amazing, but for a child to have that connection and to feel that intensity was a lot for Sarah to take in. She had met River for such a brief time but knew some of what Joshua had said was right about him. He may only have been young in years but there was emotional intelligence and knowledge that was way beyond that. But some of it was also uncomfortable for her to hear, some of the words were difficult for her to feel.

"Faith is a word that I struggle with. So many doubts," Sarah said after a time thinking, "it comes and goes as I lose track of what it means. If you throw the word God in as well, all that happens is I end up confused and bewildered by it all."

"God and Faith is not an easy concept for the head to understand it's true, but there's a reason for that. Neither of them is about what you think. Leave anything up to the mind and it will tangle you up in complex discussions and theories. Faith and God does not live there amongst theory," Joshua replied.

"My head tells me so many different things about them both, leaves me with a headache and very little understanding of either," Sarah said half laughing.

"But what does your heart tell you?"

"That faith and God is no business of the head, I'm not meant to understand it in that way, that I should feel them both only," Sarah replied, a little surprised at the turn of the conversation.

"The heart will always tell us the truth if we allow ourselves the time and space to listen. That is why River spent so much time sitting or walking through the forests and meadows alone. He allowed himself the time and silence to let his heart truly speak to him," Joshua said still looking at Sarah.

"But what about science, physics? The stuff that proves we came from something else other than God; that he, or she, does not exist."

"There is no science here, just nature and being. Where science does live is in the heads of man, it gives reason and meaning to a world which has one, apparently. That's the thing also about God. He allows us, gives us freedom of thought, action, word and deed. Let's us reach out, search, for answers to the things that leave us uncomfortable not knowing. Gives us the answers to deny his existence, without doubt, gives us all that we need to prove God does not exist," Joshua said, his eyes really sparkling now. "And then God says to each of us, despite all the evidence to the contrary… do you believe? Or more so not do you believe, but what do you know, what your heart knows? Faith, God is not about believing, it's about knowing; knowing that God can and will, if you ask," he finished and sat back, a smile of knowing on his face and in his eyes.

"Can and will do what," Sarah asked. Inquisitive now and held by what he was saying.

"Aaah, now's there a question," he replied sitting back in his chair, closing his eyes.

Sarah could see that the time for talking, for the moment had obviously finished. She sat back to thinking about what Joshua had said and about what River had said to him. River, his name, pulling at her heartstrings. She did not know where he was. But the air felt suddenly heavy and hard to breathe and in this uneasiness she bowed her head and prayed. Something she had not done for some time. Her prayers went out to River, wherever he was. She felt inside her heart that he needed them, right now.

CHAPTER 19

Time reduces life to dust...

The voice was laughing, loud, really loud. It seemed like there was no other noise that existed, before and now, except the sound of the voice laughing; relentless, non-stop. It was the only noise because it was so loud and because it just would not stop.

River was leaning over Tony, his small body, his sheer presence so out of place. He did not belong to anything that existed or was present in that place; the voice, the misery, the despair and desolation, the emptiness – in that Abyss. River was trying to put a blanket around Tony as he sat huddled up in the corner, rocking and crying. The blanket kept slipping off and River kept on picking it up and putting it back on Tony's naked body. Time after time the same thing happened but River would not give up until eventually the rocking subsided enough for it to stay put, half-covering Tony. River had patience and determination that knew no end and even in the place that he was this still shone through.

River knelt down as the voice changed to talking, moving away from the laughing, to an incessant monologue. Lines and sentences taken from Tony's writing, constant stream delivered in the same loud way. River appeared untouched by the noise and where he was. The markings on the wall, the voice screaming now, Tony half-naked and sobbing seemed to bounce off him, reflected away by the faith that he carried, that he had got from days laying in the fields of flowers looking up at the sky. The faith he obtained there carrying him through the seconds as they slowly ticked by.

Tony had been dismayed and broken at the same time by River's arrival. Of all the places he would have picked to meet again with this boy, he never would have bought him there. The pain he felt now knew no bounds it held sway and power throughout his whole body, his heart wept as the tears continued to fall from his eyes. Apart from when River had first arrived he had not been able to look at him again, almost as if by not looking then it was not real, it was all simply a nightmare. But reality had kicked in and he knew that River was there and that he was not hallucinating. The thought of River having to be there and come to this place was bad enough to see it actually now was almost too much for him to bear.

River had not said a word since he had been there. His whole focus and intention was on letting Tony know that he was not alone, that someone else was there. There was little need for words to see the pain that Tony was in anyway. He was broken, physically, emotionally and spiritually. It was clear that he had desperation in and on every part of him but it certainly was not a gift for him. River may not have said a word but in his head there was a different voice, it was the calming and loving voice of the woman he had left before he got there, Princess. Her laughter and the vision of her next to him was running through his mind, he was aware of the voice screaming at Tony and him, but was also unaware of it. There was noise but no content as far as he was concerned.

Tony's crying had started to subside, he was shivering as the blanket failed to fill the purpose it had been made and bought for. He was gasping for breath and struggling to speak but even more so to turn round and face River. The voice was silent out loud now but inside Tony's head it continued, taunting, reaching in and holding onto his heart, asking him why did he bring the boy, River, there? The twin spectres of shame and guilt rose up from his stomach and he felt himself shrink and curl up, attempting to lose himself in the corner more. In the end it was all too much and he turned quickly round, shocking River a little as he did so.

"Why did you come? Why here? You just couldn't leave me alone, could you," he spat the words out at River.

River had not expected this response from Tony, did not think that this would be the first words they spoke. For a moment he was taken aback, the ferocity of the words and their intent was something he had never experienced. River, unusually for him, felt himself draw back from Tony physically, his arm around the shoulder simply becoming a hand on it.

"Wish you hadn't come now don't you? So do I, there is nothing you can do here, it's all over and you are too late. I don't want to be saved, by you." Tony spoke again, fully turning round now to face River head on, in the process pushing River's hand away from his shoulder.

River was still kneeling but now there was space between them physically and in that space, doubt and confusion arose within River. He could no longer hear Princess's voice, see her face, feel her touch and he suddenly felt alone and lost. He looked quickly round and felt as if the walls of the room were moving in on him, getting closer. The voice which he had been unaware of suddenly became a focal point of his attention, the words spat out towards him, their focus moving away from Tony onto River. For the first time in his life River became aware of his own physical size, how small he was and how big everything else was. The doubt and confusion which had risen up moved on to be replaced by anxiety and the beginning of fear. His heart, so slow in pace normally, began to beat a little faster and his breathing intensified. All of these symptoms eating away at the innocence inside of him, new feelings and new thoughts first experienced with no knowledge of how to ease them. He felt himself move further away from Tony, he no longer felt safe around or near him. He no longer felt safe inside himself. For River this was something that he did not expect.

The voice spoke and River hear it, *"Did you come to save or come to stay? You bring with you innocence and faith, but they are so easily forgotten here. There is nothing to hold onto here except... nothing."*

River moved away from Tony, into the corner opposite. He sat down and pulled his knees up to his chest, head bowed. From the opposite corner Tony sat watching him, in exactly the same position, head bowed, knees up to his chest.

The voice laughed, again, and started to speak. This time River could hear it, *"Trace the figure and outline a shape; Shadows lengthen on what is made, time reduces life to dust, as icy hands reach down to touch."*

River started to cry as Tony looked on, rocking back and forth. The Abyss had them both.

CHAPTER 20

Hearts quiver in response to the pain...

Ty burst through the tree line. He knew he was close, he could feel her presence now. He had expected to come through the latest line of trees and find her there. The ground he found himself on certainly looked familiar, it had been in the vision he had when he was at Joshua's house. The trees, the streams, the whole thing was exactly as he had seen, with the exception of her being there. He stopped, confused, uncertain for the first time since he had started off again looking for her. He looked around, a complete circle of where he was and could not see her. His heart told him that she was there, so close, but he could not see her. The call he had responded to, her need for him beat strongly in his heart, and she was here somewhere. He breathed in deep, an attempt to re-focus and look again. It worked as he found himself drawn to an area by the stream, hardly lit by the moon which had become hidden by clouds which had built up suddenly overhead. He moved towards it slowly, afraid of being wrong, afraid that he would miss something, afraid he would miss her. His eyes became more attuned to the light, the half-light, and he found himself able to see things clearer. He saw her.

She was lying down, her head slightly raised resting on a part of the grass slightly higher than the rest. Her mother sat next to her, holding one of her hands in her own. He walked the short distance over softly, afraid to simply come unexpected. He had waited for so long for this time, before it had always been a dream and now reality had turned that dream into here and now. But now, having waited for so long, he was filled with fear and apprehension, he knew that things were not right when he heard her call, but now coming on her here he knew that they were worse than he could even have thought. Her lying down, eyes closed and no visible sign of breathing, his thoughts turned to the worst it could be.

"She is sleeping, it's not what you think," her mother said before he had even finished or got to the end of his thoughts.

He knelt next to her and looked down at Princess. Her face had changed in colour and she was pale as if she had never seen the light of the morning sun. His hand came out to touch it and swept away some stray hairs, which had drifted across her forehead. He could see that she was breathing but the sound was not audible, just a slight raising of the chest with each breath that she took. He looked swiftly across at her mother but did not get a response. Her focus and her concentration were purely on Princess and for her nothing else existed in the physical sense, even Ty being there.

"How long has she been like this," Ty asked his words barley registering in the air.

There was a silence and a space before her mother answered, "Long enough now."

"I don't understand, what happened?" Ty said, although he was aware that he may not get an answer.

Her mother again remained silent for some time before replying, "River is in danger, she can feel it, she can feel it. Until he comes back she will not return. His and her fates are linked now. Doubt and fear exist where they did not before and uncertainty reigns," she said, her voice faltering as she finished speaking.

Ty's eyes widened as his heart collapsed around him. He did not understand. He had not seen this coming, this ending when they met. Now here he was and she was lost, physically present but it was only a shell. Her spirit, her soul, had gone. It too was searching and reaching out for River, trying to find and bring him back, to rescue him as Ty had set out to rescue her, protect her, hold her. His sadness knew no bounds and fear and the possibility of losing her overtook all his emotions as he knelt over her and bent down. He held her head with one hand, and kissed her softly on the forehead, her skin cold to the touch of his warm lips. He stayed like this for some time, willing her to return, for them both to return.

"Come, step back, leave her. She knows we are here, she knows that you are here and that brings comfort, but it will not bring her back," her mother said, gently pulling at the sleeve of Ty's coat.

He lifted himself up and looked towards her mother to speak but found that she herself had got up and walked slowly away towards the stream. Ty looked once more down at Princess and saw that she quivered and a frown come across her furrowed brow, before she returned to her shallow breathing state.

He walked across to her mother and found her sitting down by the water's edge, cross legged, seemingly in reflective thought, her head bowed. Ty sat next to her, fighting the desire to get up and run back to the side of his Princess.

"River is her son."

The words were the last thing he expected to hear. Ty was shocked, not because of the idea, but because it was so unexpected. His shock obviously showed on his face and he went to speak but she spoke first.

"She is his spirit mother, soul mother if you like," she said as if it was the easiest thing in the world to say, just a normal happening, "that's why they are like they are, she knows but River doesn't although he may have some kind of idea," she went onto add.

"And his real mother, his birth one," Ty said, purely for the sake of saying something such was his shock at the initial statement.

"No one really knows. River came here one day and it seemed like he had been here for ever, part of everything, connected. No one questioned or thought about it," her mother said.

"Princess knows though," he said.

"Princess knows everything, so yes of course she does. They are connected through compassion and love. Their hearts quiver in response to the pain of others, they sense and feel in much the same way; that is why she is feeling what he is now. Despite the distance, wherever they are, she will always know. The more time they spend together the stronger it becomes. You have never met River yet have you?" she said looking at him and feeling for him in that moment.

Ty was bought back from his own thoughts by the question, "No I haven't. Princess spoke of him but that was in my dreams and I thought it was all just part of it, unreal. I take it their fates are linked then."

"Interwoven and connected at every level. If River does not return then she will live on physically but she will never be the same. She will be lost to us all, out of sight and sound and nothing and no one will ever be able to penetrate it. As she lays there now she is trying to reach him but even that may not be enough. She is fighting against something of which even she has no real sense of the depth and intensity," she said moving her eyes over to where Princess still lay.

"Why did she call out for me then. If I can't help, why did she call," Ty asked, confused now.

"Because she knew you would come and that she would need you here. Although she reaches out to River she needs to have one foot here and remember a reason to come back. If she didn't have that then she would have gone herself and that would only have put them both in danger. She cannot help River whilst she fights to save herself. None of us can, we have to give up ourselves and let go," she said her eyes watching Princess for any change.

"So what happens now," Ty said following her gaze and getting up to return to her side.

"We wait and we hope and we hold onto our faith. We are powerless in which way it goes," she said watching Ty walking slowly over to Princess, unsure if he heard or not.

Ty reached Princess and sat down next to her. Very little had changed in the time he had been speaking with her mother. He looked down at her face, its beauty hidden slightly by the shadows of the night, her smile missing whilst in sleep, her eyes closed so he was unable to see their peace and stillness. Her eyes had always captured him, from the moment they had first met. He longed to look into them now, to feel her breath on his chest as she slept but knew that this was not the time. He took her hands in his and prepared to do what her mother had said; to wait.

CHAPTER 21

A ripple becomes a wave…

The water had risen and gone past the saplings that had lived and existed on the edge of the forest, it crept further inside, reaching out and inwards through and around all that stood in its path.

Once water finds a way it will not be denied. When its driven by a force, pressure, it will seek out a crack and be through it before it's known and seen, before anything can be done, it needs no route or path, it flows and it goes, through and around, consumes ground and moves at rates which cannot be matched.

The water which had risen up over the banks of the clearing had a force behind it. A drive and a purpose to seek out and cover new ground, ground it had given up over the years. The trees, flowers, grass which had flourished under rain's touch now disappeared.

Water gives and it brings life; it takes and denies dreams and scatters them like leaves in a storm. Tossed and thrown aside, torn away from their hosts, holds them, turns them round and *uses them against each other. A ripple becomes a wave, the wave becomes two and before you know, realise even, the storm is upon you, it has arrived.*

The water made its way through the forest; winding and flowing, twisting and seeking paths which had been worn down by feet. The steps of lovers, the soft prints of angels, covered and hidden as it moved further in, rising up and reaching out; small trees gone, flowers drowned and it kept on. It followed no rhyme, had no reason except to cover, consume and destroy.

There was no wind, no rain. It was silent. Water driven by silence still holds the same power, if not more; it simply flows.

This water flowed out from the emptiness created by years of isolation; by too much time thinking, letting thoughts run alone inside rather than letting them go, out into the world.

The Abyss can come in many forms – it came in the shape and form of water, across all that had been beauty and innocence. Where life had existed it took it away; in just one day.

As time waits in the wings, so does water.

What was left was time and water.

CHAPTER 22

He stood in his own light for too long…

"Where is Tony's book?"

The words and sounds of Joshua's voice came as a shock to Sarah. They had been sitting there, him seemingly sleeping. The earth had moved, time had gone and Sarah had sat and looked out at the lake, at the fields and then at the sky. All of it had somehow bought some peace and stillness to her heart. She found her grief in there bearable and little less uncomfortable, manageable for a time. Even the view of the lake had not crushed her insides. She could look across it and see the beauty on top and beyond its surface without having to look into the depths and feel alone.

"In my bag, how did you know I had it and also how do you know Tony?" Sarah replied after getting over the initial shock. She moved towards the edge of her seat and half-turned towards him.

He sat, eyes closed still. His head was back and the words that he spoke were said as if it was the most natural thing in the world to be speaking about, "The whole world is sitting and waiting on what happens with Tony. I am no different and the book is why you are here really, isn't it?"

"What do you mean waiting on what happens with him? He jumped and disappeared, he is gone. So is River, both of them gone," Sarah caught herself up after she said the words. Her words seemed so cold and matter of fact. She said them so easily, she was worried, but tried to hide this.

"He did jump its true and physically he is no longer here. But relationships don't end when someone disappears or leaves in a physical sense, the relationship continues," Joshua said, eyes still closed.

"The relationship continues. How does it continue?" Sarah asked, interested now.

"Your dad leaving, passing, is that it then? Your relationship is finished," Joshua said, treading carefully with the tone of his words.

Sarah didn't answer straight away. She had not expected the direction the conversation was going in or how quickly Joshua got to the point. She was also aware that any mention of her dad would stir up emotions, spilling over into those laying on the surface about River.

"Sorry Sarah, I didn't mean to bring him up," Joshua apologised before she could reply.

"It's ok, I know you don't mean anything by it. Relationships, whatever they are, friends, family members, and partners they just confuse me. I can't seem to work them out or find a way through them which brings the right outcome for me. I always seem to be left feeling alone and left out, they never are what I imagined them to be in my head," she said looking out at the night sky, hoping for some kind of sign to guide her.

"Your head again eh," Joshua said sighing as he finished, "what does your heart tell you about your dad though and your relationship now," he added, again careful in how he spoke when saying this.

"That I was lucky… to have him for so long. That I was there when he died, at his last breath. He was there for my first one and I was there for his last. Exactly how it should be. Some people don't get that chance," she said, surprised at how the words came out. They bought softness from deep inside and she felt her words hold her heart.

Joshua felt them to and opened his eyes, turning to look at Sarah. His eyes filled with the same softness, a mirror of her heart in that moment, "They don't indeed. Some parents have to watch their children die before them and they are left with that unbearable pain. Others have people taken from them without being there, ripped away and gone in the blink of an eye," he paused slightly before continuing, "What you have is a memory of something that brings comfort and peace when you need it too; when you miss him physically."

Sarah nodded, her eyes faintly moist at the image of him in her head. She knew she would never get over the physical side, the not being able to hug or see him right when she needed it. But what Joshua was talking about was something else, an emotional and spiritual attachment which could not be broken. Something bound in love and compassion, an innate sense inside herself of what and who he was.

"Love and compassion are things Sarah which are not easily bought. You heart quivers and responds to pain, Tony's and River's, and love for your father shines through in your eyes now," Joshua went onto say, "if its innate and inside you and you believe it to be so, maybe there is something else there also."

"What else?"

"That word again, the one you say you struggle with," he said letting her provide the answer.

She knew what he was talking about, "Faith," smiling as she said it.

"Exactly. Move out of your head, step aside from your thoughts and you will always find it. When you come to the edge and feel like you are dropping off, or about too, Faith will always provide you with what you need, at the time when you need it most," Joshua said reflecting her smile back to her before he set his head back and closed her eyes again.

Sarah sat back in her seat also, for once any thought of grief and loss gone from her chest. Her mind felt still and her thoughts which normally jumped around at rest. She looked firstly at Joshua and then out across the lake again. For the first time she felt she could look at it and see the beauty and stillness of the water rather than glancing at it and moving her attention elsewhere. It was water, pure and simple. It simplicity bought its beauty and within it, beneath it, who knows what lay. But in that moment it was not about what lay beneath but the peace and stillness which existed on the surface. Sometimes that was enough to see and that digging or going deeper was not the answer. The most important thing was to be present and to appreciate the things which you were grateful for, in that moment. She felt herself move from one thought and feeling to the next, not attaching, no focus specifically until she found herself drifting across the surface of the water, similar to how she felt at the beach.

"You can hear it now... see it now... that sound, shape and colour... of a feeling," the voice from the beach was back.

Sarah responded to it. in her head, not out loud, "I can see a shape and the different colours also, but the sound escapes me, I hear none."

"Then you hear it then... There is no sound to a feeling, only silence."

Sarah liked that, there is no sound to a feeling. When it was put like that then every feeling had a sound of its own, within that silence, for each person. Her feelings had always left her bewildered and confused, the sounds of any of them would have been them smashing into each other, a bam and a crash as she fell down in tears.

But silence allowed them to be something different, something she could relate to for herself, she didn't need to have anything else or anyone else just to feel something through silence. She enjoyed the silence she had found whilst sitting with Joshua, it held her grief in such a warm and comforting place. It was beautiful and still and she felt looked after.

She remembered the book, from nowhere it came and touched her thoughts and she asked him, "Do you know what's in the book?" Sarah asked.

"Not the actual contents. But the themes and feelings behind it, yeah I do," Joshua replied without a pause. "I know them only too well."

"What do you mean by that?"

"I stood where he stood. Stood exactly where he stood, same place, just a different time," he said for the first time with something approaching sadness in his voice, "Seems such a long time ago, another lifetime even."

Sarah was startled by this news. The last person she had ever expected to be where Tony had been, was Joshua. "Do you really mean that, literally," she said after a time.

There was silence. She looked at him trying to scan his face for anything else apart from the peace and calmness she had quickly come to know. She thought she saw a flicker of shadow appear across one part of his face, but it soon disappeared, leaving her thinking it had just been her imagination.

"Yes literally. In the clearing day after day, left by myself, just me and my thoughts and they took me to a place which is best forgotten about, by me at least. There is a saying 'he is standing in his own light. All he can see is his own shadow'. It's a description of where I was. Where I stood for too long. I lost all perspective of the world and myself. Clarity and normality left me. My mind became dark, broody, and resentful. Any gratitude I had before went and left," Joshua said, his tone regretful and for a time sombre.

"What does that actually mean though, standing in your own light?" Sarah asked, inquisitive, but respectful of opening up wounds which may be painful.

"That I cast a shadow over my own happiness and gratitude for life through my thoughts, trying to solve things I was going through by myself. I was getting in my own way, stumbling and falling over my own thoughts and feelings. I couldn't, wouldn't ask for help. Maybe I was incapable of asking. When you stand in your own light for so long only one thing happens," Joshua said in the same tone of voice.

"What happens? What happened to you?" genuine care obvious as she spoke.

"You live in your own shadow. It's all you can see and all that you become. There is no light or day, no sunshine. All the good things in life disappear like dreams in the mist. They say you should stand aside rather than in your own light. That way the light shines on you and all you do, you don't stand in the way of your own growth," Joshua said his tone changing as he finished talking to more like his normal self.

Sarah thought about what Joshua had said. She felt real sadness that he had gone through those things and understood a little more about Tony and the obviously similar feelings he had. Her empathy and thoughts grew inside her for Tony and it felt better for her to have them. She looked at Joshua, such a kind hearted and gentle soul and thought about where he had come from, the depths and pits of despair. It showed anyone could come back, could turn themselves around, they just had to hold on, "What stopped your jumping, falling off the edge?" she said, more as an afterthought really.

She didn't need to hear his answer. It was written on his face, long before any words came out of his mouth. His face lit up, all over it, any lines or wrinkles of age fell away and a smile spread from one side of it to the other. His eyes shone like opals in a sea of rubies as he turned towards her to answer.

"It was River wasn't it?" Sarah said before he could open his mouth.

She just knew, could see it and felt it between them. If Joshua's heart could reach out and touch hers, it did in that moment. As despair and desolation can reach out and enter into others hearts so can love, faith and hope. At that moment that is what entered into Sarah's. He may not have been there physically, but both their relationships with River held fast, giving them both so much.

"River came along and everything changed. His innocence was more than enough but it was his laughter, which cast away the shadows and bought light back into my heart. He bought with him some hope, a chance of redemption and a chance to change things. It's when we first met. He bought me back and now he goes to bring someone else back except its different this time," Joshua said his smile dissipating a little.

"Why is it different this time?" Sarah asked, worried by the sudden change in his face.

"No one has ever been bought or come back from so far down. Tony jumped and that is an unknown. River followed him, again an unknown. Where they are going and what they face is the third unknown. So much to think about and so many unidentified factors. All hopes are pinned on the fearless innocence of a child. It's a lot for him to carry, maybe too much," he said with deep emotion.

Sarah understood what he was saying. It was a lot to carry for anyone. The unknowns were mysterious and dangerous because they contained so much fear. River was a child and who knew how much he could deal with. He seemed invincible but experience says that children grow up at some point and they discover fear and what it can do. They find terror and mistrust and they suddenly feel alone and different. Unknowns are that for a reason, no one knows how they will respond. River was no different in this.

Joshua uttered the longest of sighs and closed his eyes again for a single moment before speaking, "Get the book, Sarah, we can at least help River in any way we can."

The book was full of what had bought Tony to the brink and what had made him jump. It contained shadow and darkness and the meaninglessness of life when looked at from this standpoint. She got up slowly and went to go inside to collect the book. Something stopped her and she moved swiftly back to Joshua's side and flung her arms round him, holding him close as he responded in the same manner. It felt so good for her to do this, to hold someone again, even for a short time.

She stayed this way until it felt natural to break away, "I will get the book and we will help River, and Tony," she said striding away with purpose. She walked away with hope at her side and faith holding her hand tightly with each step.

CHAPTER 23

There is no end to the void evoked...

The Abyss had stopped talking now; there was no laughing either. All that was left was silence.

In one corner sat Tony and in the other River, silence between them too.

They had never sat that way together. When they had been in the clearing there had always been noise, laughter from River mostly, and silence was something, which had never existed between them or in their relationship. There, in the Abyss, conversation and laughter had died alongside hope and dreams; all that was left was silence. River was used to time spent in this, it gave him a peace and a sense of stillness that he used to hold dear. Here it did not create similar feelings. He felt out of place, as if he didn't fit, with doubts and uncertainty running round in his head like clouds in a storm. The vision and memory of the stream and the fishes nibbling at his toes was disappearing, clouding over. He was trying to remember other things, which he had left behind, but they too were growing thin and less clear. Words that had never been present inside his thoughts started to rise up, kicking and screaming to be heard – desperation, endless, nothingness, desolation – these words flicked in and out of his head, a moment here and then a moment gone, moving onto the next. They were words and thoughts that had never entered into his consciousness before. His head was thumping and his heart was racing, again all new experiences, neither welcome. He put one of his small hands up to his head and started to rub, hoping it would ease some of the pain. It didn't.

Tony had not really moved the whole time from the moment when the voice and laughter had stopped. His eyes and focus was totally concentrated on River, his gaze never leaving him. He did not recognise anything in River that he knew. His mind was empty and his heart cold as stone, with no end to the void evoked inside himself. It was a void and a chasm, which he knew well and lived with for so long back in the clearing. Here in the Abyss it was even more a part of him, it was all of him. Nothing else existed and memories of anything else totally dissolved.

"Silence is nice sometimes. Other times its unwelcome. The head has too much time to run away into places it rarely visits," the Abyss had spoken.

Tony lifted his head to hear more clearly whilst River continued to sit with his head bowed. The only sign possibly that he had heard was an increased rubbing of his head.

"You like silence don't you River. Do you like the silence… HERE?" the last word directed straight at him, by-passing Tony who had now become a secondary attraction to River's presence.

Tony moved his head, down and around, to look at River. His eyes narrowing as he tried to capture any movement on River's face that showed what he was going through. River moved his other hand up to his head. Both of them rubbing his head in an attempt to be rid of some of the pain. His thoughts were changing constantly, different ones flashing in and out, moving and flowing, back and forth, from one to the next. None of them bought relief and a sense of freedom.

"Are you still glad that you came River. Came to save him, who doesn't want to be saved; he who is beyond saving?" the voice continued, trying to manipulate and get into River's head even more.

Tony kept on looking at River, but apart from the rubbing of the head, there was nothing else showing which would have let him know about what was going on for River at that moment. He decided to move, a little closer, and shuffled himself over towards the corner where River was. It was not done to bring comfort or let River see he was not alone, but to try and get closer just to see if he was missing something.

"Leave him be, he hears well enough and is just at the point where he will let go. He doesn't need you near him now, your lost already. Let him find his own Abyss," the voice spoke as Tony started to move.

Tony stopped abruptly, the voice controlled his thoughts and feelings and it was a natural progression for his movements to be directed and controlled also. River seemed to flinch a little, maybe not, with Tony's movements somewhat closer. The boy who never struggled in other's company outside could not seem to bear the closeness of anyone else near him. The influence and effect of the Abyss was growing on him, time was running low, and the voice sensed this subtle change, even if Tony did not.

"Maybe we should help things along, allow you, River, a canvas to write on. Do you want to write now, let it all out, feel the power of letting go and letting us in."?

As the voice finished speaking there was a loud crash, like the coming together of thunder and lightning. The walls turned round on their axis's, the writing which had covered the walls previously was removed, blank, gone all sight of what was previously there, Tony's words. What was left was four blank white walls, empty, and four blank canvasses.

"Here you are River. Enough of looking at that other stuff. After a while it gets boring looking at the same thing. None of its original anyway, he simply borrowed it from someone else's head. Isn't that right?" there was no doubt in whose direction the last part of the sentence was directed. Tony looked up and then down very quickly, pulling his legs back up to his chest.

River had not yet moved his position, although the rubbing of the head had ceased. It wasn't doing any good anyway and only seemed to increase the pressure and intensity of the thoughts going on in his head. He was aware of the voice and some of the words being said and also that something had changed in the room they were in but not exactly what had happened. He was trying to reach back into a memory that was good, a treasured moment, a playful touch or smile but it was not really working. Everything inside him seemed to be flipped around, turned upside down since he had arrived. All of his intentions had been on something before he came but even now that was a distant afterthought. He was forgetting not only why he had come and for whom but where he came from also. All of these when added together and multiplied by the passion and desires held within the voice created only one thing which was rising inside of him, out of control – terror. River had no idea what it was, never heard or experienced it before, and here his previous virtue and innocent naivety was no match for its hold.

"Ready yet to give us your thoughts River? Writing them down can help you know, allow you let go of what has gone before," the voice laughed. "River we are waiting. I would say we don't have all night, but that would be a lie. We have all the time in the world," the laughter continued, a demonic sound born in the depths of the world when darkness ruled and held

sway over the day.

Tony laughed also, an exact copy of the same laugh, without the same volume and intensity provided by the voice. The sound of both of them in unison seemed to have the desired effect and River finally moved, starting slowly to rise from his seated position that he had been in for so long. He looked so small and fragile as if the merest breeze would knock him over. It was the opposite of how he moved and stood when he was in the forest. There he seemed part of all that he touched and met, he belonged to and was a part of everything. Here at the doors of the Abyss, with darkness knocking and calling out, he was completely out of place. Like a lamb being led to the market for slaughter he walked slowly up to one of the blank walls, standing still before it.

He looked around for something to use to write with. Nothing caught his eye on the cold and uninviting floor. His eyes glanced at Tony who was looking at him suspiciously. If River had been able to see such things anymore he may have found a tinge of jealousy in his eyes. Tony had been replaced as the object of the Abyss's affection and he was not used to it. For so long it had just been him and the Abyss. Now River had come along and he had been left behind, cast aside. Despite this and without hesitation he held out the pen for it to be used. River looked at the pen for some time before moving forward to collect it from Tony's grasp. As he reached him and leant down to take it, they looked directly into each other's eyes from no more than a foot away. River's hand stretched out as they held each other's gaze. He grabbed the pen but Tony held on, they grappled until River won and snatched it from his grasp. Tony withdrew more into the corner and River looked at him with contempt, flickers of hatred registering on his face. Hatred for bringing him there, loathing for letting go of happiness so easily and disgust for what he had become. These feelings were new to River but in the place that they were it was not easy to be rid of them or relate to anything different.

"Very touching, very touching, but it means nothing. The pen moves on, the thoughts remain and time is running out. Let it out River," the voice interrupted there moment, anxious to get things moving again.

River moved away from Tony, turning his back, as he made his way over to the wall. He looked at the pen in his hand, the wall in front of him and lowered his head, in thought or surrender, or both. He paused, waiting for something, for anything to reach out and hold his hand.

CHAPTER 24

Saw her sitting by the rushing falls...

The night had moved on, the earth had turned, the stars rose, sparkled, and dimmed again as Ty sat holding Princess's hand in his. He had not moved, his focus and all his power concentrated purely on one thing and one thing only, Princess.

Whilst he had been sitting there his thoughts had wandered across fields and meadows and through forests and streams. The times and places he had met with her in his dreams were etched on his mind and it was these which occupied him during the minutes and hours that he sat, waiting. He could do no more except hold onto the memories of times when he walked and sat with her and the world had paid no mind to their presence. Nothing else has truly existed for him for some time, since the first time she had walked into his dreams. Her beauty and grace and the way that she was had changed since then but only in a way which made him long and want her more. Each dream, each moment spent with her simply bound him closer to her and for him his search had ended from the first day they had met. He had always felt that at some point in his life he would meet the person who would change his destiny, who would become his fate. That belief had not left him despite the many years of travelling and searching. Each turn in the road had excited him in the hope that beyond it and past that corner that person would be there.

The moment he had turned the corner and saw her by the rushing falls he knew that he could rest, that the search was finished. He had come upon her unexpectedly, her seemingly unaware that he was there. She was standing in a torrent of water beneath the overhang of rocks where water cascaded down from above. The water was ice cold, crystals creating diamonds in her jet-black hair as she stood there. The water splashed over her continuing its natural progression down into the pool which gathered beneath her feet. He had stood for some time just watching her, knowing from that moment his life would never be the same. His blood ran, red hot, through his veins, his heart pumped and he longed to reach out and hold her underneath the water. Embrace her and feel her next to him, the water adding to the passion even under its icy touch. When he had got to know her better and they had spoken about that first meeting she told him that she knew he was there all along, looking out from underneath the lids of her eyes with her dark set eyes. The eyes told him that the affect he had on her was exactly what she intended to do. The passion, the intensity, the wanting was all in that moment. She already knew her own destiny and that he would come but it did not stop her from playing with his heart. They laughed about it afterwards but for Ty the moment would always be just as intoxicating in his memory.

He sighed long and loud at the memory and looked down at her once again. For the time nothing had changed and she still lay silently, only the slightest movement occasionally from her hand or legs to show that she was still in this time and place. He knew that her sleep was fitful, her face showed it. When he had laid with her on his chest and she had fallen asleep her whole features were different. Her mouth always turned up at the side, a hint of a grin, her face a picture of peace and grace. Today was different and her mouth was set, her forehead showing signs of disturbance and pain as she lay there.

"It may be some time before we see any change," her mother said, returning after spending some time away from them both. She knew that she had left Princess in safe hands, she trusted her daughter's judgment despite never having met Ty. Princess did not cry out for help easily and in calling for Ty her Mother knew what he meant to her.

Ty moved a little, changing position on his knees to allow her mother to kneel beside him now that she had returned. They were so alike in manner and the way they both held themselves and spoke and Ty felt it as a source of comfort to have her there; like a part of the Princess that he knew being left behind to hold onto and see close up.

"She has hardly moved in the last hour, nothing at all. What does that mean," Ty said as they sat there together.

"It may mean a lot but it may also mean nothing. We cannot know for sure," she replied touched by the tenderness that Ty displayed towards her daughter.

Ty looked up at the night sky aware of the changing colour from dark set black to the onset of purple and the hints of orange across the sky. Somewhere the sun was rising and soon it would cast its gaze over them. He felt for some reason that if nothing had changed and she had not returned by daybreak then all would be lost. That both River and she would be gone, forever.

Her mother sensed a change in him, inside him, and bought her hand over to rest on his arm, "Do not give up hope whilst hope remains inside her. She will be able to sense this through you. It may not seem like it but she can feel and hear you. It comforts her and she will need it before this is over."

Ty was grateful for the warmth of her touch and the feel of her hand on his arm. It bought physical comfort but he was waning in hope and she knew this, a tear came to his eye and he felt the start of its journey down one cheek.

"Hope can seem like the smallest of things at times, sometimes a brittle thing. Easily crushed or pushed aside when life hangs from a thread. But its strength comes from that holding on despite all that your head may try and tell you. Where breath remains, hope sits close by also. Do not underestimate the courage and faith that exists in both River and Princess. What is seen on the surface is only a glimpse of what they both hold. Together it is power that is not easily matched," her mother spoke again, her hand still on his arm.

Comfort spread through Ty's body, his heart regained some sense of composure and his breath itself returned to something resembling normal. The tear continued on its journey down his cheek but it was not followed by others. Alone it fell from his cheek onto the smooth contours of her face.

Princess awoke.

With a start she sat up and reached up first to touch her hand to Ty's face to wipe away the residue of his tear and then to move her hand towards the waistband of her skirt. Ty and her mother were both startled by this sudden change and were unsure of what to do. They knew she was aware of them both but the set of her eyes and the concentration in her face showed them that something was going on inside her.

Princess sat up more now, moving onto her knees her hand pushing more into the waistband of her skirt, she was searching for something, her attention focused solely on one thing only, whatever was in there. Both Ty and her mother moved away slightly not wanting to get in the way of what she was doing. It was obvious from her fevered actions that it was important in that single moment to find something hidden in there.

From deep within the waistband, hidden only to her, Princess pulled out what she had been looking for. She held it in both hands, for the present still hiding it from the view of them. Her lips moved in words, not audible to them. She held whatever it was to lips and bowed her head, rocking back and forth as she did.

The bright light of the morning sun had started to light up the mountains on the far side of the horizon. Soon the sun would start to travel and would reach them all.

The time when all would be revealed was close at hand.

CHAPTER 25

Capture beauty one day…

The water had travelled inland across the clearing and into the forest.

Its travels to begin with had been full of force and passion, pushed from behind by something which would not be denied.

As it moved further into the depths of the forest its progress had been slower, but it had not been stopped. It wound its way through the trees like a snake across the branch of a tree, sensing and seeking out its prey. In places it was deeper than the rest, creating pools which were seemingly bottomless. If anyone had fallen into them they would never have returned, there was no bottom to those holes.

It carried on relentless, moving forward, without a pause until it had covered nearly every part of the forest. All that remained was an area of ground slightly higher than the rest. A place which overlooked the rest of the forest. At this highest point two rocks sat, next to each other, a single tree, not large in size but covered in blossom grew close by. The view from there on a summer's day was breathtaking, beyond words.

It was the final destination of the water. It knew why it needed to get there and cover all that it found. It was where River and Princess had first met and sat together. It was the last semblance of all that was pure and beautiful. When it was covered nothing would be left, nothing would remain.

The forest would be gone, River would be gone and Princess would spend her days roaming in grief for the boy she could not save.

The tree and the rock were the only parts of the forest which had allowed the new days sun in. The sun shone through the boughs of the tree and illuminated a small circle on either side of the rocks. A solace and place where beauty still existed before it was covered before it was gone. The flowers on the ground reached up and out to the light aware of the threat that was winding itself up the hill.

Slowly with little effort the water made its way up the rising ground, the force behind it incessant and constant, as it moved and snaked its way up the hill, words came from the lips of its progression, "Capture beauty one day."

CHAPTER 26

In the days that follow ...

Joshua had continued to sit outside after Sarah had left to go and fetch Tony's book. He looked up at the night sky, as he had so many times before and let his thoughts wander across them. So many nights he sat there alone and travelled from one star to the next, hopping across them laughing and smiling at the image and what that would feel like.

But tonight was different. His talk with Sarah and the understanding of what River was now facing had left its mark. He knew what it was like to face something which consumed and reached into parts of the soul which were best kept hidden from view, best kept hidden from the outside world. It may have appeared that Joshua had moved way beyond that place and time when he had stood at the edge. The years had gone by and he had moved far enough away from it for it not to impact and affect his life on a daily basis. However, as Tony had written and what Joshua also knew, when you stand at the edge long enough a part of it always remains, deep inside, locked away. Even when you manage to pull, or be pulled by someone else, away from that edge.

It had taken a long time for Joshua to move further away from the brink. It had involved a lot of love and care, given freely by the world and others to help him move forward. At times it was easy and life flowed and he felt the true nature of freedom and acceptance as the softness of life returned to his heart. On other days his thoughts were less easy to navigate. On these days if felt hard to breathe and the past sat heavily on his shoulders, weighing him down and leaving him tired and devoid of energy. At these times he slept fitfully and any sleep was interrupted by dreams, more so nightmare, which woke him up, head thumping and the sheets dripping in sweat. The only benefit of these nights was the chance to see dawn break across the mountains and the sound of the bird's dawn chorus. He hated the nightmares and the days it took to erase them from his mind but the flip side of the dawn's colours helped heal some of the scars over time.

He heard Sarah returning and moved away from dwelling of the past and the memory of nights long and dark. He returned to the present and turned his attention to the matters at hand and what could possibly be done. All of it in the name of River, all of it done in the name of hope. Sarah came back out onto the balcony holding the battered cover of the book in one hand and the light from the fading moon reflected off it for a short second. The light bounced up and flickered across his eyes and he was taken back for that second, his heart skipped and his purpose hesitated. In a similar space of time it was gone again and both had returned to normal.

"What's up, Joshua?" Sarah said aware of a sudden change in him.

It had only been fleeting but Joshua was back, "Nothing, Sarah, nothing at all," he said, moving quickly on, "I see you have it then."

Sarah looked down at the book and bought it up to eye level, surveying it once again, "Yes I do, although there is a large part of me that wished I had never seen it, let alone looked inside the cover."

"I know that feeling very well. But sometimes you have to look, intrigue and fascination won't let you leave it alone. It's like the flame of a candle, inviting and mysterious, every part of the body wants to reach out and feel its warmth and light," Joshua replied, "and then you do and wish you had never done it."

Sarah sat down and held the book in her lap, face up, although it was not easy to tell which was the right way up, "So what now?" she asked brining her gaze up to Joshua's.

He looked at her and saw in her face the need to help. A real desire to make a difference and do whatever was needed to assist River, wherever he was. He could not find it in his heart to tell her that he did not really know what to do and even if he did if it would help in any way in changing the outcome for River and Tony. Something had spoken to him inside his soul and he had asked for the book. Now it was here, close by, there was no plan. Any voice inside had been silenced and all that was left was their intuition and faith. Even then it may not be enough.

He breathed long and deep, exhaling for what seemed an eternity to Sarah, "Sarah, it would be wrong for me to say I knew. I don't. I asked for it because it felt the right thing to do and I felt guided to by something inside me. Now, we sit here and all I can think is that somewhere within there may lie a clue, a path to guide and direct us," he said honestly.

Sarah could see that it pained him to say it, genuine warmth for this man who had cared for her and given so much already, "We will look inside together. I feel safe and secure enough here to do that at least," she said.

She tentatively opened it and let it fall wherever fate decided. At first the sight of the writing and the way it was just written tapped into the memory of when she first read it. The grief which had been stilled and hidden rose momentarily to the surface and she felt her skin tingle with the pinpricks of sadness and loss. It was only a moment but enough for her to pause and adjust her composure.

Joshua sensed it as well as seeing her reaction, "Sarah they are words, black ink on white paper, nothing more. There is no connection to that feeling for you and I anymore, not here. Remember past is past, it does not have to drag us back to it. Nor do we have to walk back and pick it up."

"I know, thank you," warmth spreading back into her body.

She turned the pages, one much like the next, rantings and scrambled message from Tony's head to the paper. Some flowed and others just didn't fit into any scheme or belong to anything in particular. She did not know what she was really looking for and did not feel able to concentrate fully on any page, skipping through them quickly, trying to reach the end. She did remember, however, the page where the writing was not that way. The poem that she read out to River at the clearing. She concentrated and focused her attention on looking for that page, where it was, front or back of the book. She couldn't find it and started to look again – it was not there.

Joshua saw her searching change from distracted to fevered, her mood become unsettling, "What is it Sarah?" he asked, moving forward in his chair towards her.

"It's not there, it's gone. I can't find it," distress evident as she spoke and continued to look.

"What's gone?"

"The poem I read to River, the one Tony wrote for him. The only thing in here without darkness and pain attached," she replied, quickly glancing up, then back down again.

"It's ok, you must have just missed it," Joshua said softly, "I'm sure it's in there somewhere still."

"It's not here, I tell you," Sarah screamed out, frustration and despair echoing across the valley, "What does that mean, what does it mean?"

Joshua stood and moved across to her, kneeling down at her side and taking the book from her hands as he did.

She looked up at him and started to cry, to sob, grief and loss rising once again to the surface, consuming her, "What does it mean?" she said quietly once again before falling into his arms and chest.

Joshua held and rocked her, comforting her in her grief, as a stray cloud slipped across the falling moon's face. He felt that he knew what it meant, possibly, but stayed silent and kept his thoughts secret. He did not feel that it was the time to speak and that Sarah could not deal with what the valley had screamed back and the silent night had hidden in that moment.

Joshua felt a sense of uneasiness and unrest sweep across his body. He looked up at the night sky as it tried to break away and find a place to sleep. The sun was growing in the sky to the east, although still hidden from view by the rising slopes of the valley and then the mountains beyond. He felt that today's dawn was different, something inside him would not sit still and rest, or be at peace.

He closed his eyes in an attempt to force the issues and find all of that within himself, he couldn't. The only images that came into view was of water rising and pushing its way across forest and fields. A girl frantically searching in a lake, her face hidden, screaming out across the heavens. Then the image of a boy from the back, so small and fragile, so lost. His blonde hair falling uneasily on his shoulders which sagged under the weight of something which could not be seen. He knew who the boy was without seeing his face.

Joshua felt his tears start to fall as he held Sarah closer to him. Both of them lost in the sweeping winds of despair that gathered around them.

CHAPTER 27

We don't need anyone…

At the same time as Princess held her hands to her lips and spoke words which no one could hear, River stood facing the wall, his head bowed.

He had been that way for some time, swaying slightly from side to side, back and forth. He had still not said a word since he had left Tony's side when he first came to the Abyss, the sound of the voice, its words and laughter had not moved or provoked him into speaking. Anything that Tony did, speak or move, had resulted in the same, no words from his mouth. Even the walls changing and the writing disappearing, leaving four blank white walls had been met with the same result – no words or sounds from River's mouth.

From a distance he would simply have been viewed as a very small boy standing at a wall. On closer inspection, from inside the room it was clear that a small child stood alone, battling something going on inside every part of his body. It could be seen from the swaying and the pain and confusion written across his face and the way his shoulders seemed to sag under the force and weight of a heavy load. A boy at the crossroads; a child far away from home and a human soul standing close to the edge of a cliff, maybe to close.

"So here we all are. It's so nice to have you both here, especially you River," the voice broke the spell of silence which had been there for a while. *"Shall we begin or just continue the charade until the inevitable happens?"* it added the words echoing in the room, filling the emptiness of the moment.

River turned away from the wall, something which was unexpected, and lifted his head to look at Tony. Their eyes met across the room and they held each other's gaze for what seemed hours but in reality was no more than a few minutes. River looked for all the world as if he was going to speak. His mouth opened slightly and Tony's eyes widened in anticipation, waiting, pleading even for a word. None came. River closed his mouth again but continued to hold eye contact with Tony for a little longer. They may have spoken across them, words which were not meant for anyone else, but the most important parts, their hearts and souls stayed silent. Both of them closed off to the call of the other. There was no connection, no spark and no identity that they seemed to share now. Two separate bodies, two separate hearts and souls, un-hinged and disconnected from the other's needs, even maybe from their own needs. They were together in the same place and time but each was very much alone. River's eyes flickered and blinked twice and he turned away from Tony, back to the wall.

"Very touching, moving even. But it's too late for goodbyes and too late for the touch of a saviour. There is nothing left for you here except more time and nothingness," the voice of the Abyss rang out.

River moved in closer to the wall, glanced down at the pen in his hand and gripped it tighter, bringing it up to eye level against the walls surface.

"Let go River and begin the healing; forget the past and

write out your destiny for all to see," the voice spoke but only into River's ear, Tony did not hear it. "Forget about him River, he was too weak and is now broken, we don't need him anymore. I only went through him to bring you here," it added again only for River to hear.

For the first time River spoke back, through his thoughts, since coming to the Abyss, "We don't need anyone."

"You're right my child, my son. Let go and create your fate, exchange that faith for fear."

River put the pen against the wall slowly, with care and prepared to write. River prepared to let go of the past, forget faith and enter into darkness.

CHAPTER 28

Remember them now...

At exactly the same moment in a place so far removed from where River was it did not even exist in the mind of the Abyss, Princess sat crouched on her knees. Her hands were to her lips and it held to them something which could not be seen.

Ty and her mother were at her side but she paid them no mind and seemed totally unaware of their presence. It could be said blissfully unaware but there was nothing blissful about Princess's state of mind and the place where her heart was. Her sleep had been restless and her dreams full of dark and empty places. The world's she had travelled to, and through, in them was not something she did easily. Even for someone like her it took a leap of faith to trust that she would be able to return. In dreams there is normally no sense of time and space but in hers she knew that time was of the essence as she travelled alone, searching for clues to where River was.

In her dreams she had come upon barren desolate wastelands where the air was foul and not a living thing grew. She searched across deserts and over sand dunes so steep and high that she struggled to reach the tops, exhausted when she did. At each peak she would scan the horizon for some sign, a signal in which way she should then travel, but for the most part she found nothing. Even the stars failed to shine and help her, hidden under a dense blanket of cloud which even the moon was unable to penetrate. Her dreams carried on and she found nothing to help her and no sign of River in them. She was lost and even worse for her to carry as she struggled forward was the thought that River was lost to, maybe forever. All through her dreams she carried with her another thought which never left her side, reaching in and pulling at her core, "I should have gone instead of him, they should have let me go."

Ty watched Princess sitting there on her knees waiting for anything from her to acknowledge that she knew he was there. He had travelled to find her after hearing her call and once he had found her, waited by her side for hours. Now she was awake, seemingly, it was like he was not there. He struggled to deal with the feelings rising inside him. He had also travelled through many miles and dreams to find her and now in the last hours of the long night he had spent with her, he too felt lost. He wanted to help but knew not how; he tried hard to hear what she was speaking but could not hear. He felt helpless and alone sitting next to the girl that he had longed for all his life. His heart and his soul dropped in despair and he found the pain of love.

Princess had awoken because in her dreams she had come upon something which stirred a memory which now held the key. She had thought that saving River depended on her finding him physically and pulling him away from where he was. She was a spiritual being, as was River, but she felt drawn and consumed by the physical need to hold him and bring him back. At the most important point of her life, the very point when she needed it most she had been drawn towards the physical nature of existence rather than her own spiritual home and the connection she and River had through that. A memory had triggered that connection and bought her back and she had woken up, scrambling and looking for the thing that she now held to her lips.

Princess continued to speak whilst she was kneeling, her body rocking, as she did now that she had awoken. The words remained inaudible until slowly, above the sounds of the night, they could be heard by all who wished to as Princess spoke them. She spoke them out loud as she felt time slipping away and River slipping away into the mist of the darkness as she knelt.

"River do you remember what I gave you on that day? The words that we said together River. If you remember them now River say them and come back to us again. Let go of that future, let go of the pen. Come back to us now River as you remember that day together and the words we said to each other. If you do and you can remember me say my name and then say the words… Come back to us River, come back to your home."

CHAPTER 29

Forever and beyond...

River hesitated as he stood at the wall, the pen touching the face of it. His body flinched and his eyes narrowed in what seemed either pain or a concerted effort to pull something out from his past, a memory or a voice maybe. He closed his eyes and breathed in deep. His lungs filled with air and his chest expanded with this. A long drawn out pause as a memory chased him down to where he was. A memory and a voice which had travelled across the breeze and through the miles to be there with him in this moment.

It was a memory ignited by the words of Princess. As she reached across the void, over the edges of the darkness with words and thoughts sent out on the back of a warm breeze, her heart and soul following on close behind. The downy hair on the back of River's neck stirred with the memory as the hair on his head moved and he felt the feather like touch of her hand on his cheek. The memory returned like it had never left and River remembered it all, as he both heard and pictured her face. A single phase came from his lips, the first time anything had whilst he had been there, "I hear you, Princess."

He dropped the pen with one hand and with the other reached inside the red jacket that he always wore. His hand felt around for a while before he pulled something out and looked at it, bringing it up to eye level to examine closer. As he looked at it further his eyes changed colour and moved back to the peacefulness and stillness that they always used to hold inside. He moved whatever it was around in his hand, feeling the smoothness and texture of its surface, as he also closed his eyes to see it clearer, like a jeweller with a precious gem. He held it to his lips and kissed its smooth surface the full memory returning with every second that passed and the person who had sent it to him. He put the thing back where he found it and looked around on the floor for what he had dropped, the pen.

During the time that River had been re-connected to Princess and the memory which she had sent out for him, all sense of time in the Abyss had stopped. It was as if the whole scene had been stuck on pause as River and Princess exchanged their message over the miles. Her power had been able to penetrate even the darkest of places as it held all else in check so that nothing could stop it reaching River. Now as River looked around the floor searching for the pen, time had returned and the voice was aware that something had just changed.

"Why do you hesitate? Start writing now, where is the pen? Why have you dropped it?" questions fired out in demand in anger at River.

River was searching for the pen but did not answer back to any of the questions. He searched but couldn't find it and was bemused as to where it had gone until he realised. He looked over at Tony who had witnessed River's change and the direction that things had now gone in and had scrambled for the pen when River had dropped it. He now held it in his hand looking back across the room at River, a smile across his lips, sneering at him.

"Looking for this are we," he said, spitting the words out.

167

River looked at him, his face changing with the pain that he saw in Tony's every word and movement. He had forgotten for a moment that Tony was there and why he came but now his attention had returned to Tony and the purpose of him coming to the Abyss. River's face had changed from the moment that he had heard the words of Princess in his ear and heart. It had returned to the warm, peaceful and loving features of the boy that everyone knew. His eyes had also returned to the normal dark brown chocolate colour and they reflected back the peace and stillness of all that he was. He held Tony with these eyes and moved over towards him slowly, keenly aware that any sudden movement could possibly affect Tony and his state of mind, already fragile by where he was.

He reached Tony and moved down to kneel next to him, slowly moving his hand forward to try and take the pen, "Let me have it Tony, you don't have to do this anymore. Let it go," he said in a soft and loving tone, the sound that he had felt inside himself for so long.

Tony held onto the pen and tried to resist, even moving another hand towards it to increase the force he was using. River looked at him lovingly, and moved his other hand up and loosened the grip of Tony's hand. He may only have been a child but he was not acting alone at that point, the whole force of another place, spiritual place, was behind him. Tony let go and River put one hand up towards Tony's shoulder to offer comfort. It was not allowed and Tony shrugged it off and simply bowed his head. Unwilling and still unable to accept River back into his life and back into his heart and soul. It would be a long journey back for him; if he ever made it that far.

River got back up to his feet and moved over to the wall and breathed in deep. He felt the soft touch of Princess at his neck, her loving kindness in his ear and he began to write. In bold letters on the wall, speaking each word out loud, almost singing them, he wrote,

"The divine in me reaches out and touches the divine in you; bound together in time, forever and beyond. With love, faith

and compassion. I will always hold you near," adding as he finished, *"I will always remember you, Princess."*

The Abyss screamed out, a long and piercing sound which penetrated the depths of the earth and the solitude of the mind. The walls cracked, long and haphazard lines spreading out and across all of them. From outside came the crash of thunder and the flashes of colour from the lightening which lit up the sky. The clouds rolled across the sky, filling it up, loading it up. The wind blew that had no equal as water rose up from the depths of the earth, bubbling and steaming as they rose, covering the land, covering any life outside.

River did not seem to be aware or hear any of what else was going on. As he wrote and said the words out loud he had been taken back. He remembered the whole of the memory sent to him by Princess, it flooded back, overloading his senses, reaching into his mind, and he dropped to his knees, closing his eyes. He was taken back to that day, taken back to her loving arms.

CHAPTER 30

Let your heart hold them ...

It had been such a beautiful day. The sun had stayed high in the sky throughout it. Not a cloud in it, not a sign of one for as far as the eye could see. River and Princess had been together since sunrise when they had found each other walking through the forest. They knew they were walking towards each other through the whole of the night but neither rushed to get there. There was time and nature they both knew and fate cannot be rushed as it is observed by two souls walking through it. Every step bought them closer whilst every breath held the beauty and stillness of the forest air inside it as they walked. It was night in the forest as they travelled but neither harboured nor held any fear. River may have been a child but life, animals and the forest never bought anything else apart from safety and love. He had been raised that all of it was a part of him and him all a part of it. None of that would ever change.

They had spent the day walking, sitting and just being with each other. Sometimes River would run off, especially when they were in the forest, chasing butterflies or other animals that Princess could not see. He would just take off, shouting as he ran, laughing, such a loving sound that it seemed to Princess that both the trees and the flowers bent towards the laughter, its warmth inviting. She would hear him off in the distance, the sounds of his voice and laugh echoing throughout the day. She smiled as she walked hearing River's voice, filled with life and reaching out towards everything he found. He would sometimes shout out for her to hurry as he wanted to show her something and she would run towards the sound and him. He had always gone by the time she had got there, hearing his laughter and voice ringing back through the trees to her, "You're too slow, got to be quicker than that to catch me Princess." She knew this was going to happen but was more than content and happy to play along with the game which he found hilarious.

It had come to mid-afternoon and they had broken through the tree line into a meadow where there was a herd of wild horses that roamed. They both knew they were there and River had got more excited the closer they came to being with them. He loved horses and would spend hours walking quietly through the herd as they grazed or stood still. She always marvelled at how gentle and soft his approach would be despite the excitement bursting through his body. His approach never startled them or caused them to run off, they felt the presence of his placid nature and calm soul and they were always ready to be stroked by him. He would walk up softly and place his hand gently to the head of each of the horses, reaching up with his small hand. All of them moving their heads down and nuzzling up to his face trying to lick it. He always tried to avoid this, not because he didn't like it, but simply because it tickled him and only created fits of giggles. He would spend the same amount of time with each of them, all of them seemingly queuing up to feel his touch and spend moments with him. Princess followed him through the herd, again all of them gravitating towards her grace and beauty after the innocence and playfulness of River. She would run her hands down their side, feeling the smoothness and the life in each one. It filled her with peace and tranquillity and she never left the time with the horses unmoved. This day was no different and they had spent some hours passing through the herd until both theirs and the horse's needs were satisfied.

"Come on, River, the sun is drooping and longs for rest and you need to eat," she said as they moved slowly away, both of them watching the horses as they left.

"I don't want to leave the horses. I never do. I want to stay here and live with them," he had replied looking wistfully back at their departure.

Princess watched them leave and put her hand down to his shoulder, holding it there for comfort, "And they would love that, but that's for maybe a different time and place, not today," she said momentarily feeling his sadness.

River sighed, longing to walk off with them, "Yeah I know, it's just that they are so beautiful, so peaceful."

Princess bent down and turned him to face her, looking directly into his eyes, "As are you River. The things you see in others are simply reflections of you, like a mirror, let your heart hold them even when you're not with them."

River smiled at her, his eyes flooding with peace, "It does hold them, like it holds you when I'm not with you."

They stayed this way for a while looking into each other's eyes and smiling, the moment full of love and warmth. It was River who eventually gave in and flung his arms around her neck, throwing himself at her. She received his embrace, his almost bear like hug, with ease and they again stayed that way for a while until she spoke, "Come on, let's go and get some food and eat by the stream. The fishes would have missed you."

He let go and playfully pushed her over, despite his size and height, "Come on then, race you slow coach," running off whilst she sat there laughing at his cheek.

She started to get up, "You just wait until I catch you. I'm going to throw you in that stream this time," beginning to run after him, not quick enough to catch him up.

They eventually settled down next to the stream after collecting all the berries from their normal place and River eating a hatful in the process of doing this. He could not get enough and their juices ran down his chin as he tried to eat and talk at the same time. When they had sat down he then settled down and they ate in perfect silence, content to be next to each other and enjoy the peace and serenity of the surroundings. The sun was falling, the moon was rising and the whole day had been perfect in every way.

They had been by the stream for some time and had finished eating and now lay on their stomachs over the edge of the bank watching the fish swim and the water flow by. River's hands were stretched down towards the water, his fingers reaching down to dance across the surface. It was not deep and they could see the bottom through the crystal-clear water's and he drew pictures and wrote words across the top as he did so. His fingers twisting and moving across the surface as the fish moved quickly away from them. When they were too slow and his fingers touched the slimy back of one of the fishes he giggled to himself, a sound that seemed to enter into the water and dance alongside his fingers. Although the stream was not very deep the current and flow was strong enough that it bought all matter of pebbles, gravel, stones and weeds along with it, dragging them along the bottom like a fishermen's nets in the ocean. It carried and washed all of them along the bottom, back and forth, coming and going as the fish swam by without a care. The fading sun reflected into the water and through the layers, drawing the colour of the stones out. A rainbow assortment finding their way up and out, spreading up and out into the inquisitive eyes of both River and Princess as they lay there. The colour drawn across their faces along with the water's reflection like a painter's brush and strokes across the top of a canvas.

They both saw them at the same time, two stones being pulled by the force of the current, tumbling along the bottom of the stream. Princess reached her arm in and plucked them up before they were lost and had gone past. River had seen them to but his arms would not stretch as far as hers and he was glad that she had done it and they had not been allowed to carry on their journey and be lost. Princess moved to sitting up and River followed her movements until they sat cross-legged facing each other, so close that their knees were touching.

"What do they feel like? They looked so beautiful tumbling along," River said excitedly.

Princess was still in the process of drying them on the hem of her skirt, taking her time to make sure they were completely dry and all the grit wiped away they may have had, "Hold on, let me just finishing drying them first," she said as she continued to do this.

"Hurry up then, I've seen milk turn quicker than you drying them," he said playfully, reaching out to dig her in the ribs.

Princess half giggled and moved away slightly, finishing what she was doing, "Maybe I will just keep them myself and hide them or throw them back in the stream to carry on their journey," she said fainting to throw them back, covering them in her hand.

"No don't," River shouted reaching up to try and stop her if she did. "Please, Princess, let me see them."

She moved her arm down and held it out to him, opening up her hand as she did. Inside there sat two perfectly round stones, opal colour. So smooth, so flawless, as if they had just been picked up from a shelf in a jewellers shop. They shone from the drying and polishing she had completed and River reached down to take one, bringing it close to his face so he could study it more closely. She did the same with the one she still held and together they sat there bewitched and dazzled by the gift they had found. As they did the sun, with the last of its brilliance shone down and hit the stones, reflecting back a myriad of colours from within, each brighter than the last – green, red, blue, black and an orange that took their breath for a moment.

"They are the most beautiful things I have ever seen, even more beautiful than you, Princess," River said after a time spent studying them.

Princess could see why he said that, they were indeed stunning. She looked into the one she held and felt a feeling pass over her eyes, a dark feeling from where she did not know, although it soon disappeared. For a moment she faltered before speaking, "They are indeed a gift, a treasure, something to remind us of today. a special day," she said lifting her eyes from the stone and looking at River.

He felt her gaze and lifted his head also, staring back into the coal-coloured eyes that always held him, "They are a gift, a very special one at that," he said matching her thoughts.

From somewhere inside Princess felt something stir her to say the words that then followed, "I think we should keep one each, keep them on us at all times, to remind us of this day and to hold the memory in when we may need it. When we may need it the most, in the darkest of places even."

River looked at her, puzzled slightly, by her change in tone and the words she said, "What do you mean darkest of places?" he asked.

Princess felt it again, a cloud passing across the front of her eyes and heart. She knew intuitively that it meant something but failed to capture its full extent. She tried to skip over her previous words, "It's nothing, the wrong words, just forget I said them," she smiled at him before adding, somewhat hurriedly. "We should do that, keep one each. Maybe even add to yours a little bit?"

"We should keep one each but what do you mean add to mine?"

River asked her intrigued.

"Well what about this," she said, taking one hand and placing it at the back of her head pulling as it returned to the front of her face a lock of her hair, made up of 5 or 6 strands from the darkest parts of it. "Give me the stone you have."

He was more than intrigued now and handed her the stone, trusting her completely. She reached out and took it and slowly began to wrap the hair around the stone until a band of hair ran across and round the centre of the stone – black against opal. She finished by tying the ends together and handed it back to River, "There, how does that look now?" she added after she had passed it over.

River's face showed exactly what he felt about it, he was in awe. He loved her hair and always played with it when he could, wrapping it round his small hands until they got lost in it. The stone itself was enough of a find, a gift, but with her hair now round the middle, it was a treasure to beat all treasures. He bought the stone up to his nose and her unmistakable smell filled his senses. He inhaled long and deep and smiled, the biggest smile she had ever seen from him, before offering the words, "Thank you, Princess, thank you always."

She smiled back and a thought came that despite the addition that something else was also needed, "Maybe we should have some words as well, to go with the treasure we have found," smiling across at him, "what do you think?"

River nodded, his smile still wide, "I think that would go really well; complete it all perfectly."

They sat there looking at each other for some time, the silence between them comfortable and easy. Many of their best moments were spent this way, they happened naturally and were totally unscripted minutes in their time together.

It was River who spoke first, "The divine in me reaches out and touches the divine in you," looking at her for guidance.

She heard the words he said and felt their beauty across her skin, adding quickly yet naturally, "Bound together in time, forever and beyond."

"With love, faith and compassion," he added on when she had finished.

"I will always hold you near," she reached over and took his two hands in hers as she completed the last part of the sentence, bringing them and hers up to her chest and holding them next to her heart.

River let her do this and felt the beating of her heart as she held them there for a time. They looked into each other's eyes with love that had no boundaries or limits, it was endless and no words were needed. The smile on his face and in his eyes was unique and belonged only to him. Only River could smile with equal measure through face and eyes at the same time. It was his gift to the world and the world was in awe of it and this boy whose innocence shone through in all that he did.

Princess felt the smile and was grateful for its presence in her life, for River's presence in her life. It would never change, her love for him and she knew that she would give up all she had for his safety and comfort. But it was not the only thing that came across her soul in that moment. A sadness and a cry for release came from deep inside her. She had never felt such an overwhelming feeling of powerlessness in her life and for the first time she experienced a fear which hit through her courage and stuck her in the middle of her heart. The significance of this moment and what they had just shared was not lost on her and she felt the need to try and signify this to River without alerting him to her feeling.

"Make sure you keep it safe, River, look after it and hold it close to you at all times," she said after a while.

River nodded and said, "It's going right here next to my heart," putting the stone wrapped in her hair into a pocket inside his coat,

"My heart that belongs to you."

She smiled back and felt touched by his emotional awareness, "And I will keep mine safe here," reaching down to push it into a pocket inside the waistband of her skirt. "I have no pocket there like you and here it will be safe and never be lost."

She hadn't finished with trying to ensure he understood the importance of what they had just done and said and took his head in her hands, one either side of his face and pulled him towards her until their foreheads touched and they sat close.

"Remember the stone, the hair and the words River, through the days that follow. Hold them close to you in your heart. When you need them, in times of sadness or uncertainty feel them and say the words and I will be there. Promise me," she said sadness knocking at the doors of her heart.

River smiled and leaned forward to kiss her on the cheek, "I will remember them Princess and if I don't, reach across and tell me, then I will remember them and I will be safe."

The wind blew across them as they stayed that way for a short time before holding each other close. River's head on her shoulder, his nose close to her hair and the smell that lit his life. The smell that always saved him from his own sadness.

CHAPTER 31

Didn't come to save you...

River had finished and stood at the wall allowing the whole memory and the voice of Princess to hold him for a while. He knew that it was not over and that he had things he still needed to do and most of all Tony to return to and speak with. The memory had awoken his true nature and self but as yet he knew he was not strong enough to carry on and complete what he came to do – to take Tony back.

He reached inside his jacket and retrieved the stone. Despite the gloom and the darkness of the room and where he was, its colour had not faded, nor had the colour and intensity of Princess's hair wrapped around the middle of it. After that day he had often fallen asleep with the stone clutched close to him, held in his hand as he drifted off to sleep. When he lay in the meadows he often got it out and held it up to the sky, a jewel in his hand outlined against the blue jewel of a summer's sky. Now he looked at it closely and saw reflected in it, again despite the gloom, his face and her's sitting by the stream in the moments before he left her the last time. He bought it up to his face and breathed in deep and long. The smell of her hair and the scent of her grace filled his nostrils and he felt refreshed and alive for the first time since coming to the Abyss. He sighed and kissed the stone wrapped in her hair which bought him back from his own Abyss, before placing it carefully back into his inside pocket. He turned to face Tony, ready now to deal with whatever he needed to, ready to reclaim Tony from his own personal hell.

The Abyss had continued to scream, the thunder and lightning had continued to rage and flash outside and the cracks in the wall, and now the floor, had opened wider. All of this had been excluded from River's senses as Princess reached across the miles and bought him back. Now that he was ready he was acutely aware of the chaos and mayhem taking place and the insults being thrown in his direction.

"Do you think that's it? That's it over now and you can all live happily ever after, like a fairy tale. That the memory of a day with HER can save everything, that it can save you," the voice spat the words out, mocking him when it said the word 'her'.

Although he didn't show it, River was concerned that the Abyss obviously knew what had just gone on and more importantly it knew of Princess. His natural reaction was to protect her, as she did him, and for a moment he faltered unsure what to do, the memory flickering slightly in his mind.

"Yes I know her, and she knows me. Be careful with the promises she makes to you, they are not always fulfilled," the voice tapped into his thoughts, sending further doubts across his mind.

River may have turned towards Tony but he had not yet taken steps or moved towards him. Tony was sat shivering in the corner, head down and rocking himself manically. The verbal assault from the Abyss and the nature of it had taken him by surprise and the continued reference to Princess had left him unable to move. The doubts had re-surfaced and the fears started to wake up and he felt that everything was in freeze frame, in slow motion. His thoughts and feelings and all his senses were at different points, places, none of them in tune. His head started to ache again and he momentarily put one hand up to rub against the side of it.

The Abyss saw this and felt the change in River and continued to taunt and manipulate, "She made a promise to us once, promised that she would come. She never kept it, she doesn't keep promises, so don't trust her voice," it laughed, "Maybe she sent you instead, a token sacrifice, have you thought of that."

The Abyss could have said many things at that moment to keep and ensure that the doubts and fears that had started to rise again in River continued, it could have held onto and followed many themes, but it picked the wrong thing. In mentioning Princess sending River instead it had pressed a button which River knew would never happen. The times he had spent with her, the love and care that had been sent to him across the miles from her lips carried with it one thing. It was one thing that the Abyss would never understand, the unconditional trust that exists between two souls when they know, they just know what the other thinks of them. The trust that existed between River and Princess was not one built on words but through actions. It was actions that followed the words, completed the relationship between them which had been created and forged along lines that the Abyss could not grasp or recognise. The Abyss fed on weakness and pain whilst the relationship between them was fed and watered on concepts beyond its understanding such as serenity, tranquillity, gentleness and compassion. In attempting to weaken this bond the Abyss had merely succeeded in making it stronger.

The ache in River's head decreased and he had no need for his hand at the side of his head to ease it. This hand dropped back down to its side whilst the other moved to cover his small heart and to feel the presence of the stone, wrapped in her hair underneath his clothing. It was there and River kept his hand there for a short time, composing himself, confirming his strength of purpose and breathing in her beauty as if she was standing in front of him.

He lifted his head and raised it to look at the ceiling, speaking out to the Abyss in a way that no one had ever dared,

"Forever and beyond means beyond the realms of time and space. It means beyond the passage of time and in that it means beyond you also. Princess and I are not controlled by your will, we move in step and to the beat of our own hearts; hearts that beat together, twin souls connected. She would never give me up. She is my mother and I will always be her son."

There was nothing in reply, no sound at all. The thunder outside ceased as if God had just put a hand out and grasped its breath; the lightning no longer flashed and lit up the sky as the wind itself ceased and there was stillness. There was no sound, a pin could drop and both River and Tony would have been able to hear it. It seemed that the Abyss did not know everything, that it could be moved to shock and silence. It did not know about Princess and River and the bond which existed, until now.

River knew it would have this effect, even though it may only be short lived. He knew time was short but shared this with the Abyss to try and give himself some time, to give him and Tony some time without noise and without the voice which held and manipulated Tony's mind and thoughts. River looked over at Tony who was in shock himself from the appearance of sudden silence. It at least provoked him to lift his head, peeking out from between his knees to see why there was suddenly nothing when there had been so much for so long. River stayed standing and did not move for a while. He looked at Tony sitting in the corner and his heart sank a little. He wondered how things had ever come this far and got so low for Tony to be sitting here surrounded and filled up with so much loneliness and despair. What had happened to the future of Tony when he was a child that had bought him to this place? River sighed, his heart quivering in response to the pain of another, to Tony's pain, a sign of his compassion.

River moved over to his side, aware of time ticking and the shock that may only keep the Abyss silent for a short while. Tony's head was still between his knees but it had moved slightly to the side so that his eyes could see River as he came towards him. River bent down and moved himself slowly onto his knees directly in front of Tony's eye line. They held each other's gaze, one set of eyes filled with peace and compassion and the other set of eyes filled with nothingness. They were empty, blank, devoid of sparkle and life and they held no hope around them.

Unexpectedly it was Tony who spoke first, very quietly, "Why has the noise stopped? I liked it?"

River paused, thinking before he spoke, "For a while it has gone, to give us time to speak."

Tony looked puzzled, "Why do we have to speak. I don't have anything to say. I don't want to listen to you."

River moved in closer so he could speak quieter, it was words for Tony's ear only, "There are things that you have forgotten, things that you lost maybe. If you knew about them it would possibly change how you feel."

Tony's eye's, freed slightly by the silence of the Abyss's voice, flickered in a sign of what River took as interest, "I have forgotten nothing because that's all there is – NOTHING," emphasising the last word to River.

River knew from the start that it was not going to be easy and hearing Tony now did not change that sense of feeling for him, "There is always more than can be seen or remembered," he said, putting his hand on to Tony's shoulder adding even more softly, "If you knew them."

Tony shrugged River's hand off, not for the first time and began to rise up, causing River to shuffle back slightly on his knees, "From you, a mere child. There is nothing new that you can tell me. It is I who can teach you," on his feet now towering over River, his size threatening.

River did not feel afraid. He was more concerned that the Abyss would be woken from its silence and that would simply make things more difficult. At least Tony was responding and up and moving rather than sitting in the corner with his head down, that was positive. River himself did not feel compelled to rise, instead moving so he could sit cross-legged with his hands comfortably positioned in his lap. His whole posture and demeanour relaxed and natural. He was out of place there anyway but this simple movement and his position now seemed to exaggerate the fact even more and even Tony was distracted. He looked down twice, a double take of River, as he started to walk around the room.

"Maybe we can teach each other and be there for each other," River said watching Tony carefully as he walked around the room.

Tony moved to one of the surfaces of the walls and followed the line of the cracks across one of them with his hand as if it was a line on a map, "I have no intention of being there for you or anyone else. Why should I do that? I don't even know why you came," he said moving to another wall now to do the same thing, uninterested in River or what was really being said.

"Are you not interested in where I came from?" River asked without allowing a gap between their exchanges. He knew that time was ticking and had to move faster to try and reach Tony, if that was possible.

Tony did not seem interested and walked and moved as if he was not listening, following the cracks still, "Where you come from is not interesting at all," he said and turned to look at River as he continued, "What you then become is far more important, don't you think?"

River listened, his heart heavy, at the resentment and past hurt in Tony's words. It was evident in all that he said, "Where you come from and what you hold onto from there – love, care, kindness and peace – shapes what you then become. That is unless something happens that makes you forget or want to forget," he paused allowing the words to move in-between them, back and forth, to lay in the air, "What made you forget Tony?"

"Life made me forget, life did that," Tony said turning angry and moved now at River's persistence and need to talk or question him, "You're a child you have no experience of life and what rejection does – heartache, loss, isolation, abuse, grief – all of that makes you forget or want to. It makes you learn not to trust," he had moved as he was speaking and now stood again directly over River, looking down at him. His eyes smouldering with rage and emotion.

River could see the emotions and the anger, the rage burning inside the eyes of Tony but he also saw something else beneath and beyond that. He could see that behind those surface emotions there existed and lay a level of fear, anxiety and doubt, and it was this that River was trying to tap into. Most of all River was trying to reach the vulnerability behind them, all which fear had kept hidden for so many years. Tony's response was a step in the right direction and River was lifted.

"It depends sometimes on where you put your trust and who you give it to?" he said with Tony still standing over him.

Tony's emotional state reduced slightly, his eyes closing and then opening again quickly, "Are you saying that I should trust you. Trust you, who I do not know. Is that what you are saying?"

"Yes. If there is anybody that you should trust then that is me, yes," River answered without a pause or hesitation.

The air, confidence and assurance of the boy sitting cross-legged at his feet threw Tony and forced hesitation in himself and his train of thought, "I should trust you even though I don't know you," he said, the rage gone but his anger still simmering beneath the lids of his eyes and inside his body.

"Yes you should trust me. That is if you want to be saved," River said, the words escaping softly from his lips.

Tony's rage rose again, his anger boiling over, "That's the thing little boy and why you should never have come here," he paused and got down on his knees to ensure his eyes were level with River, looking straight at him, as he added, "you forget. I don't want to be saved."

River felt the words and the intensity of what Tony was saying. He looked at him, holding his gaze as he said, "That's the thing that you don't know. I didn't come to save you Tony."

Tony stayed where he was, his eyes alive and listening as he said, "Who did you come to save then? There is no one else here to save."

River paused before he spoke, aware of the importance of what he was about to say and the way that he had to say it, he choose in that moment simply to be honest, "I didn't come to save you," reaching out to put a small hand on Tony's arm, as he added, "I came to save us," gripping the arm now so that Tony could truly feel the touch in his words also.

Tony heard the words and looked at the hand on his arm and felt the grip as it tightened. For the first time he did not try and pull away or push River's hand away, "What do you mean when you say us?" he said still allowing the contact between them.

River knew that he had reached him on some level, he was getting somewhere, but also felt the hands of time at his neck breathing steadily faster now, pushing him to move and act faster now, "I mean us. The connection we have, what we share, the history – don't you get it yet?" aware of the Abyss at the door now knocking and waking up.

"No what about us?" Tony replied, the hand still on his arm, something deep inside him keeping him from brushing it away this time.

"I came to save us because we are the same. The two of us are the same," River said, the other hand reaching out to touch the cheek of Tony's face.

Tony still not fully understanding, and a little bit frustrated, shouted, "What do you mean the same?"

"We are the same person. I am you and you are me," River said, "We are the same person and that is why I came and why I was sent, to bring you back."

Tony's eyes narrowed in an attempt to understand but all they found first was more confusion. His thoughts unclear, his mind cloudy and he felt unsteady on his knees. He fell to the floor and River's hand fell from his cheek, although the one on his arm still remained. Everything had just been turned upside down by what River had said. None of it fitted; the same person, connected, save us? All of it just created more questions. He looked at the boy who was now looking down at him and tried to recognise a glimmer even of himself in River. He couldn't see anything and his eyes closed in pain and confusion in attempting to recognise his past childhood.

River could see all of this and knew that this part would be the most difficult for Tony to understand and get through. It was a lot to take in especially considering not only what Tony had already gone through but also his fragile state of mind and emotional state. River could hear from a distance away the sound of thunder moving ever closer. He knew it was the Abyss rising and waking from the silence it had been sent into by shock. Time was of the essence and he was running out of it. He knew that trying to keep Tony where he was in a place where he could reach him and also to deal with the Abyss and all that was about to be thrown at them was something even he could not manage.

A voice came into his ear, a feeling in his heart which he reached out to listen to, *"He may remember if he holds what you have, use it River and use it fast."*

River knew where the message came from and who sent it. She had seen his need and provided the means to hold him and Tony again. River gently lifted Tony's head and put it in his lap as he reached inside his jacket and removed the stone. The colours of it seemed to shimmer and flicker despite the gloom inside the room and he knew it was the power of his Princess reaching out to help them. He placed the stone into the hands of Tony who now lay shivering on the floor and tightly held them together so that they enclosed the stone inside them.

The thunder outside had been joined by lightning and it was moving closer now, knocking at the door, the cracks on the wall widening as the walls shuddered under the approaching storm. River looked down at Tony, at his hands clasped around the stone and in his heart, the very core of his body he reached back out to Princess, "I don't know what else to do? Show me the way and guide me. We can't lose him now."

The storm outside entered the room, the Abyss had returned. River held Tony's head in his lap and looked down as a voice they both knew entered back into their life.

"It matters not what you say. As you are the same it means only one thing – you will both die and she will not be able to save you. Your mother will not be able to save either you, as you are now and as you were."

There was a difference now though. The voice was the same but from where it came had changed. River looked up aware that the sound and the words seemed closer. He looked up right into the scarlet eyes of the Abyss. It had now moved into physical form and stood above both Tony and River now.

"Nothing has changed except now you can see me," it said as it continued to stare at them both.

River knew that's things had just got a whole lot worse.

CHAPTER 32

The time for that has passed...

Princess had finished speaking, her words clearly audible to all, and she was still on her knees, holding her stone from that day close to her heart now with both hands on it. She had done what she could for the moment and the effort she had put in had left her exhausted physically and emotionally. It had not been easy trying to find River through the obstacles and barriers that had been put in her way and it was only by forgetting about the physical searching that she had been able to do anything at all. Even then she did not know if it was enough and she knew that there was so much that still had to happen before River could return with Tony. If that ever happened.

During the time that River had been speaking with Tony she had stayed on her knees with the stone to her lips for a while until the exhaustion took hold and she fell back. She would have crumpled and hit the grass behind her but for one reason – Ty. He had been with her through the night and had seen her rise to her knees and heard her words. Words that he knew were meant for River, wherever he was, and were said in an attempt to find and reach him and hold him safe. Ty's arms held her safe now as she fell, her eyes flicking in and out of consciousness as she lay in them.

Her mother was on her knees next to Ty and he looked at her, for guidance or reassurance, "It's not over yet, is it?" he said still looking at her.

Her mother did not look at him even when he spoke, her eyes and her will were solely on Princess and trying to connect with her, hold her, she did not ignore him though, "No its far from over. She has managed to buy some time I think but it is out of her control now. River has been pulled back from the edge but there is still much to do I feel," she said, her hand moving to smooth the hair away from her daughter's forehead.

Ty heard the concern in her voice and recognised that all things were still in the balance. He did not possess the gifts that they did but it did not mean that he was not needed there, "How long will this go on for?" he asked her, a plea concealed within his words.

"That cannot be known. Even Princess does not really know that although she may have a better understanding then us. She is bound to River and her heart and his beat in time – mother and son. It will feel any uneasiness that he feels and that will be the surest indicator for us all," she said, her eyes still firmly on her daughter.

Princess was falling in and out of sleep now, her eyes flickering and moving continuously. Her body and her head did the same and she could not settle. Words formed on her lips as she opened her mouth to speak but just as quick they closed and the words fell back into her throat. Even when a noise came out and she managed to say something they both knew it was directed not for them, but for River.

Ty felt completely powerless sitting there with her head in his lap. Since he had arrived it had been all that he had done, sit and wait. He held onto her head and held onto hope at the same time. The hope that she had been able to reach River and allow him to return. Hope that she would then return to him and his arms and the dreams that she had walked in for so long would no longer be just dreams but their reality and life together.

As these thoughts ran through his mind, Princess woke and he looked down at her face. It was contorted and her eyes showed the one thing that he had never seen in them, raw naked terror. Her body fitted as she attempted to move to an upright position and Ty fought with her slightly to make sure that she did not injure herself. Her strength was too much and her body tore itself away from his firm grip and she raised herself upwards, the terror still evident on her face and her eyes wide awake to something that was out there. She looked around hurriedly, as if she was searching for the cause of her fear, or at least be eased from it. Her eyes moved quickly taking in the surroundings, the sky, the sun which lay hidden still behind the blanket of clouds and the trees of the forest close by, none of it eased her obvious pain. They moved onto Ty and a flicker of recognition crossed them but they did not hold and stop there. They moved quickly over to her mother and finally stopped, finding something that she needed. Her mother looked back and knowing her daughter so well was instantly alerted to the fear and anxiety which was mirrored in her eyes. They held each other's gaze, the intensity even spilling out and over into all that lay outside, for some moments before Princess dropped back again and Ty caught her just before she hit the floor. Her eyes closed now, her breathing erratic and shallow.

He looked at her mother and saw that she too had changed and her face betrayed the feelings that were obviously going on inside. A mixture of pain and anguish and again this was something new for Ty to see, "What is it now? What?" he asked, imploring, feeling hope loosen its grip slightly on him.

She did not answer immediately, still lost in her thoughts and emotions and the obvious anxiety which had suddenly surfaced between her and Princess, finally she spoke, "She has seen what River now faces. The Abyss has taken on physical form and stands over him and Tony now. She is battling now to hold on, she wants to go herself but knows that the time for that has passed. There is nothing else she can do now, except what we are doing now, waiting."

Ty felt a heaviness stretch in and grab his heart, reaching in to hold it in its icy grip. A cold wind accompanied it and it made him shiver alongside her mother. He looked down at Princess and felt the doubt rise inside that they and she would be able to get through this. His dream so close yet so far. He moved one hand over and away from her head to reach out and grab the hand of her mother as he heard her begin to weep next to him. Ty knew then, if he did not before, that everything now was in the hands of small boy, one he had never met. All his future happiness rested with River and he reached out in his own thoughts to aid the boy she loved. He knew that the fate of Princess rested now in the arms of her son, River.

CHAPTER 33

Then there was the water...

The water had for a time been slowed, almost stopped, in its track up to the top of the hill where the two rocks sat under the tree covered in white blossom. It was always that way, covered throughout the year, as if it had been made to sit there and be the same every time River and Princess came to be there. The view changed with the seasons but the tree, the rocks and the surrounding areas remained abundant and full of life, even through the winter months.

The water had been slowed at the same time that River had heard her call and the Abyss had been moved to silence, leaving River with Tony. If someone had even been looking at it close enough they may even have said that it had fallen, slipping back downwards, its intensity and passion dimmed. The small area of sunlight which had pierced and illuminated a circle either side of the rocks had also seemingly grown, widening out and moving even further towards the water, pushing it back down maybe. The flowers seemed refreshed and their colours exploded out, casting shadows on the tree, the rock and even into the water. Everything had seemed brighter and hope lay in and around all that existed there.

This had all now changed. The flowers retreated back into the earth, their vibrant colours hidden by the shadow of a cloud which slipped across the sun and stayed there hiding its light. The colourless grey of the rocks became even more so without life and the tree itself seemed to wilt under the pressure and force of the air that came from nowhere. It was carried on the back of a wind which blew icily across the hill top. This wind even bought the first flakes of snow which began to settle quickly on the grass, turning green into a blanket of white.

Then there was the water. A new vigour and force had entered into it and where it had been almost still, even retreating slightly, it now moved forward again. The head of it snaking further up the hill towards the tree, the flowers and the rock. It pushed forward in its relentless pursuit of beauty, its pursuit of River and Princess and the whole world that they inhabited. As it moved onwards and upwards words again from the lips of its source, *"And through the days that follow, we find our back to you."*

CHAPTER 34

Find the meaning inside

Joshua had continued to hold onto Sarah who at that time seemed inconsolable. Joshua's tears had finished although the overall sense of sadness and loss still remained, winding itself around them both. The day was threatening to break free of the night but the clouds above held it at bay. A bank of rolling grey clouds that swept across the sky like an army of ants sweeping through the jungle.

As he stood there and looked up at the sky his thoughts turned to River and what he was going through, or at least what he thought he may be going through. The image of River lying in the fields of colour that surrounded the hut and the lake staring up at the sky for hours on end filled his mind, the look of contentment and the smile and the radiance given off by him never failed to capture Joshua. He used to watch him from the hut, River so relaxed and comfortable with all that he was around, nature and people, they were all the same to River, something to be enjoyed and loved. It was an image that always bought Joshua a sense of peace but today the image simply bought regret and fear and feelings associated with the loss of him from his life at that moment. He felt his insides change and the outsides respond to match this change. His body lost some of its warmth and his hold on Sarah reduced to something less than it was before. The chill in the air eating into his bones, turning him icy cold. It came from nowhere, this physical change and he was so attuned to all that existed around the place where he lived now that he knew it meant something else, something significant.

Sarah was not immune to the change also as her body felt the icy blast and its intensity. She pulled herself out from his arms and wiped a sleeve over her face to rid herself of some of the tears, still falling, but less so now. She looked up at him standing there. So strong yet so tender, filled with courage but also a gentleness which bought comfort and strength also. He did not look at her but more so surveyed the sky and the bank of cloud which descended across the valley, she was anxious and could tell that he was too. He sighed and bought his attention back to her, his heart heavy and his thoughts still lost in the clouds that he had been watching. He tried to hide his feelings but Sarah knew that he was somewhere else, not fully present with her.

"What is it now? It's something else isn't it?" Sarah asked looking up into his face for any sign of an answer even before he responded.

"I do not totally know Sarah. But the blanket of cloud. The lack of the sun fully appearing and the night still hanging on are signs that something is moving," he responded after a while.

"Moving where, there, where is it moving?" she replied quickly, anxious for an answer to quell her rising fears.

"Time moves on even when we are not there Sarah. In places far away, in places best not spoken about here, River stands and holds faith in his hands. All we can do is provide the hope in his heart as he stands there," he answered, aware of not only her fears, but his also rising.

"Does hope still remain though?" she said flatly.

He looked at her and smiled softly, "While life remains and breath exists there is always hope Sarah, always," his eyes warming up as he spoke.

197

"Then I must find it again and send it..." Sarah's words were interrupted by a loud, huge, crash of thunder which came from out of nowhere and rumbled on in the distance, its noise less but the force and what it left behind no less than the initial sound.

Joshua was startled and Sarah no less so. It was unexpected and it was followed up by more claps and crashes of thunder which came from beyond the valley yet still managed to fill the air with its intensity. Joshua dropped his arms from around her and turned full circle, 360 degrees, taking in the noise as he did and looking up to the sky's. He had not seen it coming and he knew intuitively that it held a significance within the scheme of all that was happening.

Sarah watched him intently, following his eyes and looking for any sign that everything was alright. She knew intuitively that it was not, that hope made her feel it was not important, whilst her heart told her something else, "This is not good is it?" she said after some time still watching both him and the sky.

The thunder continued in the distance, reaching back towards where they both stood. Joshua knew that it signalled a change but was still searching for the actual content of that change. His eyes, so warm and inviting had changed, they now held within them an intense and concentrated look,

"There has been a shift, the thunder tells us that. Things lie in the balance and River is facing a challenge he did not see. Something that none of us could see," he said after some time.

"What does he face now?" she asked, pleading for some relief.

"A physical form, the Abyss has taken on this and stands next to River and Tony now. It is here that the issue will be decided, it is now that the fight will truly begin," he said, his emotions kept in check by the need to remain calm and focused.

As he said this the book which had fallen to the ground in the time that they had been standing there holding each other was whisked around by the wind that followed the thunder, its pages opening and closing as the book itself was lifted up into the air and thrown towards the lake. Sarah ran after it and chased it down to stop it disappearing into the water. She managed to place a foot on it just as it reached the edge and held it firmly underneath it as she bent down to pick it up. She walked slowly back towards Joshua holding the book gingerly in her hand, the pages still flapping with the force and power of the wind which had now increased.

For Joshua nothing ever happened without there being a reason involved. He had heard the sound of the wind through the book, seen it take off and then watched as Sarah chased it down and stopped it falling into the water. As she walked back towards him with it held in her hand, a light ignited inside him, a soft voice came up through the darkness and gloom and whispered in his ear, *"Inside lies the gift of both yours and our salvation, seek it and find, move beyond the words and find the meaning inside."*

Joshua felt a single moment of peace walk across his soul and called to Sarah as she came walking back, "I need to see inside that book now Sarah, it's time to re-visit that which I promised never to do again."

CHAPTER 35

We will always stay together...

The Abyss still stood over both Tony and River. He had taken on physical form to meet the threat but it was not something which could be seen as permanent and apt to description as a person could be portrayed. The outline was shady, the colours mixed between a purple and a black but with hints of red and grey thrown in all around. It could certainly be seen and River could see its shape and colour as the outline moved and shimmered. One moment it took the form and shape of a man then another it changed to the shady outline of a ghost. It was neither one thing or the other, its shifted in texture and depth, filling up the room then decreasing to the size of a boy, a child, someone similar to River's age and height. Only one thing could be said whatever form it took, whatever size it was, it bought with it doubt, despair, grief, loss and nothingness.

River knew that the silence which had been in place was only temporary and that the voice would return, the Abyss would return, although he did not know it would now take the form it did. Despite its return and presence in the room River's heart remained even, the rate slow, and inside he felt held and comforted. The effect of Princess and the memory which was still at the forefront of his mind was enough to dispel any fears and doubts. It was enough for the moment to keep the Abyss at bay and hold it in check.

The Abyss was aware of this also, and simply circled the room, moving up and down through the air, touching the walls, following the cracks in a similar pattern that Tony had done. Tony himself still lay in River's lap, the stone still held in his hands, although his eyes were closed and he was shivering uncontrollably. River tried to warm him up but for the moment this was not succeeding as he lay there, drifting in and out of the room.

The Abyss came and stood directly over them both, its form now a man wearing a long black coat which reached down to his ankles. His arms were placed in the pockets at either side and his head was covered in a long mane of black hair which reached down past his shoulders, swept back at the front so the face was clearly visible. The face itself was chalk white, there was no colour in it at all, not a hint of anything else. The scarlet eyes even more pronounced because of the whiteness set as its back drop.

"He looks in so much pain and discomfort, so small and defenceless lying there with whatever is within his hands. He was fine before you came. Look what you have done to him filling with false hope, here," the Abyss motioned his head around the room, *"A place where all those who have lost hope come. Hope does not exist here even when its bought by someone who should not have come."*

River listened to what was said but did not really take it all in, "Hope always exist, sometimes it's just buried deep and cannot be seen," he replied still looking down at Tony.

"I'm confused anyway," the Abyss continued, *"I see him, look what you have done to him. But it's not him and you is it?"* it paused, more for effect than anything else, *"It's just you now. There are not two people is there? You are the same person is*

that right?"

River did not answer immediately as he knew that it was purely a game and said to try and engage him in something which would take his mind off Tony and the position and state he was in. As far as River was concerned there was only one person in the room and the Abyss could work it all out for itself without any help from him, "Just back away and be quite, no one is listening here anymore. There is no audience for you here," he said looking up directly into its eye's, holding the contact.

For a moment the Abyss in front of River was taken aback, its eyes flaring up out of their sockets, their colour ablaze with anger against the whiteness of its face. It bought itself back under some semblance of control before speaking quietly, "Do not speak in that way to me here. For a time you may feel empowered by your mother's touch but that will go and you will be left alone with me. Do not overestimate her power and her reach, and she would do well to remember that also."

The word 'mother' did not fit coming from the mouth of the Abyss, certainly in reference to his mother, Princess. River smiled in response before speaking, "You have no idea of her power and her touch," continuing to smile as he finished speaking.

The Abyss laughed, long and loud, "Touch, power, faith and hope – it's all very sweet and in itself very touching but neither of you will leave, or sorry YOU won't leave, and we all know what that means for her," throwing the words out at River, "Don't we, River," reaching in close, its face up against his.

River knew what the Abyss was trying to do, to lead him and force him into a confrontation, to forget about himself and those he loved and be consumed by anger and rage and strike out and back at that which provoked him. He would not be drawn and stayed calm, "We will leave together, and we will return to her arms," not moving away as he spoke, "There are greater things in life than you, far greater."

The Abyss stayed close in next to River's face before changing into the shape of a ghost or spectre which wound itself around River as he sat. It twisted itself round him so that it covered his whole body, close enough for River to feel it but not quite touching. Its presence around the back of his neck was cold, like liquid ice, as it stayed that way, and continued to circle him, almost as if it was looking for a weak point where it could attack. It found none and returned to the physical form which it had been before, although this time it sat in front of River and mirrored his seating position exactly.

"As I was saying neither of you will leave here," it said staring at Tony now. "He is broken and you cannot save him. What remains is an empty shell of what he was before. Sorry I mean what you were before. I have a question for you – Tell me River when did it change for you and you came to be the person that lies cradled in your own lap?"

For a moment River felt it rise from deep inside, the feeling to strike back, to react as the Abyss would have wanted, but it soon fell again and peace returned, "This is not about what happened but about now. The past is past and our future is not ruled by your empty promises. We will together remember all that we need to," he said calmly before adding, "And we will forget you and this place."

The Abyss smiled back, "So you think but you will not forget. Too much has passed between us to go back now. All of us three are in fact just one. We will always stay together, we will always be as one, living here."

"We are not as one, we never have been and never will be. What has passed is your control and your poison over us. We found something different and it does not contain you in it," River said not backing down, keeping hold of his faith, there faith.

The Abyss thought for a while and shifted his head to one

side to look at *River*. *He contemplated the child opposite him trading words and not backing down. He made a good advisory and the Abyss was enjoying the discussion and what was passing between them – a thought came to his mind, a plan, "What about a deal then, River?"*

River eyed it with suspicion, this was not a place for deals or making pacts and he knew it, and he laughed, his only response.

The Abyss continued, "I see you are suspicious, but you will like this one maybe," it paused to let the words move across and sink into River's head, "What if I let him go? Just let Tony go now. In exchange."

"Exchange for what," River replied quickly wanting the rest of it out in the open.

"In exchange for you, River. He can go but you have to stay!"

If River was shocked or surprised by what had just been said, he did not show it. In truth he was neither. Before he came he knew through Princess that he would eventually be faced with a decision that he would have to make which would decide all their fates, Princess included. This time had come and although he did not show it, the question sat heavy across his fragile shoulder, as well as across his soft and loving heart.

"I know what you are thinking, River. What will happen to Princess, to your mother?" the Abyss spoke before River had a chance, throwing it out again. "If you and Tony are in fact one then is she not his mother also? Does it matter which one returns, as long as one does?"

River had listened to the deal and knew that the time had come when he would need to decide. He looked down at Tony's prostrate form still shivering and showing no signs of waking. He thought of his options and apart from him simply picking Tony up and trying to leave then they seemed few and far between. He could never carry him anyway and looking around it was not like he could simply drag him out, there were no doors anywhere. His thoughts turned to Princess and he closed his eyes trying to feel her within him, the Abyss knew and moved in closer towards him.

"Don't try and ask her, this one has to be decided by you alone. It's time River to take that step and move from child to man and decide your fate yourself. Princess cannot decide or choose for you on this one," the Abyss said its face inches away from his, glaring at him.

River still had his eyes closed but could feel the heat now being emitted from the form in front of him. The iciness had gone to be replaced by a burning furnace now that the time had come for fate's to be decided. The whole scene had been set, the actors were in place and this was the time when all was to be decided, in the blink of an eye and the words of a child.

River went to speak, to agree to the deal, to what was being asked of him. He knew that there was nothing else he could do, that time had run out and there was no one else to run to. Princess would understand and she would take care of Tony. River cared little for his own fate. He came for Tony and would have achieved his goal, it was over.

River went to speak, to agree to what was being offered, to stay instead of Tony. Before he could open his mouth a hand came from nowhere and moved up to reach out and grab the neck of the form which the Abyss had taken, a hand accompanied by the strangled voice and a single word, "NOOOOOOOOOOOOOO."

Tony had woken up.

CHAPTER 36

Her faith unleashed…

"Noooooooooo," Princess lifted herself up from her sleep and screamed out into the forest. Her eyes opened and her hands went out in front of her attempting to grab or clutch at something which she thought was there. They grabbed at thin air, nothing was there.

Ty and her mother were startled and sprang back from their kneeling positions next to her, giving her space. Both of them had been in the process of dozing off, their heads dropping as they had sat there waiting. Now they were both wide awake and despite the initial shock moved back in closer to comfort her.

She was now sat bolt upright, still clawing at the air and space in front of her. Her eyes were open but she also seemed unaware of where she was or indeed who was next to her. Ty tried to hold her steady as her mother reached for her hands to bring them back down to her sides and between them they eventually managed to calm and placate her. Ty leant her backwards onto his chest and she lay there breathing heavily, her own chest rising and falling in rapid succession. She had not said anything else apart from the "No," and it appeared that for the moment it was all she was going to say.

"Who was she speaking to and what was she trying to grab or reach for," Ty asked whilst holding her tightly to his chest and in his arms.

Her mother had been alarmed by princess's sudden movement and the cry out but had relaxed slightly now that she was at least lying down, "I can't be sure but I can only presume she was crying out to River, trying to stop him doing something or someone doing something to him," she said in reply.

"How can she see or know what's going on? I thought she had done all that she could before," Ty asked worried at this new turn of events.

"Princess has powers and gifts way beyond what can be seen and felt by both you and me. She does not reveal everything to anyone, she always holds something back," her mother answered. "She has always been that the same way even as a child. She is stubborn and beautiful in the same moment, wilful and graceful within the same smile, filled with peace and passion in a glint of her eye. All mixed together; well it's a potent combination and very powerful. No one should under estimate the range and extent of what she can see, move and influence. She could make clouds disappear if she wanted to, never forget that."

Ty listened carefully and felt he knew some of what she said from his own personal experience. Even in his dreams, Princess could often show all the things her mother had mentioned in a blink of an eye. She was often headstrong and would even walk off from him in his dreams if she had been crossed. She always came back and forgave and showed the other peaceful sides of her. But the undercurrent, the passion when confronted, which simmered underneath the surface often erupted like lava from a volcano. She could unleash a fury to match that and something more, of that he had no doubt.

They both looked down at her again as they heard sounds coming from her mouth. Her lips had started to move and her breathing and heart rate rose as she attempted to reach out and communicate with something or someone. Neither could hear what she is saying or even guess at it but it was clear that she was trying to speak with someone across the breaking dawn. Princess was using every inch of her power and the gifts she had to reach out once again to River.

She would never stop reaching and give up on him, to both of them it was the one thing that would always remain. She would never give up hope. Her faith unleashed she continued to speak, and they watched over her. She reached out, through the air, using all her powers in a concerted effort to reach her son, her River.

CHAPTER 37

You will meet before the end…

Joshua and Sarah sat on the small steps of the balcony in front of the hut. They had moved there from there standing position with the book sitting for the present on a step also between them. He had been looking at it for some time and she had just been looking at him. From what she could visibly see there had been no real change over his face. They had been sitting there awhile and she was unsure why he had wanted the book and what was going to happen now.

After some time she felt she could contain her anxiety any longer, "So are we just going to stare at it then, is that the plan?" deciding on humour to break the tension that was clearly evident.

It worked, Joshua laughed loud and for some time, the light returning to his eyes, "If only that was the plan and what was needed then it would be great," still laughing as he replied.

She smiled and laughed with him, glad that she had chosen the right option, "So what is the plan exactly and why did you suddenly change your mind?"

Joshua thought about lying but decided quickly against it, if there was ever a time for truth then this was certainly it, "Princess spoke to me, guiding me, telling me to look inside for salvation," he said still staring at the book.

"Princess spoke to you?"

"It should not really be a surprise. Her son is in danger and she will be using all the gifts she has to keep him safe. Her power is beyond any understanding to us mere mortals," Joshua replied, his gaze not shifting from its object.

Sarah did not know Princess. She had only seen her from a distance but through her travels with Ty and her time now at the lake with Joshua she longed to meet her. It was clear the impact and effect that she had on everyone was the same. She was a gift and bought so much into their lives and she hoped that one day, when all of this was over, that she would meet her. Even thinking of her bought a stillness to her beating heart and she felt a sense of calm return.

Joshua knew what she was thinking, could feel the sense of peace radiating from her, "She is aware of you Sarah and has sent blessings to you before, straight after River jumped. With God's will, you will meet before the end."

Sarah was not amazed that he knew what was in her head. She was unaware that Princess had done this but again the knowledge now bought a further sense of ease and comfort to her and she shared this with him, "Thank you, it's nice to know that she cared for me enough to do this."

Joshua nodded his understanding but knew that the time for talking and pleasantries was past. It was the time for action and his actions included picking up the book. He had said that the past and what he had gone through before no longer had any hold over him but now, right at this moment he was taken back. He was taken back to the moments before he met River and some of the thoughts that were present in him. It had been some time since he had re-visited them and for a moment he wanted to run far away, leaving them and the book behind.

Sarah saw his face change slightly, a tension come to pass, and put her hand over to rest gently on top of one of his, "Are you ok with all this?"

Joshua felt the softness of her touch both physically and in her words, bringing him back from his past and to the job at hand. He reached over and put his other hand on top of hers and squeezed it with affection, "Time to move on now, time to see what we can find inside," moving both his hands away from hers and to the book.

He picked it up and slowly felt his way across the top of it, it was certainly well-worn and battered in places, reminding him of Tony's state of mind maybe even his from the past. He knew he had to begin the search. It had to be slow, methodical and assured. He knew the importance of the moment and what he was doing. He had to try and find what was needed, somewhere within lay the key to open things up further, the chance for River and Tony to return. Somewhere inside there existed the words, a line of words even that Princess had spoken to him about, salvation. He felt the weight across his shoulders. With a sharp intake of breath he turned the cover open and began to read.

CHAPTER 38

It's not important now...

Tony's hand had reached out and grabbed the Abyss by the throat, it held on, trying to tighten its grip around it. In reaching out, Tony moved himself up from his previous lying state and was now in the process of getting to his knees, moving and twisting with the Abyss as it tried to free itself from the hand clutched tightly around its throat. Tony pushed River to one side as he did this and he fell to the floor, forgotten about in the midst of the struggle between Tony and the Abyss.

Despite its obvious power and force the Abyss had never been touched by a human hand or anything physical. The shock of this and the extent of the force behind Tony's grip had momentarily left it shocked and stunned, struggling to regain some form of control and composure, but mostly power. It eventually managed to free another arm from amidst its long black coat and bought this to bear on Tony's hand, both of them twisting and tumbling across the floor, like two crocodiles locked in the middle of a death roll, tearing at each other in their separate attempts to gain control.

Tony was screaming as he struggled to hang on, his strength

deserting him with every second which passed, "Nooooooooooooo. Leave him alone, leave us alone, I will never let you have him."

River had regained his own composure with the shock of what just happened but knew that he could not interfere, his physical strength was not enough to get involved and in trying to do so he knew he would only put them both in jeopardy. Tony would get caught up in protecting him and that was not what was needed now. He looked on, helpless, something which he had never experienced before and he felt very small and very alone.

They continued to struggle and paw at each other, rolling around the floor and smashing into the walls, causing the cracks in them to widen, sending out long fissures across each wall. All of this was accompanied by the sounds of thunder smashing and crashing across the whole depth of the room itself, lightening illuminating the scene of two forms locked in battle. The storm was inside the room in every way and the noise and the accompanying screams from both Tony and the Abyss rang out long and loud.

In the end, after minutes of wrestling with each other, Tony's strength gave out and the Abyss pulled his hands away from its own throat and in a last-ditch effort threw Tony across the room. It sent him flying across the width of the room and bought him crashing into the wall, leaving him draped on the floor in a heap. River rushed over to his side to be of aid but Tony lay unconscious from the throw and could not be woken.

The Abyss stood there triumphant, wiping its sleeve across its face to wipe away the saliva that had formed during the struggle. It removed its coat and threw it also in the direction of River in a show of contempt towards them both,

"Here give him this, wrap him up, he will need it when he wakes," it said scowling the words at River. "When he leaves and you stay, he will need it."

The coat had landed a few yards away from them both and despite not wanting to River reached for it and bought it across to lay over Tony's prone body. River had never seen anyone fight before and seeing it for the first time had left him a little dazed and shell-shocked and he took the time to care for Tony but also care for himself. In this moment and in an attempt to find some solace he remembered the stone, wrapped in her hair, and then further remembered that Tony had been holding it before he woke. He looked down at Tony and around the immediate area but could not see it. He felt a sense of panic and looked further but could not see it.

"Looking for something are we?" the Abyss spoke.

River turned around slowly, trying not to let his head run to what he already knew. The Abyss stood there, defiantly, triumphantly holding the stone between two bony skeleton like fingers. The black band of her hair clearly visible across the middle.

"I have to admit it's very pretty, lovely even," it laughed sarcastically, "Although this black stuff round the middle does ruin it a bit. Not sure I want that on it."

River felt a force inside rise up from the middle of his being, his stomach, a rage and anger that he had never know, it threatened to continue to rise and to come out but as it reached his throat its force died and it fell again, back to where it had started, calmly he spoke, "You cannot hold or take everything. There are certain things that you will never understand or defeat."

The Abyss snapped back, anger rising in it, "I will take and hold and then possess all that I want. There is nothing you or her can keep from me – Nothing. You would do well to remember that."

"There is nothing that you will ever say that I will remember," River replied before pausing and adding, reflecting its words back for effect, "Nothing."

The Abyss was for a moment ready to strike back and continue the rage in its words but decided to go back, back before Tony woke up, "So I was forgetting in the excitement where we were exactly," pausing for its own amusement, "Oh yes, you were just about to answer I think."

River knew it was coming but the Abyss had misread the time and the signs. If it thought that River was waiting to say yes then it was mistaken. River was looking for time, waiting for time, biding even for just some more moments when it could hold the Abyss and concentrate its efforts on him. The longer its focus was on River and the answer to a question the more he was blind to other people and what was being done outside to aid them. The Abyss was so intent on what was in the room that it was forgetting what lay outside which exerted influence and held sway at times. The walls of the room were not immune to Princess and could only hold her at bay for a certain length of time. The Abyss was forgetting this and River aimed to continue the charade for a little longer. River looked down to check on Tony once more and there was no change, He got up from next to his body and walked across towards the form in front of them both. The Abyss was surprised and it showed as its eyes flashed in acknowledgment of this.

River's eyes were on the stone and it was this that he turned to, "It's nothing really, it's just a stone with hair round it. I keep it more as a lucky omen more than anything else."

The Abyss eyed him suspiciously and looked down again at the stone in its hand, the colour fading as it did, "Really, is that so. Then if it's destroyed it matters not to you," it said keeping its eyes fixed on River for any sign that was different to his words.

River turned away and walked towards a wall on the opposite side of the room, "Do with it what you want, it matters not to me," running his hands along the cracks as Tony had done earlier.

"River please, dishonesty at a time like this. It's not you," the Abyss pouring scorn on his words, *"I felt the anger rise in you and then fall. You should have let it out, it would have been more interesting than this."*

"Your right I guess, I'm busted," River laughed, the sound of his innocence so out of place, "It means everything to me, without it then there is no point."

"Aaahh – there's the River we know and everyone loves," the Abyss continued with its scorn, *"What's it like to be loved so much but in the end let them all down?"*

For a moment the Abyss struck at something, a chord and thread inside that felt like a hammer blow to his soul. River continued to run his hands across the cracks on the wall and did not answer immediately and the Abyss knew it had hit the mark.

"That one hurt didn't it," laughing again, *"It's just the truth River seeing as that's where we are at now. But don't worry. I'm sure they will forget you when you stay. You are going to stay aren't you?"*

River sensed the opportunity and turned to face the Abyss who itself had moved towards the centre of the room, again sensing the moment arriving, "Maybe they will, it's not important now," walking towards the Abyss, meeting it halfway, "What is important is that you return the stone to me. Here's a deal for you, give me the stone, let Tony go and I will stay."

They eyed each other from only a few yards away. The Abyss towering over the blond-haired boy who dared to come and demand a deal. They glared at each other with contempt and disgust for what the other stood for. The Abyss contemplated what River had offered, tempted beyond words but wanted one other thing also.

"Tony can go, you can have the stone back and you will stay here; that is all fine," it said after some time thinking.

River looked up and acknowledged and signified a yes with a nod of the head.

But the Abyss was not finished, "There is one other thing, a small thing really," pausing, bending down to look River directly in the eyes, close in, "you disown her. You can have the stone, but the hair stays with me. Let go of her, let go of Princess, your Mother and then we have a deal."

River's heart sunk to the lowest point, his soul screamed out and he fell to his knees, sobbing as he did.

CHAPTER 39

You could have saved him...

Joshua had been going through the pages of the book for some time now. It was a slow process and a painful exercise and one he would not choose to do of his own accord. There were so many emotions, so many raw feelings inside a single line let alone a whole page – "Fearing the dark... reeking of self-doubt... tears at the hole... submerge into dust... all vision fades to black... it lives in shadow" – line after line, sentence after sentence, endless page after endless page. The torment and misery written down just went on and on. He thought that he would be able to deal with the experience but it was as painful for him as it seemed for Tony at the time of writing. As he continued to read he found himself hoping even more that Tony would be saved, returned and in time recover. All the focus had been on River and amidst it all Tony had somehow gotten lost. He paused for a moment and looked away from the book simply to reflect on this and re-connect with the world and the area around where he lived. He wanted to feel the simplicity of life in all its beauty.

Sarah had been sitting next to him when he first started to read but as time went on, she got up and walked away leaving Joshua on the steps of the hut going through the book. She wandered down towards the lake, its presence losing some of its effect the more she spent time around it. She looked out across the water and thought about all that had happened since she heard the voice in her head at the beach. She didn't even know where she was really and if she would get back to there. Her normal life seemed just that, a 'lifetime' ago. If this was a dream then she hoped that when she woke up she would remember only certain parts of it, she would happily forget some things. She thought of her brief time with River and longed for that back again. It had only been short but she could see why so much was being done to get him back safely and quickly. She herself would give up anything just to see him once more and to hear him laughing and seeing him running towards her.

As this thought and the warm feeling came into her head, a voice seemed to rise up from the depths of the lake. She knew immediately that this was a different voice, it was cold and flat, not the voice of something she knew, *"What would you give up Sarah? Would you give yourself up for him, give yourself up to me for his safe return to those who love him?"*

Sarah froze, rooted to the spot. Her heart started to race, beating faster as if it would tear through her chest. She instantly felt fear rising inside her which continued as the voice spoke again, *"You could have saved him yourself, but you didn't; you let him jump into my arms."*

Sarah was totally frozen now. The grief which had been stilled and silenced began to rise up, knocking at the doors of her very existence. She struggled to breathe and the emptiness and heaviness rose with it, threatening to overwhelm her as she felt unsteady on her feet. Her eyes began to well up, the memory of her frantic search for River in the water returning and re-surfacing to haunt her vision. The voice continued, *"Come and join him, join us. He is here with me now, jump in and you can be with and see him now."*

Sarah buckled falling to her knees, the tears openly falling down her cheeks like leaves ripped from the branches by an autumn wind. She began to sob and tried to call out to Joshua but the words would not come, drying up in her throat.

He was there anyway, catching her before she totally dissolved and fell to the floor in a heap. When he had looked up from the book for a moment he had seen her by the water and noticed the change in her whole body as she stood there. Intuition kicked in and he had thrown the book down and ran to her aid, crossing the distance quickly.

He held her as she sobbed, her whole body heaving with the outpouring of emotion. As he held her Joshua looked up towards the lake and saw wide ripples snaking out from the centre, as if something had just disappeared under the centre of it. Something had certainly disturbed the surface and who knew what lay underneath but he was sure that whatever it was it was linked to Sarah and her current state.

He did not want to push, hurry or leave her there but he was aware of time moving on, time which they did not have to spare. He managed to get her to her feet and also get her walking back towards the safety of the hut, consoling and persuading her with every small step they took. They arrived back there and he got her inside, still sobbing, moving her across to the bed and laying her down, covering her with a blanket in the process. She curled up instantly into a ball and pulled the blanket further around herself, as if she was aiming to hibernate like a hedgehog in winter. He looked down at her and wanted to stay with her but time was ticking and wanting had been pushed to one side at the expense of what was needed, "Sarah, I have to get on and find what is needed, you understand?"

She looked up at him, lost and alone written across her face, but nodded her understanding and motioned for him to go. As he left she pulled the blanket tighter almost to make up for his leaving her.

Joshua walked outside with purpose and commitment in his stride.

He could see that everything was moving at a pace and that something had used that speed and the moment to reach out and try and take hold of Sarah. He needed no confirmation from her to know that, his insight and experience of the world taught and showed him that. The lake had also left its mark in the distortion and change in the nature of the water's surface, leaving him in no doubt.

He got back to the balcony, picked up the book and got ready to sit down when something stopped him. A sound, at first hardly audible, moving closer now, becoming clearer with every second. It moved quickly eating up the distance, entering into the valley and towards Joshua.

A voice reached out to him, *"The Lake, the water – you need to be closer to it to feel the source of what you seek. Move towards it and let it back in."*

He knew instantly that it was the voice of Princess, soft yet forceful in his head. He had heard her voice many times to know that when it came it always came for a reason. The words rebounded and knocked around in his head and he got up slowly, the book in his hand and started off towards the water.

As he walked down towards the crystal waters he found himself thinking of a time which he thought he had forgotten. Many years before something called him to walk towards the edge of a bank, another voice different to Princess's, but as alluring and demanding. It pulled him close on that day and asked something of him. It asked him to trust it and he had without regret until that fateful moment when he climbed up on the rock and prepared himself to jump. His state of mind had changed since then but he thought about the similarities between the voice then and her's now. They both called him to the water's edge and he jumped to their call. They were so different but he continued to think that despite this the outcome was the same – he was now at the water's edge because of their influence and power. Had he really changed that much over the years or was all of it purely on the surface and superficial, still so easily manipulated by the voice and will of another?

It was with these final thoughts in his head that he arrived at the water's edge and he looked first across it and then into the blue colours of the water in front of him. He still struggled to look into the water and until this moment had never actually done it. He had always looked across and never focused on a single spot, aware that to become fixated creates an attachment to a feeling or a thought and any attachment, he had come to learn, only bought pain and in the end suffering. He had gotten used to simply allowing his thoughts and feeling to come and then go, experiencing them but not holding onto them. Fixation on one thing had led to pain and now he was having to revisit many of the places that had bought him that pain. It was not something which sat easily or comfortable on his shoulders. There was a part of him that wanted to put the book down, turn and walk away. Let others deal with what was needed to do, it was too dangerous for him. The thought of doing this surfaced steadily and threatened to consume him and define his actions but one thing came and cancelled them all out, an image, a boy, a child needing his help – River.

He sat down without any further ado and opened the pages again. His search began and this time he moved through the pages quicker, because he knew there was no time left to play with. It was not also the place to get consumed by the thoughts written down and the feelings expressed. He knew he could identify, empathise and sympathise with what Tony had written, but now was not the time. Not here at the water's edge the memory sitting below the surface of his emotions but ready to strike up and out at any time if he weakened. It was the time only to hold River at the centre of his thoughts, keep him in focus but not to fixate and steadily work his way through what was in front of his eyes.

He pushed past the pages he had already read and onto those he had not yet visited. He had not read them but the writings and their themes continued, never ending and never changing as it became clear that the further he went into the book so did Tony's eventual steady decline into the arms of what was waiting for him, the Abyss. He scan read much of it, passing over and onto the next line or the next page, hoping that something would itself 'jump' out at him or be guided by the voice of Princess which stayed in his head.

He had gotten through most of the book, towards the back end of it without any luck and without finding what he was searching for, the writings themselves, here, became even more disjointed and lacked any kind of rhythm or flow. They just seemed to simply consist of abstract thoughts written down one after the other. In any one poem there seemed to be three or four others twisted across the length and breadth of them. It was hard to follow and Joshua had brief thoughts and memories of being in that same place but skirted around those quickly and tried to stay focused on the search and on River.

He was reading across the top of one page, nearly at the end, when something drew his attention to a set of smaller line written diagonally across the page on the one opposite to what he was studying. There was a slight difference in how they were spaced out and in the style of the writing itself. It was nothing that could have been easily noticeable and Joshua could easily have scanned over them without any due regard, but something wouldn't let him. A voice, mellow and soft returned to his head and he heard her words, *"Slow now, miss nothing which cannot be missed, time runs short and the hour glass is full."*

He turned the book slowly around in his hands to look at the words from a different angle. As he did this he noticed that all the words seemed to turn round with it, moving in alignment and shifting across the pages as he did. They were moving into something else which wasn't there until only a few simple lines remained, staring boldly at him from out of the page. All the other letters and lines that were not needed to fill those words had gone, vanished, disappeared. All that was left was a number of words that re-arranged themselves as he looked. Eventually all that was left was six sentences which sat evenly in the middle of the page, as if they had been there all along.

Joshua read them once, twice, three times and then once again just to be sure. As he read a stillness removed the past, wiping it clear from his mind and leaving him lighter than he had ever felt before. He got up, exalted, and turned starting to run back up towards the hut, shouting as he did, "Sarah, Sarah, come out. I've found them. I found what we needed for River."

CHAPTER 40

We will find peace inside each other...

River was still on his knees but had stopped crying now. He had been this way for quite some time, but the Abyss seemed in no hurry to move him along or complete the deal. It walked around him as he knelt or at times simply sat back and waited, bending down and trying to look up and under River's head to the eyes beneath. River's long blonde hair covered this and his eye's remained shut tight, so that the Abyss could not look into them and see what lay behind.

Tony had woken up a short time ago and at present sat with his back against the wall of the room still recovering. His head was groggy and he felt weak, almost too weak to even stand and any knowledge of what had happened to leave him that way had been wiped clean by the blow to his head. Blood trickled down the back of his neck where he had sustained a deep cut which had now congealed over. He held his hand to it to try and stem the flow even more and the sweet taste of his own blood was present in his mouth where he had bitten his tongue as he had been thrown against the wall.

River was aware that Tony was awake and had seen him, from under the cover of his hair, pull himself up and rest against the back drop of the wall. The cracks rising from under his body and spreading out across the wall, as deep and as long as the hours that they had been there together. River knew that he could not stay this way for ever and now that Tony had woken up and hopefully regained enough energy to leave then River knew he had to do something to move things along. Although the Abyss had made a deal and offered to let Tony go, River was not sure that this would always be the case and it would not go back on the idea at any point. It was best to move forward and get Tony out of there before the Abyss changed its mind.

River lifted his head and opened his eyes and found himself looking first at Tony and then moving over and up to the eye line of the Abyss. There was a haunting and chilling presence in its eyes, a mark of victory, a warning of wanting more and a distinct lack of warmth or compassion. They were the eyes of hell and they blazed with defiance and aggression, their colour darkening as they did.

"Well then, time to make the deal complete. Shall we shake on it then," it said, *half smiling and putting a bony hand forward in expectation and leaving it there for River to take.*

River looked at it and then quickly away, getting up at the same time and ignoring the Abyss and walking over to Tony. He bent down and moved Tony's head slightly so he could see the back of it where the blood still ran, darker now, "How does it feel now, your head?"

Tony tried to smile and nod at the same time, "I think it's stopping really but I do have a little bit of a headache – what happened?"

River moved past the question, "Nothing really you just slipped and fell, that's all. Can you stand up yet?"

"I think I can, I don't feel as dizzy as I did," Tony replied easily enough, his words slow but sure.

"Let's try and get you up then, see how it feels when we do," River said trying to lift his arm underneath Tony's and assist him as he did.

Tony used River as little as he could aware that he was not only a lot bigger but also a lot heavier and he did not want to rest all his weight on the boy's shoulders. As he rose, with River's help, he looked at the boy next to him and wondered how he got to move so far away from being that boy. If it was true, which he knew it was, that River was him but just as a child then in the case of looking in a mirror he could not understand why he would want to change any of what River was. Looking at River now made him smile and feel lighter inside but it was also tinged and tainted with shame, regret and remorse for putting him through all of this. What had happened to his future bright when he was River's age was anyone's guess. Who knew what happened and why he moved away from that path and it was possibly a question for somewhere else and not the time and place they found themselves in?

The Abyss had watched them together, allowing them a moment, but was starting to get agitated and impatient with their closeness and bond, "Yes all very touching, moving again, but time to just get it all over with. Now River we have a deal then?"

Tony looked down at River surprised at the words which had just been spoken, a question forming on his lips and in his eyes.

River did not allow him time to speak and answered, "We have a deal but I will shake or touch no part of you, not now and not ever. Give me the stone and let him go and then we will do whatever else you want to do."

Tony was appalled by what he had just heard and said, shouted more so, "What do you mean let me go? I am not leaving here. I stay and you go, there is no other deal to be done," bending down towards River his head next to his.

"You have no other part to play. You have fulfilled your purpose and bought him here to me. Go and be grateful that I

do not make you stay also. The torment and suffering you think you have gone through is nothing to what it could have been," the Abyss responding before River.

River looked into Tony's eyes and saw the fear and terror inside them. At that moment they did not mirror each other's, they were poles apart. Despite the time and what was about to take place River's eyes had returned to their natural colour and depth. They shone more now than they had ever done, sparkling with love, shining with hope and filled with a peace that rested only in those who knew fully what it was to be complete. Tony saw this and his heart was stilled, his soul, previously restless, comforted and eased by the sheer magnitude of what he saw in River's eyes.

They were eyes which spoke as they rested on Tony's. *"Trust in my son, he knows the way out of here,"* it was the voice of a woman speaking out from behind the eyes of River, *"He knows the way out of here for both of you."*

River smiled at Tony and bought his face close to his, pushing it forward until they were touching, "Be not afraid anymore, we will find our peace together, we will find peace inside each other," he said and kissed him gently on the cheek.

"Enough of this, enough time wasting. Fine if it gets things moving you can have the stone and then he can go and you and I can have that little chat," the Abyss fired the words across the room towards them both, pulling the stone out from inside one of the deep pockets of its coat.

River and Tony looked at each other one final time and smiled. Their eyes locked in an embrace which said so much without the words. They pulled apart from each other and turned to face the Abyss. A face off across the room as the Abyss held up the stone. Her hair could be seen clearly bound around the middle of it and the sight of it made River homesick for her arms and her loving touch.

"So you get the stone and I keep the hair River, that was the deal," the Abyss said as it slowly undid the small ties on the hair and started to unravel the lock of hair.

The sight of his hand on his mother's hair and the significance of it was hard to watch for River and he struggled with the emotions coursing through his veins. He wanted to walk over and grab the hair and the stone from the hand which he had come to despise. It belonged to a voice which he hated and a place that he did not understand. The Abyss continued to unravel the hair as River and Tony watched and seemed surprised itself at how long it took to do. Even River was and felt sure that when she did it in front of him that it was not that long or thick.

Finally it pulled the last threads clear of the stone and finished wrapping the hair itself around its wrist, again the mere sight of her hair against the pale skin disgusting and appalling River at the same time. The Abyss saw this and started to laugh, "Not easy to see this is it River? I never imagined you thought this is where it would end up when she gave it to you?"

River ignored the question and was about to speak when Tony did first, "It's not important now. Pass over the stone and be quiet," speaking with force and power for the first time.

The Abyss was moved towards anger, and took a step towards Tony. "Found your voice again have we. Do not speak to me here like that. Remember that some deals can be changed."

River intervened between them, "Let's just have the stone now and we can move on."

The Abyss ignored River's response and held Tony firmly in his gaze. The scarlet eyes brimmed with loathing and anger and it burnt a line up between them, "Here take it and be happy," *it said tossing the stone in the direction of River whilst maintaining eye contact with Tony, anger still burning a hole in its chest.*

River caught the stone lightly in one hand and looked down at it. He used the cloth of his jacket to wipe it clean and try and return it to its natural state. He also tried to wash away the thought of where it had been and the touch of the Abyss on its perfect shape. The colour seemed to have faded and dulled slightly and River continued to rub across its surface until he was satisfied.

"Get him out of here. He is boring me now. He can be gone and be forgotten," the Abyss said, turning away finally from Tony and looking back again at River, moving towards him.

River looked directly at the Abyss and smiled, "I think it is you that has forgotten something."

The Abyss stopped walking, held in check by River's response, "I do not forget anything," it said staying still, doubt rising.

"You forget the book and what is in it. Not what you know that's in it but what you can't see," River said slowly and calmly to let the message sink in, and allow the doubts to rise further.

"The book is his head and I wrote what was in his head. I am the book and all that is inside it. Don't try and buy time here. Time has run out," it said although a hint of doubt rising into its words now also.

"No, Tony wrote most of the words that you put into his head in the book. But I wrote in it first, before you had even thought about Tony, or thought about us," River said taking a step towards the Abyss now, Tony following.

Doubt had now been overtaken by anxiety and with it fear knocking on its shirt tails, "You wrote what in it," the Abyss said, hesitation walking inside the words.

"I wrote the way out for both of us. You forget that fate cannot be changed and when we were born that was written also. We were always meant to end up here but it's how we leave which was always in question. I just played with fate a little, evened things up, hope that you don't mind?" his smile widening now.

Anxiety had been pushed aside for the Abyss now, fear and terror present in its every breath, "Fate cannot be changed even the outcome."

"That's normally the case yes, I agree. But there's one small thing that you forget," River said taking another step towards it.

"What?" the Abyss spat back.

"I am your fatal flaw. I am your destiny. I am what you loath and despise. My mother knew this day would come and did not come herself because she knew that your fate was in my hands and not her's. She could have come herself but did not. That is called love," River responded, Tony right next to him.

The Abyss felt trapped by the words that River was saying and also by what he was explaining to him. It had forgotten with its arrogance and ego that sometimes things that are not explained hold more power than those that can be explained. By reaching out and holding onto Tony, filling his mind with nothingness and despair that it would change all the fates of everyone. It knew of River and Princess but did not know the bond. Something not spoken about openly, simply existing between the two of them and her mother. The Abyss felt it could enter into and shape and colour the tone of life in every way but it was finding out that some things always remain and that something's will always win through.

River held the stone up towards the Abyss, it suddenly seemed small whilst his hand grew and reminded the Abyss of the strength and faith of River. It started to glow, and give off shimmering colours, illuminating the darkness of the room and sending colours spinning and twisting across the walls where the cracks had started to shrink and reduce, their depth gone. The walls returned to their natural state and the light continued to bounce across them, a myriad of colours which bought a welcome sense of relief to both Tony and River.

Along with the colours from the stone came a voice, "All is in place and the words that you left have returned and been found. It is time to change destiny."

It was the voice of Princess. The voice of their mother reached into the room and held their hearts as River held the stone out in front of him and the Abyss took a step back.

It was time.

CHAPTER 41

He feels your love for him...

Princess had woken up from her fitful sleep, slowly got up and walked bare footed over the dewy grass to the edge of the forest. She walked with beauty, poise and grace and it seemed that the Princess they all knew and loved had returned, just when it was needed.

Both Ty and her mother let her go, doing nothing to get in her way. She did not acknowledge them when she got up, it happened quickly and without warning. They both knew however, that she was neither ignoring them or unaware of their presence but was simply concentrating on something else. It seemed that she was being pulled or gravitating towards something that they could not see. It was obvious that it had something to do with River, her whole thoughts and being had been focused on him since he had left and that would not change until the end came. It was an end which was still uncertain and hung in the balance.

As she walked it became noticeable that some of the clouds above lost some of their darkness and the air itself felt lighter, less heavy on the chest. The sun which had been hidden by the dark blanket of cloud appeared briefly between a gap, a break, in them and its light seemed to capture and follow the path she walked along. Her dark hair fell loosely down her back and the sunlight caught it inside its rays, sending out tiny diamonds of colour as she walked. They rose and fell scattering themselves around her as they walked, like rose petals being thrown in the path of an empress.

Her eyes were open and their colour and shine had returned, reflecting out the overall beauty that she carried within her. The whole time she walked her lips moved, speaking out words of direction and encouragement towards someone – River, Joshua, Tony, Sarah, the universe – it was unclear as to whom. She came to the edge of the forest and stopped right at the exact place that she had seen River disappear from. She held her hands open in front of her, palms facing upwards, revealing the stone inside one of them. The stone that she had which held the memory of the day with River. It glowed brightly, shining its opal colour back up into her eyes, the coal black there mixing with it and sending darker shade up and out into both the forest and the sky. She started to speak, bowing her head as she did, sending out blessings, thoughts and prayers to those in need, her two children Tony and River.

At the same time she was doing this, some distance away, Sarah was being woken from her sleep by a voice shouting out to her from outside. It was the unmistakable voice of Joshua although she would have sworn she heard a women's voice telling her to wake up also from inside her dreams. She scrambled out of bed, wiping her face and untangling herself from the blanket which had wrapped itself around her during her sleep. She rushed out of the door and onto the balcony, still half asleep, and forced herself to look towards the direction of the voice, towards the lake. As she did she saw Joshua waving and calling for her and for a moment her fears faded as hope began to rise again inside.

Joshua was looking back towards her and shouting, "Sarah, come down, you are needed here, come down now."

Sarah hesitated slightly before she rushed to him, not quite wanting to leave the safety of the hut for some reason. For a moment it seemed too hard to take that single first step. It may have been a step to salvation, a move towards healing and away from fear but it was proving too much for her to easily do. She closed her eyes for a second and felt a slight tug and pull at her heart and the first words River spoke to her came quickly behind it, "Will you play with me now?" It proved to be the push she needed, the final shove and she stepped off the balcony running towards Joshua, running towards the water.

Joshua had watched her pause at the edge of the balcony, for a split second he himself thought she may falter and not come down at all. In his heart he willed her to take the first step knowing that the others after that would be easier. He spoke softly back up towards her in his head, "Just one step Sarah, everything always starts with the first step, after that its nothing to worry about." He repeated the words again until she did take that step and started to run towards him. He watched her coming and smiled knowing the big obstacle that she had just overcome.

She arrived, panting and a little breathless from her exertions, and he put a caring arm around her shoulders, speaking softly to her as he did, "It has been revealed to us. All that we need now is here as it's the time."

She spoke through her gaps for air, "What has? Where is it? Where?"

Joshua showed her the book and the pages that still remained open, "River hid it so well," he said smiling long and deep, "but then again he was always the best at hide and seek," laughing now as he finished.

His laughter was the tonic that she needed, lifting her spirits as she looked at the pages open in front of her and read what was written,

"There's not much there. Are you sure that is it, that it's enough?"

"More than enough and exactly what River would write. He is a child and for him less is more. He never uses fifty words to describe something when ten will suffice. It's just his way," Joshua replied.

Sarah had finished reading it but read it again for good measure then looked back at Joshua. His whole face was alive, the eyes sparkling as he stood there. His whole demeanour was infectious and Sarah could feel with each passing moment the true nature and beauty of life being renewed inside her. For the first time since she had witnessed River jumping she felt the rawness and intensity of hope throughout her core. It burnt a hole through and crushed the grief and loss that had held her for what seemed an eternity. There was a real chance now she felt that she would get to see him again, that he would return.

She felt a stillness wash over her as she spoke, "So what happens now?" looking into Joshua's eyes.

"We wait here for the sign. We wait for River and Princess to call us and then we destroy all that is and all that would be," he replied, adding, "We walk into the water Sarah without doubt and leave fear where it belongs, behind us on the bank."

Sarah heard the words and felt the last part more as it sank in. She knew it was the time to move past and beyond what had been and retake and reshape the future. She looked at him and said, "I will walk into the water with you," taking his hand in hers and clasping it tight. "For River and Tony, I will do that."

He looked down at their hands joined together and then back up into her eyes, "I know that you would Sarah. Not only that but River knows too. He feels your love for him and it touches his spirit, even now he feels it – trust and know that."

Sarah knew he was right. Every bone in her body and every breath re-enforced all that he was telling her. She knew at that moment

River could feel her courage and touch her love for him. It bought him renewed strength and faith and was needed right then. Sarah would walk into the water with that image in her mind. She would walk into the water with River always.

CHAPTER 42

Power enough still lives on within it…

River still held the stone out in front of him moving closer towards the Abyss with every second that passed. Tony was next to him, close by his side, the two of them locked in battle with what lay in front of their return, there release from torment.

The colours within the stone had continued to change and move throughout the time they moved forward – green, black, blue, red, orange, purple – back and forth until it finally settled on and emitted the most stand out white colour that there ever was, almost diamond rather than white. It was stronger than the nearest star, brighter than the fullest moon and it projected this diamond colour out and around the room. When it hit the eyes of the Abyss it temporarily blinded it and it shrieked in pain and terror.

The voice of Princess which had entered 'its' domain had rendered it speechless, its voice silenced once again although it was unsure if this would remain permanent. She knew it would give River and Tony some space and time for them to do what they needed to. The Abyss tried to speak, opening its mouth to reveal a gaping hole, a cavern in which the ends of the earth, the chasm of its soul could be seen. It offered nothing from that hole but despair and nothingness. The Abyss was the same on the inside as it was on the outside, without light, colour or beauty. It was dead inside of hope and dreams.

River left Tony where he was and circled the Abyss, the stone still emitting the same powerful white light from its centre. Any outside would have been transfixed by the sight of the small blonde haired boy walking round what it was, slowly and carefully as if he was walking through the forest on a summer's day. He did not seem perturbed or afraid and just gave off an air of peace and confidence which was echoed in his words.

"You forgot the power of love, faith, compassion, beauty and kindness when it's all combined. It conquers all. It is not me that renders you speechless but the power of all that is good in this world. All the world stand with me and we will prevail," finishing now to stand in front of it staring straight up into the scarlet eyes deep within its skull.

River knew that the Abyss wanted to reply and spit out, lash out and destroy the boy in front of him. As with anyone his eyes spoke volumes but he could not yet speak again and the frustration made it worse. River lifted his head slightly, trying to hear a message that was being passed to him.

At the edge of the forest Princess could see in her mind's eye all that was happening. She saw, for the first time, River standing in front of the Abyss, its eyes seething with disgust and hate. Until this moment she had not been able to fully penetrate into that world. The image and the sight of her son and where he was made her falter slightly, wanting to go physically and snatch them both up, remove them from there without a second thought, not waiting for another moment to pass. She knew that everything was in place, the tides were turning and destiny being reshaped but she struggled with the natural reaction of a mother to protect her child physically at all times, to stand between him and danger. She faltered but let the moment pass knowing that if she had done it then all would have been put back in jeopardy.

In her other mind's eye she also saw Joshua and Sarah. They were at the lake, at the edge of the water, the book in their hands, ready and waiting for her signal, her voice to direct them, she spoke, "It has been silenced and it is time to enter into the water. Walk and tread with care for power enough still lives on within it."

Joshua heard her voice and for the first time since the night she had met Ty, so did Sarah. It was strong, assured and confident yet carried a softness within which helped still her racing heart. They both looked at each other and started to walk the ten or so paces to the water, holding each other's hands, whilst Joshua also held the book. They reached the water's edge and slipped their shoes off, their toes catching the first touch of its icy feel. Sarah felt it through her veins, running up her legs to her rapidly increasing heart. A large part of her wanted to turn and run, never to return. Joshua sensed this and clasped her hand tighter, whispering, "Hold firm and keep your faith. Without this it does not work."

The tightened grip and his calming words served their purpose and it was she who took the first full step into the water, through her fear. He followed close behind and they moved carefully but also quickly forward until in no time at all the water had reached just above their waists. He still held her hand firmly, above the water line now and carried the book carefully with the other hand.

"This is far enough, Sarah, "he said, "I need to use my other hand now, ok?"

Sarah's anxiety and fear had lifted after taking the first step and it returned momentarily as he gently let go of her hand. She managed to reassure him, "It's ok. I'm ok," spending energy in doing so that she hardly had to spare.

He bought the book over to in between them so that she could see it, holding it in two hands, "Are you ready, Sarah?" he asked turning to look at her.

She returned his look, "Yes, I am more than ready for this to end, she said, her words coming easier now.

The water seemed to anticipate what was about to happen and was pushed forward at them by a power or force which could not be seen. It began to rise slightly, swirling and twisting around there legs and catching them in a tight hold, trying to drag them down. Icy hands came from out of its depths and tried to take the book itself from Joshua's hands. He was forced to move it higher for a moment to keep this from happening. Sarah began to panic and started to lose her balance alongside any sense of composure or peace that she had previously had. The hands continued to grab, the water continued to rise and spit at them, hissing almost as it did.

"Now, Sarah, now, time has run out," Joshua shouted above the noise which had suddenly come from inside the water.

Then they spoke, together, the words that River had left behind. The sentence's that he had hidden, to stay hidden until they were needed. The lines that had been written for one moment in time, this moment only.

The memory dissolves

Her hair unfolds

And 'it' will turn to dust

And through the days

That follow this

I will find my way back

To You.

CHAPTER 43

Her hair unfolds…

At the top of the hill, were the two rocks that Princess and River used to sit on when they were there, underneath the tree covered in white blossom, the water which had begun to lap at the bottom of them stopped. It started to recede.

Falling back down the hill at a pace twice as fast as it had covered the ground up the hill. It seemed to be sucked back to its source, something pulling it back from whence it came, quickly and with real force.

In the forest the water level briefly reached out to try and grab another inch from the trees and the flowers but it was in vain. The force that had driven in and been behind it was draining of all power and life. The Abyss had been silenced and was in the process of being dissected and taken apart piece by piece. Some fight still existed within its eyes but the power and combined force of what it was up against meant that it was a battle that it could not win. The water here attempted to push on but it stood little chance against its foes. It also began to retreat, falling back to whence it came, back to the stream and the place where Tony and River had jumped.

They themselves were in front of the Abyss itself. River stood holding the stone high out in front of him as it continued to shine. In his hand it flickered and glowed, seemingly brighter than before, quickly dying totally, its source and light gone. Without this source of power it began to crack and splinter from the inside, chips and shards being ripped off and flying across the room in the direction of the Abyss. It tried to shield itself from the attack it was under but the stone continued to fall and be ripped apart in front of its eye until finally with a loud crack it shattered completely, the final parts dissolving inside River's hand until it was gone, there was nothing left.

River looked deep into the eyes of the Abyss, they were burning fiercely, its anger and rage knowing no bounds, speaking out at him with their fury. River spoke with force and power towards it, "The memory has been dissolved. The physical memory at least, unlike you, both of us do not attach ourselves to things. That memory still remains inside us, we do not have to carry it around to reconnect to the emotion of that day."

Its eyes blazed and the mouth opened, a sound came out, not words but a noise which attempted to transmit something of what it was feeling. It came from the bowels of the earth and was full of the fury which blazed throughout it. The sound that came out was a mixture between a scream and a roar; a symbol of defiance, of confrontation and something else. Time was ticking and that the voice was returning, slowly maybe, but it was returning and River could hear and feel this.

Tony started to pull at the arm of River's sleeve, aware also and filling with anxiety, "River it's time to move on please, it's too dangerous to wait longer."

River knew he was right and acknowledged his awareness, "Yes I know, don't worry we are moving on now to the next stage," looking at the Abyss he spoke, very matter of fact, "Her hair unfolds."

River and Tony looked directly at Princess's hair tied around the wrist of the Abyss. They had not tried to take it back because they knew the importance of it to what was to happen. The Abyss watched their eyes focus on it and stare directly at it and he followed their gaze.

For a time nothing happened and then it started, slowly at first and gradually increasing in pace as it found its way. The hair that had been tied around its wrist began to unravel, strand by strand, lock by lock, uncurling itself from around the wrist of the Abyss. The mere act of what it was doing, apparently unaided by any other force held all of their gaze. The colour seemed to shine with an added intensity as it continued to unravel. When it had been wrapped around the stone that River had held to his lips it seemed a simple band of hair, not long or particularly thick. It had grown and it now consisted of enough length and strength that was a surprise to them all. As it uncurled it moved snaking itself from the wrist of the Abyss up its arm moving slowly but with sureness and a firm of purpose. Further up the arm it travelled past the elbow and up towards the shoulder and then beyond.

The Abyss watched it, feeling a slight burning sensation across its skin as it moved, a prickly heat left where it had been a sense of anxiety and nervous anticipation of what was to come. It had completely unravelled from its wrist and the end of it followed the rest and made its way upwards until eventually all of it fell loosely around its neck, bound around it and then it stopped moving, laying there ready.

River had realised as it made its way what the intention was, looking into the eyes of the Abyss who stared down at the strands hanging loosely around its neck, the intention had obviously just registered also. They looked at each other for a while, silence between them, hate in its eye's, faith and a deep sense of knowing in his.

The Abyss spoke, its voice returning slowly as realisation hit home of what was passing, "This changes nothing you understand River. It's purely a pause in what will be."

River listened with curiosity rather than interest. It was not a time to enter into a discussion about the future. River never did, he was only interested in what the now would bring, "It changes here and now. That is all that's known," bending down and placing himself on his knees, Tony following his lead.

The Abyss looked down at them both, a laugh trying to come out from its misery, nothing came, "Look at you two, still on your knees in front of me. As I said nothing changes."

River spoke with Tony, ignoring what had just been said, "We kneel here in reverence to what we hold dear, in life and death, love, faith and compassion will always hold us."

Tony looked across at River, so small yet so big, so fragile yet full of strength and felt himself lifted by the boy that he used to be. For a moment regret at what and where he had led that boy entered his mind but he brushed it away, time for that was past as the memories were also, "He holds no power over me anymore. When he goes then all that has been will go to."

The Abyss spoke, loud, almost in a last show of defiance, aiming it at Tony, "I will always have power over you. Do not listen to the boy who kneels next to you, at the end he will betray you. I never did and remember that when he does."

Tony, like River before him ignored the voice, speaking to River once again, "Can we go home now please River. I'm tired of all this."

River looked at him and smiled his understanding, "Yes Tony lets go home."

At the sound of these words the hair around the neck of the Abyss quickly came to life, wrapping itself tightly around its neck, digging in and holding onto the neck which it had completely absorbed. The Abyss struggled and tried to free itself from the binds of hair that would not let go. It used its hands now free to attack the hair, pulling and grabbing at the locks and strands that dug ever tighter. It tried to scream, shout, taunt, but its voice was unable to get out. Its breath, the dark toxic breath catching in its throat as the last signs of life started to leave its body, its form, the room and their lives. It fell to its knees directly in front of River and Tony who had simply listened and not watched what was happening in front of them. It was not something they wanted to see and their heads were bowed as they knelt silently, protected by the power of what came from outside to hold them at that point.

With one last scream, a final cry out, the Abyss still tried to pull at the hair which now covered the whole of its neck and had moved even further up to wrap itself around its mouth, any chance of it catching air and living being extinguished. It fell to the floor, exhausted, broken, only the last signs of life left in its body. It lay there, unable to remove the hair from round its neck, its eyes staring across the floor, blinking in and out of consciousness.

It was not over and River pulled Tony quickly from his knees and ran with him to the other side of the room, tightly pressing himself and Tony against the wall, "Whatever happens hold on tight, and don't let go of my hand."

Tony did not understand, confused, he thought it was over, that was it, but now this was not the case, "What now, what?" he shouted at River.

Despite him shouting the words got caught up in the noise and mayhem that now consumed the room. A storm returned outside which had no equal, thunder crashing and drumming at the walls, anything that was outside thrown at the room they were in by a wind which came from nowhere but blew with a ferocity and intensity not previously know. Then there was the sound of water rushing and pushing itself to try and get in to where they were. They could hear it outside, the wind forcing it into waves which smashed against the outside, knocking at them until it was answered. The storm, the wind and the water unleashed as a final attempt to get to what was inside, to take River and Tony with the Abyss into the depths of hell.

They were both huddled together, keeping close to each other as the storm raged outside and threatened to burst inside at any moment. River knew that Princess would be doing all within her power to hold the storm at bay but even then it may not be enough. His mind tried to stay as calm as his heart but he struggled to keep it in check. Other plans and ways out went through his brain, but he knew that if the walls fell and the water came in, they would be swept away on the dying tides and breath of the Abyss.

The Abyss itself was still lying on the floor and any attempts it had made previously to remove the hair around its neck had long since gone, resigned to its fate. Its defiance came through the storm outside. It was all it had left and even that was failing although the wind still continued to provide the force to take them all. Its eyes opened, the colour and the rage dying inside, and looked across the room at River and Tony. It was a look of pure hate fuelled by a loathing of all that was good and what River stood for. Inside the resentment burned towards Princess and the part she had played in bringing River back from the edge. He was so close to slipping over, so close to falling that the Abyss could smell River's fear and taste his doubts in its throat. It had been ripped away by Princess, taken back from him, and even now as it stood on the edge of its own death the hatred still festered deep inside.

Its eyes caught River's and through them it spoke, "The scars you have will not heal, she cannot sooth them. Nothing can and nothing will and you will remember me more as time passes."

River heard the words and Tony didn't. He knew that they were words which were said to scare and leave doubts in his mind, to rise again at a later date and time. He went to reply but before he could there was a roaring from outside, a rushing so loud it overshadowed everything else as it crashed against the walls from outside. This and the continual bashing the walls had received was enough and the cracks returned to them but this time they were deeper than before and the water slipped in and through them, quickly beginning to fill the room.

River knew that it was the last acts of the dying form in front of them but as the water began to rise quickly, sweeping up past their ankles, he wondered if the end would come in time before he and Tony would be submerged and unable to escape. The Abyss half on its side now was beginning to be submerged itself but life still existed in it. Time was running out and River knew it. One final thing had to be done and he sent out his thoughts to the two people who could end it now, Joshua and Sarah.

It was Sarah who heard the voice of River in her ear, "The book must go now, and it's the final act."

She turned to Joshua who was back on the shore with her after they had said the words that River had left behind. When they had said them the water had returned to its normal state and they were able to make their way back without its icy hands grabbing at their bodies. When they were back on dry land they had stayed close to the water's edge as Joshua said there was one thing which may also need to be done and they would have to wait and listen for the call.

It had now come and Sarah turned to Joshua and spoke, "He said its now, destroy it now."

Joshua did not question how she knew or where she heard it from, time was gone for questions and only answers would suffice. He walked to the water's edge with Sarah at his side and then looked down at the book. The cause of so much and the reason for where they were. It had no power anymore over any of them and he was happy to let it go and to throw it into whatever opened its arms to receive it.

He looked at Sarah, "May this be the final act, may they return to us now."

He threw the book out, high and long into the sky and across the top of the lake. They watched it sail off into the distance carried by the breeze, its pages flapping as it went. It came down and hit the water and for a moment lay on the top of it before it began to sink. As it did they saw a bony hand, white in colour reach up and snatch it before it could be taken back and drew it down under the water.

Finally, the book had gone.

In the room where River and Tony were the effect of this was dramatic. The Abyss's body rose up above the level of the water, unaided, floating in the air as the last flickers of light and rage left its eyes. The hair tightened a little more and there was a loud crash of thunder and lightning from outside which caused River and Tony to put their hands to their ears. In front of them the Abyss arched its back and then the whole of its body just simply fell away. Bone, skin, hair turning to the finest dust which hovered in the air for a short while before it dropped into the water. The water around River and Tony's feet just slipped away, disappearing into the cracks and holes which had been formed and ripped by its entering the room. The Abyss had departed and they were left alone at last.

River fell to his knees in relief and bowed his head as Tony joined him.

Together, speaking to no one in particular they said, "And it will turn to dust."

Finally, the Abyss had gone.

CHAPTER 44

It's not goodbye, just see you later...

With the Abyss turning to dust and the book destroyed a sense of normality returned to all things in dramatic fashion. It was as if nature has just been waiting in the wings ready to reclaim at a moment's notice what had been given up. The natural beauty of the trees, flowers, meadows and hills regained what had been hidden by the vast expanse of water that had threatened to consume all it found in its way.

The force behind the water had been destroyed and the natural balance and flow of all things had been restored and with this nature took hold and the grace and beauty of all that was began to blossom and grow even more. The water which had threatened to consume left behind the ingredients for all living things to flourish. The leaves and blossom on the trees flourished as the roots of the trees used the water and what it left behind to sustain what was already there and to nurture new growth. The birds that had flown away as they saw and sensed the danger from the water returned to the branches of all the trees, contesting against each other in their attempts to create new songs to greet the new era that had come into being.

For River and Tony, the moments after the Abyss turned to dust and the book was destroyed it had been a little overwhelming. The water simply backed away, taken away as if someone had sucked it back in through a vacuum. It disappeared quickly, silently and left not a trace that it had ever been there. The walls that had cracks across them of all different sizes and shaped, knitted back together as if they had never been anything else than what they now were, four white blank walls. They looked pristine and new and for Tony and River the sight was difficult to take in.

There was still one major problem, how to get out? There were no windows and doors and with no cracks to play with or use there was no give in the walls at all. They were still trapped but for the time being as the walls returned to their natural state and silence returning it was the last thing on both Tony and River's mind. They both knew that there would be a way out, none of what they had gone through would have happened simply to leave them in a room without doors, windows or a way out. But for the moment getting out was left to one side and the time had come for them to be alone with each other and reflect on what they had been through.

The Abyss in its physical form had gone. It had been defeated by many things bought together from different sources and various places, but there was one main reason why it had gone. River had been the boy who held onto his faith and carried hope in his heart and never let it go. Its voice had left with it, it seemed eerie without the threat of it. The silence to begin with left an anxious edge on both River and Tony. It was strange that they both had got used to the chaos and mayhem and all that surrounded the Abyss and now it had gone that anxiety came from it not being there. They felt it at the same time, looked at each other and laughed together. It was a laugh that was filled with triumph and also relief. They had done what they needed to and the victory was filled with so many things, but relief dominated most of it. It had been draining, demanding and not easy to get through. When it came the relief swept through them in waves; waves that carried real emotion and could easily have knocked them off their feet.

They continued to laugh until Tony's began to die out and he looked at River. It was a look that was filled with so much warmth, compassion and gratitude. Although River did say that he came to save them both, Tony knew that he could have chosen not to come at all. Let things just go, let fate be and leave Tony, alone, to an eternity of what they had experienced. River would not have felt it fully and never had to put himself through what he did. River's laugh began to die out as he realised that Tony had stopped and was stood now just staring at him.

"What's up, it's the time to laugh and be happy, come on," River said still feeling the end of his laughter and giggling.

Tony continued to look and eventually spoke, "I can't believe that you just put yourself through that, for me."

"Us," River said, "it's us remember not you and me, us."

"I know it's us but you still didn't have to come," Tony said, staring at him with the warmth that he still felt. "I know enough that you could have chosen not to do it and carried on."

River stopped laughing, sadness entering across his eyes, "How could I have carried on knowing that I had left a part of me here, left my future here. That wouldn't have worked at all."

Tony heard his words and knew that what he said was right, River would have been lost and tormented by it for ever. It would have been the same if it had been the other way round and Tony had come to save River. They were an 'us'; their pasts, futures and the present were all woven and linked together by so many different threads. Here they were safe and had just gone through something that made them stronger and more able to carry on. What didn't kill them would make them stronger as they both knew. But they also knew something else, which did involve a death.

They knew that there was only one of them that could return physically to the natural world. There was not enough room there for them both, only one could return. They knew that the decision had to be made by them that no one could do that for them. Once that was made they could finally escape the prison that had been the room they still found themselves in, only then.

It was Tony who spoke first, "So decision time it is then. What do we do flip a coin or something or is it scissors, paper, stone?"

River was quite, deathly silent. He knew how it would play out and what had to happen, but it didn't make it any easier, "No coins and no games, it's just fate, I'm afraid," pausing as his eyes began to well up.

Tony had said what he did to try and take the sadness out of the situation but he already knew the answer and what was going to pass, they both knew. It didn't make things easier in any way.

River's manner changed and his words and tone showed this change, "I am going to miss you. I'm going to miss us actually," his eyes moistening over. "We are a pretty good team really, when you get your act together."

Tony laughed, loving River more for the bringing humour in along with the realism, "What do you mean get my act together? You took so long to get here I nearly sent out a search party; if there was anyone to send. No wonder I was angry left alone with Mr Personality for company."

They both fell about with his reference to the Abyss as Mr Personality – it was needed and broke the tension and the sadness of their imminent departure from each other. There tears now were in sadness at the loss of each other but also with the joy of their coming together and what they had done. It had not been easy and it had come very close to not working out. River had been in danger, at real risk of not coming back. It was something that could not be seen yet but it left a scar, and one that would need healing and close attention from his mother.

"So how does this work then, you're the master of the mysterious," Tony said as they continued to prolong the moment.

"We get down on our knees," River said, the tears falling steadily now.

They both moved in sync and got down together, Tony crouching down slightly so that his head was level with River. His eyes had started to deepen and their colour fade slightly as he knelt, it was all happening very quickly. He could still see River but the outline of all other things had begun to fade and discolour and even on his knees he felt unsteady. He reached out with his hands and River caught him, softly but firm enough to hold him there and stop him falling more.

"It will be ok, don't hold onto the fear just let it go slowly. I am here," River said as Tony began to feel weak and his breathing started to become shallow.

"It's funny but I remember by the stream now, the poem that I wrote about you," Tony said, his words softer as time went past.

River smiled, "I remember it to. The day I chased butterflies and actually caught one," his eyes completely filled with tears now.

Tony smiled and attempted to laugh, but the energy no longer existed for it, "I think it let you catch it out of sympathy," he was fading faster now, "I didn't mean for it to come to this, you know that don't you River?" Tony said, gasping.

River just nodding, unable to speak any words, simply reaching out and putting his small arms around Tony and hugging him, holding him, tighter than ever before.

Tony used the last of his strength to hug him back, his head on River's shoulder as they both simply stayed that way, without speaking, through there tears.

In a room where they had come back together to defeat that which had taken them both they held each other. They held each other as a part of them died and was lost. Although River's innocence, faith and compassion had saved them both it could not heal and remove all that had gone before. The part of them that was Tony would have carried some of the pain and despair around and it was too much of a threat to let that happen possibly. The Abyss was secretive and cunning and could easily have lain hidden in Tony looking for a sign and an entry back through someone else – its power had been defeated for now. But it fed and lived on the edge and would have found it somewhere and in someone – at any point the edge for anyone is always present, and it knew this. Anyone can stare at it for too long and be consumed by its mistaken beauty, once that happens the outcome is unsure. It was only through Princess and River that fate had been changed but not every person could be saved by them. It was only because it had been Tony had they intervened. This time the Abyss had chosen the wrong person, next time it may not be the case.

They continued to hold each other as the moments and their time together slipped by until Tony spoke, "It's been a gift getting to know you again, sorry to know what I was again," feeling his last full breath. "Goodbye, River."

River pulled himself up and away from Tony to look straight into his eyes. He lent forward and kissed him on the cheek and kept his head next to his ear as he spoke, "It's not goodbye Tony, just see you later."

A moment later River was sat there holding nothing. There was no sign to show that anyone else had been in the room. What was left was a small blonde-haired boy who stayed on his knees with his head bowed in a mark of respect of what had passed between them. Tony had dissolved as the Abyss had dissolved, their fates connected, like twin brothers, blood brothers. There had been too much that had passed between and through them for their deaths not to be linked, it was always going to be that way.

River knew it before he even came to save his older self that he would just be left at the end, it was just how it was. He changed the words in the book one day when Tony was asleep because he didn't want all of it to end in despair. By giving himself a chance to return and save Tony he did save himself. River never lied when he said he went to save 'us', his gift was truth so he was never going to lie about himself. If anyone was given the chance to save themselves at a later date River knew that they would always take it, as he did. The only thing that was different with him was that Princess was his mother and her gifts, along with his, meant that he would always be able to start again with the knowledge of the experience. He would be able to shape his life again and not put himself through what had happened – now that was a gift.

What was left was to get out of the room he found himself in now, alone. That sense and feeling was surreal in itself. There was no one else there, no noise and the silence that River craved always had returned. But it was different, within that silence and because of what had happened he had no peace to go with it. He looked down again at the spot where Tony had disappeared, there was no sign of him even having been there. In reality there was and River knew it. He was there and Tony lived on in him. He started to smile and knew then, for the first time how he would get out from the room.

He walked up to one of the walls and looked straight up, as if he was looking for the sun in the bright blue sky and spoke out loud, "Across a cloudless sky, life was laughing at a butterfly resting in a child's hand and in that moment it found – innocence."

They were the words of the verse that River had always held dear written for him by Tony and the words had the desired effect, the walls melted away, vanished. River was taken up into the air by a gentle and warming breeze, he closed his eyes and allowed himself to be carried enjoying the peace as he flew up higher. It was only a short ride seemingly, although he had been carried quickly without him knowing it and put gently back down to earth, on his feet. He opened his eyes and found himself back in the world and the place that he held dear to his heart. He found himself delivered back into the field where the horses grazed and lived. They did not seem alarmed by his sudden appearance just started a slow trot over to feel his gentle hands on their manes.

River smiled at their coming, now only one thing was left to do, find his way back to her.

CHAPTER 45

Let him find his way...

Joshua and Sarah had got out of the water at the earliest opportunity. The book had been destroyed and it was clear that the natural state and order of the world had returned but for both of them that didn't mean staying in the water. They both felt more comfortable on dry land and as soon as they returned to it they simply turned and fell into each other's arms. The whole experience had been full of doubt, fear, uncertainty and anxiety. They felt like they had been taken to the edge of their own levels of endurance and then asked to take another step forward. At times there whole nervous system felt shredded and in danger of being torn and ripped apart. When it was needed however, they had found from somewhere a source of energy which held them and pushed them forward. They had been supported by each other at different moments but most of all the main guides, River and Princess held them and pointed the way forward. Their devotion and love for River and his safe return had kept them focused above all else. He had been saved now and they could relax and celebrate this news.

They continued to hold each other for some time, feeling the warmth and relief flooding through them both. They were exhausted from the emotional exertions of what they had both been through not just from their time in the water but also from the whole experience. It felt like they had been broken down and then reassembled piece by piece. Sarah was crying and had her head buried in the chest of Joshua who held her tight like he had done for all of her time in his house. For him it was a time of mixed emotions. The book was destroyed but with this also came something else which he knew and Sarah didn't. He waited for a while, letting the feel of Sarah on his body bring a sense of comfort to him also till eventually he lifted her head up from his chest.

"Sarah, it's over now. The time for tears is passed it's a time for laughter," he said as she looked up.

Sarah nodded and wiped her tears away with her sleeve, "I know, its relief more than anything else that it's over."

He understood fully, "Yeah after all that excitement I think we should just sit down here for a while and just look around, one last time."

"That sounds like a really good idea, it would be nice just to sit and not think about anything," she said moving to sit as he followed her lead.

They looked out across the lake, the waters still, like a mill pond. Nothing moved seemingly across the top or below the surface, the water reflecting the sky back at itself, coloured by it and enchanted by its face. The hills that rose up and away from the lake seemed to have a fresh look, as if they too had been renewed of energy, no longer hiding their colour or beauty. Over to one side the field or slope of flowers spread onwards and upwards. The colours mixing together as they gently swayed and danced in the gentle breeze which seemed to be only there. The wind acting as the conductor for the overture of their beauty and grace. Whenever they looked there were two things which ran throughout, tranquillity and peacefulness. They were there in anything and everything, a constant theme binding it all together. It really was stunning.

Sarah turned suddenly from looking out, her brain catching up finally with his last words, "What do you mean one last time?"

He didn't reply immediately, refusing to look back at her but mostly refusing to take his eyes away from what was in front of him. There was no doubt that he loved this place, everything about it had showed him so much and taught him so much. When he had come to live there he had been lost in a sea of self-doubt, wracked by anxiety and fears and still shell shocked by the thoughts and feelings that he had inside. The lake cooled them, the flowers softened them and the hills held him in when he felt like he would explode or implode. The natural beauty that lived there had eventually won over and reflected itself into his heart, slowing his breath and finding beauty where there had only been rage and anger. He sighed, long and deep, it was a sign of gratitude but also loss. It was also a long breath before he spoke, before he told Sarah.

"River will return here and he will need you. Will you wait for him here? My home is yours to have always," he said still looking out across the water.

Sarah was puzzled, "Of course we will wait here together and see him," she reached over grabbing at his arm, forcing him to turn towards her. "Why are you talking like this?"

His eyes gave him away, they still shone but there was an underlying sadness which also sat within them. It grew as he looked at her and spoke, "All good things come to an end, Sarah, this is mine and where we get to say goodbye," he looked back across the water before adding, "It's a beautiful place to say that goodbye."

She heard his words, recognised the sadness in his eyes, but tried to ignore them both, refusing to hear, "Your just being dramatic, it's all the excitement, you most likely just need to catch your breath," willing her words to be right.

Joshua smiled back at her, his eyes saddening more, "Tony has gone, Sarah, and with him going so my time has come to an end also."

Sarah sat back surprised, fear rising again in her chest, "What do you mean his gone? He was saved, they were both saved."

"Yes, he was saved, River saved them both," speaking with clearness so she understood fully. "He was saved from living on as he was, saved from himself and the Abyss, but not from an end in this life."

Sarah was totally confused and showed it, unable to take it all in and unable to speak a word, the only thing she could communicate was her sadness as her eyes misted over.

"The time we have here Sarah is only borrowed, our bodies purely for rent. My time is passed with Tony going and now the book destroyed. What you think you see is not who or what I really am," his face starting to lose some colour now.

She controlled her tears long enough to be able to speak, "Who are you then?"

"I am Joshua, but I am also Tony and River as well. All of us have been to the edge and Tony has left because there is a part of him that will always remember that. He could not stay as it was too dangerous. If you can understand that you will know why I have to go now also."

Sarah didn't understand at all, was struggling with yet another loss right in front of her eyes. It was too much and she started to sob, losing control and breaking down next to him.

Joshua felt her sadness, could visibly see it and reached for her hand, holding it tightly, "Sarah, lift your head up please for a moment."

She heard his words felt within them his need for her to do it, managing to hold on to her tears a little as she lifted her head up, trying to wipe her eyes clear.

"When River returns he will need space and time," his words soft and full of care, "Let him wander and let him drift, there is much that he needs to heal and only he and the natural world will be able to fully do this. Let him be and let him find his way, he will seek here and you out."

Everything was happening too quickly for Sarah. It was clear that Joshua was leaving and this was hard enough to take on board without trying to hear what he was also saying about River. She knew it was important as he was looking directly at her and speaking slowly so that she could take it all in, "I will be here and I will do whatever is needed. I promise."

Joshua could see from her eyes that she heard him and knew that she would do anything within her own power to be with and look after River. Joshua knew why River would seek her out and how they were connected. It was something he felt best to leave for River in his own time to deliver. But inside he smiled at what this would mean to Sarah. He knew that it was a story for another time and place.

He leant forward and kissed her on the cheek holding his lips there for a short while, feeling the warmth of her skin and its touch before pulling away, "Right come on then, time to pack there are a few things that I would like to take with me and it's a fine day to walk out in the country."

He stood up and put his hand down for her, pulling her up as she reached for it. They both turned and walked back up towards the hut, the spell broken as they moved towards it swinging their hands in unison and laughing as they did.

CHAPTER 46

From today we will never be apart…

Princess stood with her head bowed, still at the edge of the forest. All the clouds that been around her both physically and spiritually had cleared away. The sun was now out, ready to rise even further into the turquoise sky that was now as clear as the eye could see. Even the birds in the tress that had been silent during the early part of the dawn started up again. Their sounds, their songs added the final touches to a morning, which had become 'the' morning to be alive on.

She stayed where she was for a while; catching the sun and feeling its warmth brush away the coldness that she had felt for much of the night. It felt good on her skin and she felt herself invigorated and being renewed. She stood catching her breath and feeling her chest rise and fall again in a slow steady rhythm, her heart returning to its slow and easy pace. She bowed her head in gratitude and stood this way for some time, she offered a blessing of gratitude for the safe passage of her son and to those who had made it possible. It was certainly a morning to have gratitude on and the sun and skies above echoed that with their beauty. She finally opened her eyes and turned around lifting her head towards Ty and her mother. It had been the first acknowledgement towards them for what seemed an eternity. She smiled at them, a smile which came from all that she held dear inside and its light and radiance lit up all that it fell upon.

They saw and felt the richness and depth of her smile and with it knew that it had all come to an end finally. It was clear that a great weight and responsibility had been lifted from her shoulders and that she had been returned to them without harm. They felt the same warmth of the sun returning them to happiness and peace as she did. The cheerful sounds of the bird's heralding the end of all that had come to pass. Now that she had turned and smiled, everything was almost complete. She walked over to them, gliding more than walking, as if she rode on a carpet of magic. Every movement she always made was filled with elegance and grace but on this day it seemed to be added to a little more. She carried a beauty with her that existed in anyone's dreams. For Ty though this was no longer the stuff of dreams as she came to stand in front of them both. It was on this special day, this bright morning that Ty met the woman of his dreams – and she the man of her's.

Her mother placed her hand on Princess's cheek and ran it up onto her forehead, brushing her softly away as she did. They moved towards each other and embraced with warmth, tenderness and devotion. They continued to hold each other and for anyone else watching apart from Ty they may have felt uncomfortable in its presence. He didn't, watching and waiting, his eye's never leaving them both. His heart softening as he bore witness to the intimate bond between mother and daughter.

After a time they pulled back from, but not away from each other. This was done merely so that they would be able to look at each other fully. Her mother ran her hand across her cheek and up onto her forehead, brushing her hair softly away from her face as she did, "I thought that we had lost you both, that the time had come and gone. It was too late for either of you," she said as she continued to run her hand over her face.

Princess heard the words and felt the concern contained within them also, dropping her head and chin slightly, "I'm sorry to have caused you so much pain and anguish. I know it was difficult for you both," throwing a quick glance towards Ty as she spoke.

Her mother moved her hand from stroking her hair and put it to her chin, lifting it up so that she could look into her eyes, "My child no apology is needed. I would do the same for you. Rest assured of that," reaching forward to kiss her softly on the cheek and holding her lips there for a while. They held each other's gaze for a short while before Princess cast a sideways look at Ty and moved over towards him, her mother moving aside and taking herself away to allow them some space and privacy.

Ty's heart was beating anything but slow. It was racing at a hundred miles an hour and he could swear that it was about to burst right out of his chest. He felt so excited but also nervous at the same time, wanting to say so much yet tongue tied also. So many times he had dreamt of this moment and now it was finally here he was unable to speak or seemingly move. He was captured by her beauty, entrapped by her scent and he dropped his own head in both shyness and vulnerability.

She could visibly see his discomfort and felt it between them also. She moved to stand directly in front of him and put one hand out and placed it, palm down on his chest, in an attempt to still his racing heart. Despite his shyness and state of mind she could feel his strength and love and firmness of purpose through the fingers and hand now covering his heart. It travelled up her arm and spread out across the whole of her body. She kept her hand there as she moved her other one up towards his face and lay it softly on his cheek. His eyes lifted slightly although his head remained bowed for the moment.

Princess spoke, "My brave and special Prince. You came when I called, stayed by my side and held me close. Never giving up, keeping your faith and holding onto hope when it seemed lost," her hand stroking his cheek and moving down to lift his head up as she finished speaking. Their eyes finally came to rest on each other's as she did.

Her eyes always held Ty. If he had to pick one thing, if he had to, it would always be her eye's that he would never want to lose the memory of. Their depth, knowledge and understanding bought out their beauty. They sparkled and shone as bright as any diamond despite them being the colour of the darkest coal, taken from the deepest mines in the remotest places on earth. Ty was always in awe of them, and they held sway over him in his dreams and now those dreams had become reality the effect was even more so. As she stood and looked at him it was like discovering them all over again and his heart felt lifted and in awe at the same time. They were coupled with her smell, from her hair and her skin. It was as intoxicating as it was in his dreams. It inspired a desire in him that was basic and instinctual but mainly bound together by a need to always hold her near, till the end of time. She had him in that single moment on a beautiful dawn at the end of the longest of nights. He was lost yet found in an instance and he felt so at peace.

For the first time he felt able to speak, feeling his breath relax enough before he did, "I will always come to you whenever you need me. I will always be here at your side," reaching his hand forward to touch and hold her hair, breathing it in.

She smiled at him, a smile full of love and warmth, "I know that you will. But you never have to do that again," leaning forward and adding softly, "because from today we will never be apart."

They moved in slowly towards each other, pausing slightly before their lips met in a soft, full and gentle kiss. It was a kiss, which sealed their love and commitment to each other. A kiss, which would not be broken by the end of a dream and one of them, leaving. They both knew that in that moment they had truly found their hearts desire and bound themselves to each other for not only that lifetime but also lifetime's to come.

Her mother watched them kiss and smiled at what she knew Princess had found. She had always known that her heart would choose well and in Ty it had found its twin, a perfect match. She bowed her head in a blessing towards them and let herself remember the time when she had been in exactly the same moment with Princess's father. Ty reminded her of him in a lot of ways and she was glad that Princess had found someone who would bring her as much as he did. She lifted her head and turned away, walking off into the forest. She knew that there was no need for a goodbye to them both at this point, Princess would understand and know why she left. They would always continue to meet each other through the years ahead and she would always come and be there if Princess called.

Ty and Princess gently parted, feeling the sensations of each other's lips even after they did. Ty took her hands and held them in his, looking first into her smouldering eyes and then over her shoulders to what was behind her, "I think you should turn around now Princess," he said and gestured with his eyes to what lay behind.

She looked at him and smiled, showing him that she knew, what she was turning round to see. Still holding one hand of his she turned round slowly and looked towards the forest and what she knew she would find.

He walked slowly, at first not easily seen, through the thick blanket of trees that guarded his path. But he was coming, his distinctive blonde hair visible more every minute as he moved towards them. Her face lit up, her smile wider than ever as he finally cleared the trees and calmly walked into view.

As he cleared the forest, where it ended and the grass began, he stopped. He had been walking with his head down, lost in thought it seemed, but lifted it as he cleared the tree line. For the first time in what seemed an eternity they saw each other at the very place where he had left, but this time the emotions were very different.

She let go of Ty's hand, leaving him standing where he was and walked slowly over towards River. They were both smiling but it was one that contained as much relief as happiness. It also had within it shades of pain and loss and they both felt it as they moved closer. She knew what he had been through and that his emotions were still raw and exposed and that tenderness and care was needed. The distance between them reduced until they stood opposite each other, about ten paces apart.

They looked at each other for a moment, a very short moment, before he could contain himself no longer. He ran the last few paces towards her as she knelt to receive him, jumping into her arms.

Princess and River reunited, mother and son returned to each other's arms.

CHAPTER 47

Find your heart...

It was such a stunning day. The sky was so vast and deep and its colour so blue it could only have been dreamt of in dreams. The sun lay high above casting its warmth and light across the landscape, every part of the natural world reaching up to touch and feel its embrace.

In the valley everything was just how it should be on a day such as this. The lake, shimmering in the heat, its surface still like a millpond. Its sparkling diamonds reflecting back up, visible to anyone who could see it. The meadows ran out and away from the lake, its waters ensuring that the grass stayed the brighter side of green, an emerald green, bright and vivid to the eye. The hills around rising slowly up to their peaks, rising and rolling up into the sky, their colours blending as they met on the horizon. The hut was the only thing that seemed out of place, purely because it was not something which struck the eye as naturally beautiful. It was dishevelled and ramshackled from the outside; odd bits of timber and iron knitted together with a fabric of nails and mesh but it had always been solid enough to withstand any storm nature threw at it. Although it looked out of place it actually wasn't. It was the one thing that seemed to bring everything together, nestled into a dell with a backdrop of tress behind it, and inside the warmth of the fire which burnt brightly on any winter's evening. The hut just, worked where it was.

For Sarah, who now sat on the balcony out by the front the hut was something that would always provide the comfort and security it had always done, since she first ran up the steps. It held the memories inside that she would never forget of Joshua, his love and care and the gentleness with which he looked after her. He had only been gone a few days so his parting was still fresh in her thoughts and in her heart. As she sat there drinking coffee her thoughts wandered back to their last conversation on the balcony and him walking off.

He had packed a small bag, nothing big in it. He knew that his journey was not going to be a long one and had merely packed some small items which were personal and dear to him, not wanting to leave them behind. She had waited for him on the balcony allowing him some privacy and space to say goodbye inside to the place which had been his home for so long. It was somewhere that he had recovered in and she knew that the walls of the hut had provided peace and solitude at a time when he needed it most. He came out onto the balcony, his eyes sparkling, and his face as peaceful as she had ever seen it.

Sarah smiled at him, it was a smile full of warmth and held inside the arms of love that ran so deep in her for him. They allowed themselves a moment just to look at each other from a few yards away, almost as if they were taking a mental picture to remind themselves of each other.

Joshua spoke, "Sorry, I couldn't have left you a more auspicious place to stay, but it serves its purpose in more ways than one."

Sarah laughed at his use of the word auspicious, "Well, you should be sorry. I am used to more comfortable surroundings than this you know. I am a lady," continuing to laugh as she finished speaking.

He looked at her, her love and warmth of feeling reflected in what he felt to her, "Yes you are a lady. A very brave and gentle one at that. I am so glad that I got to spend this time with you, it's been such a pleasure and I would not have missed it for the world," his words ending in a choke as sadness kicked in.

She closed the gap between them and put her arms round him, holding him tighter than he had ever been held before. His arms were around her, feeling her love, her life and all that she was. They knew that they could have said many thing, sat and talked for hours but it would only have delayed the inevitable and left them feeling even sadder.

They both seemed to sense at the same time that they should let go, dropping their arms from around each other until they held each other's hand and walked to the edge of the balcony, standing at the top of the first step. Breathing in deep, feeling the air through their lungs, feeling the love of the moment which held them and always would.

"I will walk with you," Sarah said looking at him taking in the view.

"No, here is where I walk with God," he said turning towards her as he finished, "As he will always walk with you Sarah, in every step and every breath he will always hold and walk with you."

He then just moved forwards and kissed her simply on the cheek and bought her hand up to his mouth and did the same, "Goodbye my beautiful Sarah, we will see each other again I am very sure."

Then he was gone, stepping off the balcony with Sarah left there watching him walk away, she wanted to run after him, bring him back, hold him for one last time, talk with him for one last hour. But she knew that it was the time, time for her to let him go, time for her to turn her thoughts back to River and when he returned. He could hardly be seen now, merely a shadow that walked across the land, slipping in between this world and the next until eventually she could see him no more.

Joshua was gone.

A tear slowly began to fall down her cheek, running slowly as it continued its journey down. As it did a voice, Joshua's, drifted back towards her and spoke, "Faith is a wonderful thing, Sarah, but I think you know that now. Find your heart and yourself in that faith, now and forever."

Sarah smiled and knew that she had found what she had always searched for, something inside which would hold any fears and extinguish any doubts – she had found her own place, she had found her own faith.

CHAPTER 48

I need to wander...

In the days immediately following his return, River had not really left her side. He would follow her everywhere she went, hardly talking and rarely smiling, but it was clear that he had to be near her. For Princess this was something that was not a problem and she wandered here and there with him next to her, holding his hand and talking to him as they walked along all the paths that they had walked before so many times. His appetite was also very small and even the berries from the area that he loved before so much were not enough to tempt him, eating only handfuls at any one sitting.

It was his sleep that was the most disconcerting for her. It took him along time to drop off to sleep, lying awake in the early hours with Princess wrapping her arms around him and pulling him close into her chest. He always slept with his back to her and she could feel his heart racing as her hand lay over him and flat against his chest. Despite not being able to see his face she could tell from his heart that he was not sleeping and Ty would often return after nights out in the forest searching for food to see River lying there with his eye's wide open, staring into something and hardly noticing him. When he did sleep it was often fitful and he would toss and turn and speak to himself incessantly through it. Princess would lie with him trying to offer comfort from just her presence but even this did not seem to work. It was clear that he was deeply troubled and that he had not fully returned to them.

He had been back for about a week and had eventually fallen asleep one night in the early hours. Princess had spent hours telling him new and some of his old favourite stories to him. He had just listened and rarely smiled until he had fallen asleep. When he did she lay down next to him and held him, whispering blessings and prayers into his ear as he slept, willing the old River back and trying all she could to reach that part of him which she knew so well.

Princess woke up after having fallen asleep herself to find him gone. Ty was away for the night hunting and had not returned. She immediately got up looking around trying to find him, for a moment lost in old fears and anxieties that he had gone and would not return. Her eyes scanned here and there until she spotted him by the stream, his back to her, standing at the very edge. He seemed fixated by something that was in there, something had caught his eye and it was not letting him go. The old fears rose again and she got up, running towards him as fast as her legs would carry her shouting his name as she ran, the image of him at the edge of the water bringing up and stirring her scars and what they meant. Before she could get there, he jumped in, her heart jumping out of her chest, her lungs exploding, her voice screaming, "Riiiiiiivvvvvvvvvvveerrrrrrrrrr."

She got to the water's edge, unable to hold it all in, crying desperately. She was aiming to jump straight in after him, when his head appeared from under the water and he exploded back into the light and air, his fist closed and held above his head holding something he had picked up from the water.

He looked at her in surprise, his whole face aghast by the expression on her's and the tears falling down her cheeks, "What is it, why are you crying?" – then it hit him.

He suddenly realised what had just happened and all that she must have seen. His heart skipped a beat and his face went ashen. Him at the edge of the bank, the water, him jumping in and her not being able to stop him. The memories of what had passed and what she had been through, what he had been through. He looked at her with deep regret and pain on his face, the pain matching what was showing on hers. He made his way back to the bank slowly and carefully, head down and at the edge she reached down and put out a hand which he used to drag himself back onto dry land.

He stood there, water dripping down his face, his hair stuck to his head which remained bowed as he got out. She just picked him up and took him into her arms, wrapping every single part of him up in herself, squeezing him so tight that he struggled to breathe. After a time she let her hold gradually reduce and she gently put him back down onto the grass, wiping any water that was still there from his face.

"I'm so sorry, so sorry," River said after a time, looking up now and into her eyes.

Princess looked back at him, her tears no longer falling, knowing that he meant it, "It's alright, there's no need for sorry, it's my stuff."

River knew what she meant but said anyway, "Still, I should have thought before I jumped in, I'm sorry for doing that without thinking."

She brushed the wet hair away from his forehead and kissed him on the cheek, "Let's forget about it now," looking down at his hand and the fist which was closed around something. "What did you get in there anyway."

River smiled at her and opened his fist, showing her what he had found, her eyes widened in amazement, it was a stone similar to what he had previously had, to the undiscerning eye it could even have been an exact copy of it and the one that she still held.

"Yeah, I know, can you believe it? I was asleep and someone came in my dreams and told me to wake up and go to the water and look out for it," River said his eyes matching hers in amazement.

For a moment Princess' eye's narrowed, studying his face, deeply concerned, "Who came to your dreams and told you to go to the water?"

River could see her concern and knew what she was asking, and reached forward to hold her shoulder as he spoke, "Mother don't worry," starting to smile, "Tony came and told me."

She visibly relaxed, her chest less tight, her own smile returning, "Did he really, that must have been so nice, to see him again."

River sighed, it was one of loss and missing, "Yeah it was the best. I have been waiting all these nights hoping he would come and then he did. He has shown me the way forward and what I need to do now. I feel better, lifted."

She could see that he did; his shoulders seemed less tense, his smile more natural and he seemed a little more at ease around all that was there, "It's nice that he has," she said smiling from deep inside towards him.

River smiled back for a little while before he spoke, "I have to go soon; I have to go and find my own way for a while. I need to wander and just be and find my way back to Joshua's," his name on his lips causing his eyes to sadden. "Although I know that he is no longer there."

Princess knew how much River loved Joshua and that the feeling was mutual. She knew that River had saved him from a similar fate to Tony and the peace he had bought into Joshua's life, "He loves you very much, River, know that. In the end he gave himself up for you too."

River nodded, knowing what she said was true, the pain still resonating through his eyes, "I know but I need to go back there still, you understand?"

Princess did understand and River knew that she would never stop him doing what his heart and soul directed him to do, she would never hold him back and would always let him choose his own fate, however much sometimes she struggled to allow it, "I know and I do understand my special boy."

"And I will get to see Sarah there to," his eyes and smile jumping out at her.

She laughed, "Yes you will," ruffling his hair as she spoke again, "I think someone has a little crush, don't they?"

He smiled, eyes still wide, "Just a little one," using two fingers to show her how much.

She scooped him up into her arms, both of them laughing, as they danced around together, the forest hearing their voices and laughter, bending towards the sound of mother and son fully reunited. The real River returning.

She stopped dancing and set him down, her face becoming serious for a moment, River no longer smiling and seeing the change in her, anxious and worried, he spoke, "What is it, what is it?"

Princess's face continued to remain stern, her manner a little cold, "Let me see the stone again, before you go?"

River held it out in front of him, opening the palm, showing her the stone which seemed the exact match to the one he had lost. He looked at her, her eyes narrowed, knowing something was up.

Princess continued to look at it, "There is something that's not quite right with it, not quite the same," rubbing her chin as she spoke. "Something's missing from it."

"What's not right, what's missing," he said quickly back.

"Let me have it for a minute, I need to look at it more closely," she said offering her hand towards his.

He gave her the stone and watched her studying it in her palm, rolling it around before lifting it up between two fingers in front of her eyes and closing one so as to magnify it further.

"Yeah as I thought, missing something," she said after a time.

"What is it missing, what?" River jumping up and down now with the suspense.

Her eyes changed, their colour sparkling more as they softened, her smile returning and she pulled her other hand out from behind her back, revealing what she was hiding, and "This is missing of course my little Prince."

The suspense was over and River looked at what she had bought out – sparkling in the morning sun, a long dark band of gold, a lock of her hair. He watched as she carefully wrapped it slowly around the stone he had found, an exact replica of what had gone, until she finished tying the ends in a small bow, as she had done beforehand long ago. She took it and gently placed it in River's hand, closing his fist around it, locking it into his heart.

"To replace the one that got lost," reaching forward again to kiss him on the cheek, "I hope it will do."

River didn't say a word, simply stood there feeling the stone in his hand and the hair around it. He could smell her hair and he lifted his hand up to his face to breathe her smell in, its odour leaving him slightly dizzy.

"This is the best present, even better than the previous one," he threw his arms around her, holding it carefully as he did, "I love it, thank you."

"I'm pleased, we have one each again," a tear coming to her eye as she thought about him leaving shortly, knowing the time was coming when he would walk away.

River felt her loss and held her tighter, whispering in her ear as he did, **"The divine in me reaches out and touches the divine in** *you: Bound together in time, forever and beyond; With love faith and compassion; I will always hold you near."*

River remembered what she had sent to him and spoke it now to ease her pain. He spoke then to let her know that wherever he was, whenever she needed him all that she needed to do was say the words herself and he would come.

River would always come and find his mother, to find his Princess.

CHAPTER 49

I get to spend all of it with you...

The heat of the day had long since passed and the cool of the night had pushed in behind it. It bought a welcome relief and a hint of a breeze which helped take the heat of the day away. The sky had stayed clear and the stars were given a blank canvass to shine from as none of them were hidden, all vying with each other to be the brightest. None of them could hold a candle to the moon, full and white it illuminated the whole area, shining onto the water and bouncing back with the reflection that it made.

Princess and Ty were by the water's edge stretched out on the grass, her lying half across him, her head on his chest. He had one arm round her, holding her close as his other hand reached up and played with her hair. He let it run through his fingers, watching the dark strands fall, feeling its touch and its silkiness. As always the smell played with his senses, drowning him in them and then pushing him away once they were done, a tease and a toxin. It made him want to take her in his arms and kiss her with all the passion he felt inside, take her in his arms and never let her go. But it was mixed with the feeling deep inside that he always had with her, peace and tranquillity, his heart losing itself in the slowness of her's.

It was the night after River had left and although Princess had struggled through the day and needed to spend time alone walking and collecting her thoughts, she had returned somewhat lighter.

"This really is one of the best places to be," she said after a long time without any words spoken between them.

Ty looked around again and had to agree that the view and where they were was spectacular, especially under the light of the full moon, "Yeah it is pretty amazing, the moon just adds to it tonight," he said softly in reply.

Princess laughed to herself, "I was talking about lying on your chest not the view. That is one of the best places to be."

Ty laughed with her and at himself. The words hit home and he felt himself fall for her on yet another level, past all love and into devotion and ending in oneness.

"I dreamt about lying here so many times. My head on your chest, listening to your heart and feeling your hand's in my hair. That waiting, the anticipation was well worth it," she said moving her hand across and laying it flat on his stomach.

Ty felt her hand and it stirred the desire in him once again. Her touch, her hair, her skin and her eyes were more than he could ever dream of or wish for.

"When I first set eyes on you I knew in that instance that I had found everything that I had always been searching for," he said carrying the conversation and the feeling on in him.

She lifted her head up and turned to look at him for a moment, "What did you find," she asked her eyes sparkling with curiosity.

Ty looked down at her and smiled softly, "What I found was the answer to my heart's search," he replied moving forward to softly kiss her on the lips.

She held herself there, returning the kiss with a softness and fullness to match his, turning back towards his chest as it finished and laying her head back down.

With her taste still on his lips he continued, "When I saw you my heart, my whole body, my soul just stopped," pausing to let his words sink in with her. "Everything inside me just went so still, so quiet and so peaceful."

She heard his words and felt the power and the feeling and all that it meant to him. She couldn't resist though and tested him, "That's all you felt, peace, nothing else. No desire, no passion, no wanting?"

He knew she was teasing and played along, "No none at all, just stillness."

She dug him in the ribs with her elbow, causing him to wince before saying, "That will teach you to play with me."

He laughed and moved at the same time from underneath her, pulling her up as he did with his hands, lifting her up until they stood facing each other. He reached forward and cradled her face in his hands, one either side, looking deep in to her eyes. He was totally lost in her but knew that the feeling was fine in her hands. He could trust her with it and his heart would always be held.

"You know the best thing about finding you and being with you, here and now?" he said still holding her face.

She looked up at him, holding his gaze, before whispering back, lost in him at that moment as well, "No I don't, what is it?"

He moved closer, inches from her lips, looking straight into her eyes, "That because I found you now, it means in my next life I get to spend all of it with you," moving closer still his breath on her lips, "I get to be with 'my' Princess for all of my lives."

She smiled, her heart lifting and melting at the same time. She closed the small gap between them to kiss him on the lips as he returned it with the same passion.

By the lake, under the starts and the light of the full moon, in a setting and a place which came straight out of a dream, they sealed their love for each other as their souls embraced – forever and beyond and into the next life.

CHAPTER 50

That's a story for another time...

It was another beautiful morning, and she was on the balcony. Sarah stood and looked out over all that lay in front of her, again there was not a breath of wind, a hint of cloud and the day stretched itself out in front of her with its arms open, welcoming her into its warmth. She walked slowly forward until she came to the steps and leant forward, propping herself up on her elbows on the rail which ran around the length of it. She looked across the valley and smiled at the rainbow assortment of colours which greeted her eyes. She stood there quietly spellbound by the view. She had been there for over two weeks now and it was something that never failed to disappoint or amaze her. There always seemed to be something new to see, a different colour, shape or pattern. It never seemed to change from a distance or at first glance but when studied closely it did and had, in subtle ways. Like all things restlessness and impatience had to be put to one side if change was going to be noticed. Sarah had come to learn, that nature, had to be studied and observed with no eye on the clock or any other thing. It was then, and only then, could its true beauty be fully seen and appreciated. It was something else that she had got from Joshua and today she missed him more because of that gift he left behind with her.

She let her head move round and with it her gaze followed, up past the lake and across the meadows and towards the field of flowers. There colours shooting out across the valley in the bright sunlight. On any given day it was always enough to bring her face out into a huge a smile, one which covered her whole face. On this day it was nothing different and she felt the smile start to fill her face, pulling it in all directions. Her smile today though knew no bounds because of the addition of one other to the flowers. Something which seemed to brighten their colours even more as he lay there in the middle of them all, making 'flower-angels' – River.

She had woken early than normal and was sitting on the balcony drinking coffee and enjoying the gifts of the dawn. She had always had a peaceful feeling on waking up since being at the hut but on this morning it was more than normal. It was a peacefulness that had a real presence and she felt it grow inside her as she sat drinking and looking out. This peace inside which she felt seemed to move out beyond her and out into the air, across the ground and up the slopes of the valley. It was something that was clear, light, and transparent. Even the sounds of the bird's dawn chorus seemed to embrace this peace, their songs lighter and lees shrill. Her eyes followed the line of the hills and for the first time she saw him.

He walked into view and stood at the top of the hill, right in the centre. He stopped and simply stood there for some time, swaying slightly as he did, such a small figure against the backdrop of the sky behind him and its shimmering haze. She had to fight the feeling to rush out, run to meet him and sweep him up into her arms. She had been doing this in her heart and soul every day for the last two weeks, even since the day that they had last seen each other at the lake. But something held her back, Joshua's words about letting him be and find his own way repeating in her head, as she fought the feeling inside her.

He was obviously just standing there taking in the view as his head moved with his body. He turned and seemed to acknowledge every single corner and space of the valley in turn, almost like a king acknowledging his subjects, it made her laugh. After he had finished she saw him bow his head put his hands out in front of him, seemingly in prayer. Sarah noticed at that moment everything went quite. The birds stopped singing and she even felt her breath falter, or pause, put on hold by something outside of her. She knew instantly that River was giving thanks for his return but also remembering those who had made that possible and those that were no longer there with them – he was remembering Tony and Joshua. It was only a short pause, a momentary flicker, but it was poignant, moving and heartfelt. He lifted his head and she felt herself breathe again and the birds started up again in welcome to their most favourite child.

River looked over towards the hut and noticed Sarah. It may have been some distance between them but she could see that his whole body relaxed and even the gentle smile that spread across his face. It was reflected back to him by her own smile which was captured in her face, heart and her eyes. Both of them looked at each other in that one moment with love which carried with it the depth of the deepest ocean and the tenderness of the softest touch. River's smile widened and he started to laugh. It was a laugh that woke anything up that had dared remain sleeping and the whole of what lived in or around the valley bent towards the cause of the sound.

River put his hands up to his mouth, on either side of it to increase the effect and the impact. He screamed out, so that Sarah along with everyone else in the valley heard the boy they loved, "I'm back."

He finished shouting out and he was off running as fast as his legs could carry him down the slopes, rushing towards her. She was already running before he had even started, eating up the ground quickly, desperate to get to him. The distance between them reduced until they were only ten yards apart and she stopped allowing him to continue running. He threw himself at her with such a force that it knocked her off her feet, leaving them both on the floor, him on top of her.

His small arms held onto her, holding her as tight as he could as if he was scared that he would be taken from her again and that he would not be able to get back. Her arms returned to embrace, feeling his heart thumping in his chest, filled with excitement that had been building during his return back to her. They were both laughing, it was not a time for any tears, it was purely a time for love and celebration of the fact that they were with each other again.

It took a while before he lifted himself half away from her and looked down into her eyes. They were full of joy and happiness at both seeing and holding him again. She looked into his eyes and saw something else, a vision of something hidden in her past, his eyes there then, holding her heart. It was something she was not expecting.

He laughed at seeing this, "Are you remembering something?" his eyes taunting her with the answer.

"I am and you know it," she said reaching up to play with his blonde hair. "Are you going to tell me what it is then?"

He laughed long and loud, "Sarah, that's a story for another time," moving his head down to kiss her on the cheek. "Another time and maybe another place."

It was enough to hold her for that moment, he always knew what to say to keep her held, "Then I look forward to it," she said pulling him to her chest again.

His lips were at her ear, whispering softly, "It's the best story there is, much better than anything else," he paused before adding. "We spend an eternity together in that one."

They pulled each other closer still, back with each other and safe in the place that would become their home and where River would find the time and peace to heal his heart. He was with the person that apart from his mother would always hold a special place there because of what they had shared in another lifetime.

But as River said, it was a story for another time.

Across a cloudless sky
Life was - smiling.
A deep resonance
Of sheer simplicity
And as it walked
It found - innocence.

Across that cloudless sky
Innocence was - laughing.
At a butterfly resting
On a child's hand
And as they talked
They found – beauty.

Across a cloudless sky
Beauty was – infinite
Around and within
It simply 'was'
And as one together
They found – love.

Across a cloudless sky
Love was – whole.
Life, Innocence
Entwined with beauty
Bound with love.
- Inside a cloudless sky.

THE END

ABOUT THE AUTHOR

John Tweedy was born in London, lived three weeks of his life there and then moved out to the suburbs and grew up in Surrey. Bought up in a one parent family by a dad who gave all for his three children, he sought solace and peace outside from an early age, as well as the freedom. Shy and vulnerable in his teens he found that his 'daydreams' tasted sweeter than real life and he got lost, and fell deeply. Within the grips of a terrifying drug addiction, he wrote desperate and desolate rhymes. Finally, at the age of 38 he found recovery through the love and care of others that bought fresh light, creativity, and imagination into his feelings which then became his words and his actions. He found study again and went to university after living in France for 18 months and through the guidance of something 'greater than himself' created a different life, reaching out to others in need through his counselling he was drawn into writing *A Soul called River*. This was inspired by a person who came into his life at that time and the book was written in three months. It helped him, alongside his previously published poems, to find light in places where shadows lived before. He has run the London Marathon for Action on Addiction, spent summers in the Himalayas and hopes that a peaceful and quiet life surrounded by those who show him how to live, may continue. As is his hope for all those across the blue marble we all live on…

Instagram: twistypoet

Email contact: twistypoet@hotmail.com

Printed in Great Britain
by Amazon

62315496R00169